# Also by Chris [illegible] Tubbs

THE SCARLETT FOX SERIES

Book 1: Scarlett

Book 2: A Kind of Freedom

Book 3: Legacy

# CHRISTOPHER C. TUBBS

# Kingfisher

*THE DECOY SHIPS*
BOOK ONE

LUME BOOKS
A JOFFE BOOKS COMPANY

LUME BOOKS
A JOFFE BOOKS COMPANY

Lume Books, London
A Joffe Books Company
www.lumebooks.co.uk

First published in 2023 by Lume Books



Cover design by Imogen Buchanan

Cover image © iStock by Getty

ISBN: 978-1-83901-564-9

# A Royal Commission

Sir Thomas Allin, Admiral of the Blue and bane of the Barbary pirates, sat in an anteroom at Hampton Court waiting for an audience with King Charles II. He had no idea what the King wanted to talk to him about. The summons had arrived that morning.

> *You are hereby required to present yourself for an audience with His Gracious Majesty King Charles the second at the eleventh hour of this morning at Hampton Court Palace.*

It was almost rude in its abruptness, and he wondered what he had done to offend. He forced himself to relax by sitting back in the chair, his hands on his cane that was propped between his knees. He noticed a smudge on his silk stocking and was about to attack it with some saliva on a handkerchief when the door opened and a herald stepped through.

'Admiral, the King will see you now.'

He stood easily, even at sixty-five years old he was spry, and followed the herald into the audience chamber. The King had been on the throne for ten years now and Allin saw a mature man of forty-one years, dressed in a black silk loose-fitting coat, petticoat pantaloons, dark silk stockings and shoes with gold buckles. His long, dark, wavy hair hung below his shoulders.

'Your Majesty,' Allin said and made an elegant leg.

'Aah, Admiral, good of you to come,' Charles said. 'I asked for you because those damnable pirates are taking our ships in the Mediterranean again. The merchants are complaining most loudly and demanding we do something about it. But even if I had ships to send, all that happens is the cowards run away as soon as they see them.'

The shortage of ships was caused by Anglo-Dutch relations being so poor that a series of wars had been fought, culminating with the Dutch raiding Chatham and Gillingham and burning a good part of the British Fleet at anchor. Consequently, the majority of the Fleet was occupied in the North Sea. Allin knew this as he was one of its commanders.

'I was told that you have an idea how to counteract them?' the King said and looked at him expectantly.

Now he knew why he had been summoned, Allin relaxed; this was ground he was sure of.

'If your fish is shy, then you have to present him with a juicy fly to get him close enough to catch.' Allin was a keen fisherman.

The King looked intrigued, so he continued. 'The Barbary pirates are only interested in profit and slaves, so they only take ships that they can attack with low risk. They rely on boarding with an overwhelming number of men. My idea is to provide them with a juicy fly that has a hidden sting.'

'And how do you propose we do that?'

'There is a hull half raised on Phineas Pett's slipway at Woolwich for a fourth rate. My proposal is to redesign her to look like a merchant vessel while retaining her firepower.'

'I see! She will be our steel fist in a velvet glove.'

'Yes, Your Majesty, and when she is finished with the pirates she can be returned to the navy as the fourth rate she really is.'

'How much extra will it cost to make her into this... Do you have a name for it?'

'It will cost three hundred pounds and take an extra three months. I call it a lure ship much like a fisher would use to attract his prey.'

King Charles frowned, toying with the name. He was keen on shooting. 'I think decoy sounds better. Yes, a decoy ship.'

'Your Majesty is always wise,' Allin said with a bow, knowing when to give.

'Don't polish my balls, Admiral,' Charles chided although he looked pleased at the compliment. 'What is she going to be called? And do I get to christen her?'

'She will be the Kingfisher, sire. The navy would be honoured if you would christen her.'

Before she could be christened, Allin had to get her built and his next stop was Woolwich. He hailed a barge at the palace dock which took him through the City of London to Woolwich and the docks that sat on the south bank of the Thames. Woolwich docks was a sprawling set of construction yards with five slipways, ropewalks, warehouses and a navy barracks.

'Where is Master Pett?' he said to the first man he saw as he walked up the steps from the barge.

The labourer was so surprised to be addressed by such a worthy that he stood with his mouth open, hat in hand.

'Well come on, man! Where's Pett?' Allin barked.

The labourer bobbed up and down as he repeatedly bowed. 'The middle slipway, my lord,' he managed to stammer.

Allin walked away without a by your leave or thank you, leaving the astonished man in his wake. He walked briskly through the docks to the third slipway where a hull was up to the lower gun deck and shipwrights were busy shaping timbers with adzes and saws.

'Phineas!' he called.

'Admiral Allin, what can I do for you?' Phineas was the commissioner of the dockyard as well as an accomplished shipwright.

'I have come from the King. I have his commission for the decoy ship modifications to the Kingfisher we discussed.'

Pett looked at the hull and said, 'Just in time, come let us go to my office and discuss the design.' He called to his son, also called Phineas. 'Take over here. I will be with the Admiral for the rest of the day.'

In Pett's office, discussions began.

'The ship needs to look like a merchantman and be able to come to quarters without alerting the pirates that anything is afoot. The crew must be able to load the guns and be ready to fire before the disguise is dropped. The other requirement is that they must be able to change her appearance,' Allin said.

'She will carry a fourth rate's complement?' Pett asked.

'When she returns to the fleet, yes.'

'So, the modifications will need to be reversible?'

'With work, yes.'

'Is there extra money for these changes?'

'Two hundred and fifty pounds,' Allin said. The fifty pounds he diverted would go to maintaining his mistress, a bonny girl with expensive tastes.

Pett nodded and looked at the model of the Kingfisher that the shipwrights were working to.

'If we step back the hull at the gun decks and put in false bulkheads that can be dropped quickly' – he pointed to the sections of the hull that would be changed – 'that will take care of disguising the guns.' He turned the model in his hands, visualising the changes. 'I can change the model and show you what I mean. Can you come back tomorrow?'

Admiral Allin's family home was in Lowestoft where his wife, son Thomas and two daughters lived. He also kept a house in London where he had installed his mistress. He went straight there after his meeting with Pett. His personal coxswain opened the door for him. Lofty Long had been with him for years and acted as his butler when they were ashore.

'There is a Lieutenant Wrenn here to see you. He was sent by Admiral Mason.'

Allin remembered he owed Mason a favour – the modern navy ran on the exchange of favours. The navy officer class was built on patronage, so he put thoughts of his mistress to one side while he dealt with the young man.

Newly promoted Lieutenant Ralph Wrenn had been at sea since he was ten years old. He was the third son of a Bedfordshire country squire and had been put on a cousin's ship as a midshipman. Surviving the burning of the ships at Chatham by the Dutch, he had been placed on the flagship of Admiral Mason. He had distinguished himself and been noticed by the Admiral who had taken him under his wing. When he made lieutenant, the Admiral, who had no vacancies for officers in his squadron, heard about a new ship being built at Woolwich, a fourth rate, and put him forward for fourth officer.

Now here he was at the London home of Admiral Allin, a man with a fighting reputation and known for his ruthlessness. When he arrived with the letter from Admiral Mason, he'd expected to be told to come back at a later date, but a very attractive woman had met him and told him to wait for the Admiral to come home.

Now he sat on the edge of a chair in the sitting room drinking tea opposite Elizabeth, trying hard not to look at her breasts while he answered her questions. Her dress was cut as low as fashion would allow and her bodice pushed them up.

'How old are you? You look very young for a lieutenant,' she said.

'I am nineteen, miss. I've been a midshipman more than seven years and passed as lieutenant a month ago.'

'Are you really?' She leaned forward and breathed in deeply, Ralph tried very hard to keep his eyes away from her breasts and only partially succeeded, 'And when was the last time you had shore leave?'

His mouth was dry, and he was having real trouble keeping his eyes on hers.

'I…' he started to say just as the door opened and the Admiral walked in.

Ralph leaped to his feet blushing and Elizabeth giggled as she saw the effect her attention had on him. The Admiral gave her a look, but she was unrepentant and stared back at him.

'Thank you, Elizabeth, I am sure you have something to do,' he said sternly.

She tossed her head as she left, sending her curls waving and her hips swinging.

The Admiral sighed and went to stand in front of the fireplace.

'I have a letter from Admiral Mason,' Ralph said, holding the letter out as he bowed.

Allin took it and used a knife from a side table to slit the seal. He held it to the light from the window to read it.

'I see Admiral Mason thinks very highly of you. He has requested that I find you a berth on a ship no bigger than a fourth rate for you to gain as much experience as you can.'

He folded the letter and placed it on the table.

'I have a new ship on the stocks. Her keel has been laid in Woolwich. She is a fourth rate being specifically constructed to counter the threat the pirates on the African coast are presenting to our trade. She should be ready for sea in six months.'

Ralph's hopes for a rapid deployment dropped.

The Admiral picked up the letter and scanned it again. 'What do you know about ship construction?'

'Not an awful lot, sir,' Ralph said.

'Well, this is the time for you to learn. I want you to accompany me to the yard tomorrow morning. Be here at two bells of the forenoon watch.'

Ralph touched his forelock and bowed, interpreting that correctly as a dismissal. He'd reached the door when the Admiral said, 'You should visit Madam Percival's establishment on King Street. It will be the cure for Elizabeth.'

He nodded and, as he closed the door, heard the Admiral chuckling.

Ralph had spent more time at sea than on land since being ten years old, so it was not surprising he was still a virgin. He had money in his purse and Elizabeth had stirred up his hormones which were playing havoc with his libido. Without being conscious of making any kind of decision, he found himself outside the establishment. A burly doorman looked him over, then surprised him when he smiled. 'First time, son?'

Ralph nodded, blushing.

'Come inside. Maggie will look after you.'

He took Ralph by the arm and led him through the door into a palatial interior. A woman who wouldn't have been out of place at a society ball met them in the hallway.

'Maggie, this young gentleman is in need of assistance.'

'You have money?' she asked in a voice that matched her appearance. He nodded. 'Come with me then, dear.' She led him into a sumptuously furnished room with red velvet coverings on the walls, a deep pile carpet and chaise lounges. Six scantily dressed women sat around chatting, sewing and knitting. They looked up, assessing the young man as he entered.

Maggie scanned the girls then selected a woman, who was probably in her mid-twenties, with long blond hair and rouge on her cheeks. 'Daphne, would you take care of young, what's your name?'

'Ralph.'

'Young Ralph, a new customer.' She put an emphasis on new which caused the women to giggle.

Daphne stood. She was not as tall as him and was dressed in a corset, silk stockings and not a lot else. She stepped over and hooked her arm through his. 'Come with me, sweetheart.' He noticed she had a slight Black Country accent. She took him to a room on the first floor which was furnished with a bed and an oddly set up chair which didn't look like you could sit on as it had two very odd appendages. Then he realised it was for kneeling on.

'You are a sailor?' Her voice brought him back to her.

He nodded.

'How long have you been at sea?'

'Since I was ten.'

She laughed and helped him out of his coat; his education was about to begin.

At eight o'clock sharp the next morning Ralph knocked on Admiral Allin's door; he had a spring in his step and a smile on his face. The door swung open, and he was almost knocked over as the Admiral came out and set off down the street at a brisk walk. 'Come,' he said, and Ralph followed. The Admiral flagged down a cab at the end and Ralph had to quickly jump in before it set off. Once they were moving, the Admiral turned to him.

'We are going to Woolwich to meet with Phineas Pett, who is the commissioner of the dock and the designer of your next ship.' He could see Ralph wanted to ask something. 'You have permission to ask questions.'

'As she is not built yet, are there any other officers, sir?'

'No, you are the first of the crew. She is the Kingfisher and will sail to the Mediterranean when she commissions.'

'What do you want me to do?'

'Learn as much about her and her construction as you can. I expect you to guide her Captain when he arrives.'

Ralph considered that. It would be unusual for a fourth to know more about the ship than the Captain. However, his thoughts were cut short as they arrived at the dock; the Admiral led them straight into Pett's office.

'Phineas, good morning.'

'Admiral Allin.' Pett bowed and looked at Ralph.

'This is Ralph Wrenn. He will be the fourth lieutenant on the

Kingfisher. I want him to be here throughout her construction. Now, have you a new model to show me?'

Pett went to his worktable and lifted a beautifully made model of a fourth rate from its stand but, somehow, it didn't look right to Ralph. Pett handed it to the Admiral who turned it around in his hands.

'It certainly looks the part. How do the false bulkheads work?'

Pitt leaned over and pointed to the upper gun deck. 'This section of the hull is hinged so it can be hoisted up out of the way.' He used a fingernail to hook a section up revealing a row of gunports. 'I managed to work out a way to do it without recessing the gun deck.'

'Looks like all you did was remove the gunport lids and replaced them with this bulkhead.'

'It is more than that but keeping things simple keeps the cost under control.'

'I can't argue with that. What about the lower-deck guns?'

'Their covers swing up to the horizontal.'

Pett went on to describe the other alterations he had made to enable the ship to change its appearance to the rigging and masts as well as several deck features that could be moved around, taken down or erected to alter her profile. Admiral Allin hummed and hawed over them, then passed the model to Ralph.

'These changes all fit within the expanded cost?' Allin said.

'Yes, we can do it all for the money,' Pett said. 'Where are you lodged?' he said, turning to Ralph.

'At the Four Horsemen in Stanhope Street,' Ralph said.

'A mediocre establishment at best. You will lodge with my family while you are here. It will keep you out of trouble.'

Ralph's heart sank; he had been looking forward to furthering his education with Daphne in the evenings. But he plastered a smile on his face and said, 'Thank you, sir. Where is that?'

'Lord Warwick Street, a ten-minute walk from here.'

'If I may, sir, I will bring my things here tomorrow morning,' he said, making a bid for one last night of heaven.

The Admiral smiled knowingly and said, 'One last night in London, eh? I think that will serve you well m'boy.'

Pett didn't seem so keen but he bowed to the Admiral in agreement.

That night, Ralph didn't leave Maggie's until the early hours. It cost him a whole guinea but it was worth every penny. Daphne brought in a friend, Sally, a buxom seventeen-year-old brunette and the three of them had explored things Ralph had never imagined. He went home exhausted, poorer and never happier.

He arrived at the yard close to ten in the morning to be met by one of the foremen.

'Put your bag in the office then come with me.' He looked him up and down. 'Do you have some old clothes?'

'Yes, why?'

'Because you're going to have to do some work and you don't want to make your uniform all dirty.'

Ralph came out of the office dressed in clothes he usually reserved for jobs like tarring the rigging – slops from the purser's bin.

'I see you have some experience with maintenance,' the foreman who introduced himself as Pete said, as he looked him over.

'Caulking and tarring mainly. Things we have to do regularly once the ship is in service,' Ralph said.

'Ever handled an adze?'

'No, never.'

What followed over the next six months was an apprenticeship in ship construction. He worked with the carpenters shaping timbers, the blacksmiths forging nails and ringbolts, and even spent time in the ropewalk with the ropers. All this time the hull grew, the decks appeared and finally it was time to launch her.

King Charles himself turned up for the ceremony when the hull left its slipway. She had no masts, was unballasted, gun less and empty of stores. She bobbed on the surface rather than swam, rolling like a sick pig. That soon changed; ballast rocks were brought aboard and lowered into the bilges. She leaked, but as the timbers swelled the leaks lessened every day until she was a tight, dry ship.

Crew started to arrive and, as the only officer present, Ralph took command. The warrants arrived first. The purser, Aled Williams, a jolly rotund Welshman always singing in a glorious tenor. The carpenter, Finnigan Smith, a Kentish man with an Irish mother and a temper to match his red hair. Master at Arms, Arthur Grimsthorpe, a fierce Yorkshireman, scarred by fire when his ship was burned by the Dutch. They were followed by the first hands, landsmen, topmen, and waisters.

The first lieutenant arrived and Ralph met him at the side. 'Granger Felton, First Lieutenant,' he said after he saluted the quarterdeck.

'Ralph Wrenn, fourth, sir.' Ralph doffed his hat in salute.

Felton looked around at the busy ship. 'Are you the only officer aboard?'

'Aye, sir.'

'Not even midshipmen?'

'None yet, sir. Warrants are all aboard apart from the surgeon, and we have fifty-two crew so far.'

Felton wasted no time in getting settled in; he took over immediately and started moulding his ship into the shape he wanted it.

Masts were stepped and Ralph was busy aloft supervising the team reeving the running rigging when he saw two more lieutenants arrive. One stood out – tall, elegantly uniformed and obviously wealthy as it took several men to bring his baggage aboard.

As lunchtime approached, he was informed by the first that he was required to dine with the other officers in the wardroom. He hurried below and changed into his uniform.

'Ah, Mr Wrenn, so good of you to join us,' Felton drawled in his Cornish accent. A steward offered Ralph a glass of red wine. He sipped it and nodded in appreciation.

'Do you know your wines?' the elegant lieutenant said. Before Ralph could answer, the first said, 'May I make the introductions? Henry Twelvetrees, the new second, and Cecil Stockley the third. Gentlemen, Ralph Wrenn, our fourth, who has been with the ship during her construction. Now, Mr Wrenn, what do you think of the wine?'

'A rather good medium-dry Madeira.'

Twelvetrees raised his eyebrows in surprise. Ralph took another sip and swirled it around his mouth.

'Fortified with grape alcohol and typical of the type exported by the Dutch East India company. Was it taken from one of their ships?'

Twelvetrees grinned. 'It was actually, by my uncle. Captain Frances Irlingham.'

Ralph silently thanked his father for drumming wines into his head when he visited home.

'Lunch is served,' the steward announced and they sat around the table which had been laid with a selection of cold cuts, cheeses, nuts, fresh bread and an interesting green leaf that had a peppery taste.

'What is this?' Ralph asked.

'That be watercress. We grow it in Dorset,' Stockley said pronouncing it wadercress and Daarset 'I brung it up with me from home.'

'How did you get it here so fresh?' Felton asked.

'I sailed up from Poole in my father's pinnace as it was the only way to get here in time. The dolt who carried my orders got lost.'

'Gentlemen,' Felton interrupted. 'Our guns will be arriving in two days and our Captain on the morrow.'

'Do we know who he is?' Twelvetrees said.

'Captain Edward Castle, he had the Fortune before she was burned at Chatham. He has a reputation for running a taught ship and hating the Dutch. He does everything by the book.'

Ralph frowned. That didn't sound like a captain they would want for fighting pirates.

'You look troubled, Mr Wrenn,' Felton said.

'I was just surprised, sir. I was imagining that the Admiral would give the command to someone with…' He struggled to find diplomatic words, but Twelvetrees stepped in.

'More flare? Given our mission I would have expected that as well.'

'I understand he is to command the ship through her sea trials and getting the crew into shape,' Felton said.

'Speaking of which,' Twelvetrees said, 'we have a crew of just over sixty at the moment. When can we expect the rest?'

'Aah now there lies a problem.' Felton frowned.

# Shake Down

Captain Castle arrived precisely on time and was piped aboard. He read himself in after meeting his officers and took the opportunity to address the ship.

'It is a privilege for me to be given this ship. To bring it to service with His Majesty's Navy. Especially as she was commissioned by King Charles himself. I intend to make this ship the pride of the navy for its efficiency and willingness to fight. To that end we will not leave the dock until we have a full complement of men.'

He left the quarterdeck and went below, bellowing for his clerk.

'Well, that tells us a lot,' Henry said to Cecil.

'Wish they would get here before the guns. It's going to be a hard job with only half a crew,' Cecil said.

He was right; the first of the guns arrived the next morning in carts. The carriages were loaded first. The lower-deck guns were thirty-two-pound demi-cannon. These were not the biggest available but were considered by the navy to be a better option than full cannon which were unwieldy monsters. Once the carriages were sent to the lower gun deck, their eleven-foot-long barrels were carefully hauled up and over the side. This was a highly dangerous exercise as they weighed close to five thousand five hundred pounds and if one were dropped it would go right through the bottom of the ship.

Ralph would be responsible for the lower-deck guns once they were in service, so he got the job of coordinating and managing the activities down there. They were in the process of accepting their third gun when he felt he was being watched. Ignoring it, he focused on getting the boys to align the barrel with the carriage. He walked to the front end and checked the alignment, then walked to the side and checked it would drop neatly onto the quoins.

'Lower away, slowly now!' he shouted.

The barrel inched lower. 'Steady!'

He noticed a sailor had his hand on the carriage where the trunnion sat; he was intently watching the barrel, not where he had his hand.

'Norris! Move your hand!'

Norris jerked his hand out of the way just before the trunnion slotted home.

Ralph waited until the eyebolts had been fitted, making the barrel secure, before approaching him.

'Watch where your hands and feet are at all times. I do not want to see you crippled for want of attention!'

'Aye, aye, sir,' Norris said, wide-eyed at being dressed down in such a quiet way.

The lunchtime break came, and a ship's boy approached him.

'Mr Wrenn, sir, the Captain sends his compliments and asks you present yourself in his cabin.' The youth stuttered as he tried hard to repeat exactly what the Captain had said.

Ralph sighed. His midday meal would have to wait.

He knocked on the door to the Captain's cabin.

'Enter!'

He stepped inside, hat under his arm.

'Captain,' he said and touched his forelock.

The Captain was eating. He had a meat pie and potatoes on a plate in front of him and a napkin tucked into his neckline.

'Mr Wrenn, you have been on this ship for, what is it? Six months?' he said.

'Aye, sir. Almost seven now.'

'You were at the yard as it was being built?'

'The upper decks, sir, the lower were finished when I started.'

'Whatever, you are familiar with these false bulkheads?'

'Aye, sir. I helped with their fitment.'

'Do you support this kind of deceit?'

'For the purpose of countering the threat of the pirates, I think it is necessary,' he said carefully.

'Well, I don't. It is a dishonourable way of carrying out war and damned ungentlemanly. I have never used false colours and I am damned if I will hide my guns behind a hatch.'

Ralph held his tongue. If there was ever a man less suitable to Captain the Kingfisher, he would be hard put to think of one.

'But that is inconsequential. We will be getting three midshipmen by the end of the week. As fourth, you will be in charge of them. I want a programme for their education before they arrive. On another note, you did well to stop that man from getting hurt. Well done. Now go and get your meal.'

Dismissed, he went to the wardroom. The other officers knew he had been summoned.

'Ah, the sacrificial lamb returns from the alter of justice!' Cecil teased.

'Nothing like that. He told me that the new mids are coming and I will be in charge of them,' Ralph said.

'A fourth's burden, you should have expected that,' Felton said.

'I did. He wants a programme for them before they arrive.'

'That is also not unexpected and does not explain your troubled look.'

Ralph told them of the Captain's views on their decoy role.

'One can only hope that the man in charge when we enter the Mediterranean has more of a mind to use our unusual assets,' Henry Twelvetrees said.

Ralph was back on the lower gun deck that afternoon. He had got just four of the big guns down and mounted that morning and had another eighteen to go. With only a fraction of the crew, the work went slowly. In the end it took three days of back-breaking labour to finish the job; then they started on the upper deck. In between doing that he had to come up with the educational programme for the midshipmen.

The Captain was not idle. He sent a series of messages to the Admiralty requesting then demanding more men. When he got no reply he wrote to the King.

Admiral Allin arrived three days later, stomped up the gangplank and without ceremony ordered the Captain to his cabin.

The lieutenants gathered on the quarterdeck, to keep the men away from hearing what was said through the skylight of course.

'What is the meaning of this?' they heard Allin bark.

'I simply explained to His Majesty that with only half a crew the Kingfisher would not be capable of fulfilling its mission.'

'I know what it says, man! Why send it to the King?'

'I wrote to the Admiralty five times and got no answer.'

'You did what? Why didn't you write to me?'

'I obeyed the process as laid down in the regulations.' The Captain sounded indignant.

There was a spluttering; evidently the Admiral was lost for words. He eventually found his voice.

'Dammit, man, this ship isn't subject to the regulations! That was explained when you were offered the commission.'

'Even so, I need a complement of at least two hundred and eighty men to be able to fight one side at a time.'

There was silence for a full minute before the Admiral said, 'I will see you get your men by the end of the month. Good day to you, sir.'

The lieutenants dispersed before the Admiral came on deck and got the side party, who had been on standby, assembled.

Admiral Allin visibly reined in his temper by taking a deep breath and closing his eyes after he emerged on the deck; then he walked across the deck to the gangplank. Spotting Ralph, he stopped.

'Mr Wrenn, good to see you. Are you satisfied with the state of the ship?'

Ralph was aware that the Captain had followed the Admiral out onto the deck.

'She is a fine ship, sir, tight and weatherly.'

The Admiral smiled, aware he had asked an impossible question of the young officer and had received the answer he deserved. He leaned in close so that only Ralph could hear. 'She will get the Captain she deserves after commissioning.'

Ralph didn't know what to say to that and had no time to reply as the Admiral stomped down the gangplank.

The Captain appeared on his shoulder. 'What did he say?'

'That he was pleased to see me, sir.'

'I meant after that.'

Ralph thought quickly. 'That he hoped I was happy, sir.'

'He has an interest in you?'

'He has, sir,' Ralph replied honestly.

After that, the Captain kept him at arm's length and very busy. The midshipmen arrived. Fourteen-year-old Peter Highcliffe, two years sea time, fifth son of a Cheshire landed family. Thirteen-year-old Simon Barnes, also two years real sea time, his father a landowner from Dorset. And last and most definitely the least, ten-year-old Egbert Teddington-Smythe, who had no sea time, but came from a seafaring family.

Ralph gave them a couple of days to settle in, then went to find them. The cockpit was a mess. Ralph stepped through the door and shook his head at the piles of clothes, scraps of food and general debris on the floor. He went up on deck where the three were skylarking in the rigging.

'Mr Highcliffe, I want you and your compatriots in front of me on the deck NOW!' he bellowed.

The three came down and lined up in front of him. He looked them over, then grabbed Barnes by an ear and examined behind it.

'Filthy as I expected,' he said, then shouted, 'Mr Grimsthorpe!'

Grimsthorpe was the ship's Master at Arms and responsible for discipline. He was standing nearby and stepped over, tugging his forelock.

'Aye, sir?'

'I want these wretches scrubbed under the deck pump. They are filthy and, if I'm not mistaken, lousy. Once they are clean, they are to be dressed in clean uniforms while these are boiled. After that, they are to report to me.'

Grimsthorpe grinned. Soon the deck rang to howls as the three were stripped and scrubbed by willing hands with stiff brushes. The now sparklingly clean youths were dressed and paraded in front of Ralph. He meticulously checked them over.

'If I ever find you in that state of cleanliness again you will kiss the gunner's daughter. Highcliffe, you are senior, and I will hold you responsible. Your quarters are a mess. You have one hour to get them in order, now go.'

Exactly one hour later he stepped into the cockpit. The three boys were lined up by what was now a spotless table. Ralph inspected their bunks and opened their sea chests.

'What is this?' he said and held up a rather tatty piece of pink blanket.

'That's mine,' Smythe whimpered.

Ralph put it back in the chest and closed the lid, knowing what it was like to leave home young.

'Make sure it stays there,' he said. 'Now we will start your lessons, mathematics…'

The hands trickled in over the next week and they reached two hundred and eighty men. A letter from the Admiral said that was all they could have until she was commissioned. The ship was provisioned and watered, then warped down to the powder wharf.

'I want the decks sanded and wetted,' the first ordered, to prevent spillages endangering the ship.

Dusty Miller, the gunner, supervised the loading of the powder casks to be sent aboard and stowed in the hanging magazine. He inspected each one for leaks before it was placed in a net to be lifted aboard.

'Nice even-grained powder,' he said to Ralph who was on the dock to oversee the loading of the barrels into a net.

Ralph knew enough about gunnery to know that a regular grain size meant the guns fired more consistently and the finer the grain, the more power you got per pound. Fine ground, or corned, powder was used in pistols and handguns. Cannon used coarser, slower burning powder. He watched the gunner take a sample and place it on a metal sheet in a walled off area a safe distance from the store. He ignited it and watched the burn carefully. Satisfied with the burn rate, he allowed the powder casks to be loaded. They would take on ten tons of the stuff.

'Haul away!' Ralph called once four casks were in the net.

The casks rose up and were swung aboard. A gunner's mate awaited them below.

'We are taking on enough to fight proper, let alone do the shake down as well,' Dusty said.

'You never know what we will come up against,' Ralph said.

The empty net returned to the dock and the men loaded the next four casks.

'Haul away!' Ralph called and watched them rise.

'AVAST HAULING!' He walked under the net and held out his hand. A trickle of powder landed on his palm.

'Lower them down slowly! Dusty, we have a leak.'

The casks bumped down onto the flagstones and they carefully checked each one. 'Loose bung here,' Ralph said. They removed the cask. Dusty took a wooden mallet and tapped the bung. Ralph held his breath.

'Bung's split,' Dusty said. He tipped the cask on its side and rolled it so the bung was on top. 'Hold it there,' he said to Ralph. Ralph steadied it. Using a brass lever, Dusty removed the broken bung and took it into the store. He returned with a new one of the right size and placed it in the hole. He took the mallet and was about to tap the bung home when he looked at Ralph. 'You do it, I got the cask.'

Ralph took the mallet and looked at the bung.

'Go on, give it a tap.' Dusty grinned.

Ralph took a deep breath and tapped the bung.

'You need to hit it, not tickle it.'

He hit it harder.

'And again.'

He hit it again and this time the bung went home nice and square. He breathed in and let it out with a whoosh.

'Get it in the net,' he ordered the men.

'See, you didn't blow us up.' Dusty grinned again.

*Not this time,* Ralph thought.

Fully armed, the Kingfisher left Woolwich and started down the Thames. She was a picture in the morning sun as she rode the outgoing tide to the estuary. She looked the part of a merchantman, but the number of men in the rigging and on deck gave the knowledgeable observer a hint that not all was what it seemed.

A merchantman of the same size (six hundred and sixty tons burthen) would only have a crew of sixty or so men. Their warship complement would allow them to sail and fight the guns at the same time. The lower-deck demi-cannons needed twelve men each and the upper-deck culverin and demi-culverin eight to ten men each. To get the gun crews to work together would take time and a lot of practice. Even so, they only had enough men to fight one side at a time.

The river meandered east, sometimes swinging north and sometimes south and they had to avoid other ships and barges coming up the river.

Thames barges were used for ferrying goods to and from ships moored in the river. They were also used to bring stone in from places like Portland and Purbeck on the south coast, and hay and other feeds for the multitude of horses in the city. A barge filled with tons of stone was an unwieldy beast and if one collided with the Kingfisher it would be disastrous. The Captain had extra lookouts posted and the sail handlers on alert.

Once past the turn at Erith, the river opened up and everybody sighed with relief. However, that didn't protect them from a craft manned by an incompetent or drunk Captain.

'Deck there. There's a barge coming up on the wrong side.'

'Mr Wrenn, go forward and see what that idiot is doing,' the Captain barked.

Ralph made his way quickly to the bow and saw a barge approaching, piled high with hay, on the wrong side of the river – their side. By convention, ships passed starboard to starboard so ships coming up the river should stay to the southern side. This ship's Captain was either unaware or ignoring that.

'We need to steer to starboard, sir, he's not seen us!' Ralph cried out.

'Do we? Be damned! He is in the wrong. Tell him to move over!' the Captain shouted back.

*Oh Christ,* Ralph thought, but he grabbed a speaking trumpet and shouted out, 'Ahoy the barge! Steer to starboard! Get in your lane!'

A head appeared around the side of the hay – a teenage boy. He saw the approaching ship with a look of surprise. Ralph gestured that he should move to starboard. The head disappeared and a second head appeared. An older man in a cap. He looked at the ship, then at the river and disappeared.

The bow of the barge started to turn. Slowly.

The Captain arrived and grabbed the horn from Ralph. 'Turn faster, you damnable idiot!' he shouted, but the unwieldy barge could only turn so fast.

Ralph shouted for men to grab poles to fend off.

The Captain, now very aware of their peril, ordered the foresail backed to slow them, but Ralph knew it was too late – they couldn't avoid a collision. The barge was a scant thirty yards away and they were closing fast. The wheel was swung to larboard but without the sails helping it was too little and too late.

The bow of the Kingfisher hit the bow of the barge slightly to starboard of the prow. The men tried valiantly to fend her off, but she was too heavy. The grinding of wood against wood was loud and the ship slowed suddenly. That wasn't the end though. The barge's rigging got tangled in the Kingfisher's and the two ships being quite firmly entangled stared to pirouette around each other.

Ralph half expected them to lose a mast but when the two ships came to a relative stop, everything was still intact. The Captain was apoplectic, shouting at the bargeman with language commonly only heard in the docks. Ralph went to the side and looked down. He could see the bargeman lying in a heap, the lad trying to get him up. An empty brandy bottle rolled across the deck.

'Mr Wrenn, be so good as to organise a party to cut us loose,' the First said.

Ralph jumped to it and soon men were hacking at ropes with tomahawks to free them. The Captain had retreated to the quarterdeck, his face purple with anger. Now, though, another danger approached. They were being swept along on the current and a curve was approaching.

The Captain noticed and ordered all sails to be backed which bought them a little time. The last of the entanglements were cut free and the ships pushed apart. The sails now had the power to push them backwards against the current although the same couldn't be said for the barge whose rigging was severely damaged. She drifted downstream. The befuddled bargeman could do nothing other than watch the oncoming riverbank.

As soon as they were clear, the Captain ordered the sails to be reset and they continued past the stricken barge which was now well and truly aground.

'Get the name of that hulk!' the Captain roared.

'The Rose of Wapping,' one of the lieutenants reported.

'I want a report on any damage.'

The damage was an impressive scar on the bow where the two vessels had hit, a sprung plank well above the waterline that the carpenter said they could repair before they exited the Thames, and some damaged rigging. In Ralph's opinion the scar added to their disguise, but the Captain wanted it painted over.

Taking out his ire on the crew, the Captain exercised them relentlessly for days after they entered the Channel. Sail evolutions, mast lowering and raising, gunnery and man overboard were all practised until they reached his desired level of readiness. It only stopped when they came upon a lone French merchantman sailing from Amsterdam to Le Havre.

'Sail Ho!' the lookout cried.

'Where away?' the First called out.

'Two points to starboard.'

'Mr Highcliffe, please inform the Captain that there is a strange sail in sight,' the First said to the nearest midshipman.

The Captain took his time coming to the quarterdeck; Ralph assumed it wouldn't be seemly to be seen to hurry.

'What is it, Mr Felton?'

'A French merchantman, sir.'

The Captain looked around the ship at the eager faces of the crew who were anticipating some prize money.

'Maintain a course that will take us past him and raise Dutch colours.'

*Dutch colours? We don't look anything like a Dutch ship,* Ralph thought. He also noted that the prospect of some prize money evidently overcame the Captain's dislike of deception as he didn't order the false bulkheads to be lowered either.

'Take us to quarters. Load but do not run out.'

The drums beat 'Hearts of Oak' and the men rushed to their stations. Soon the sound of hammers came up from below as the walls of the Captain's cabin were removed to enable the rearmost guns on the lower deck to be used. Ralph was at his station when all lamps were extinguished. Men stood ready to lower the bulkheads and run out the guns.

All they could hear was the gentle sound of water passing the hull and the creak of the rigging. The only light came down through gratings above and that only served to dimly illuminate the deck. Midshipman Barnes came down the stairs and said, 'Captain says that we will run out the starboard battery.'

'Aye, aye,' Ralph said. 'Ready the starboard battery!'

They waited.

'Run out the guns!' echoed down from above.

'Raise the bulkhead!' Ralph shouted. Light flooded in as the bulkhead swung up causing the men to blink.

'Run out!'

The deck rumbled as the big guns were hauled forward.

Ralph looked through a port. They were coming up on the merchantman. *Warning shot,* he thought as a shot rang out from above. The French Captain knew the game was up; her sails flapped, and colours fell as they surrendered.

'Secure the lower-deck guns!'

'Haul them in, remove charges,' Ralph shouted.

Midshipman Barnes reappeared. 'Mr Wrenn, the Captain wants you on the quarterdeck.'

Wondering what he had done wrong, Ralph ran up the stairs. He emerged onto the main deck and made his way aft, the French ship wallowing beside them.

'Mr Wrenn, prepare a prize crew and take over that ship. Twelve men should be enough, the Captain ordered.'

Surprised, Ralph looked around the other lieutenants to see if any were offended they hadn't been chosen. He was met with grins.

'Aye, aye, Captain.'

'Bring around the longboat,' the Captain called.

Ralph walked down the deck. 'Simmonds, Trout, Baker, Cummings, Baverstock, Finch, Allington, Jones, Trent, Thatcher, Williams and Grey. Get weapons and your sea bags, then into the longboat with you.' He ran below to the wardroom and found their steward already packing a sea bag for him. The tubular bag with a chord to close the end was commonly used for temporary assignments to other ships and could hold a change of clothes and personal items.

He finished packing and was back on deck in time to see the last man of his crew drop down into the longboat. The Captain was waiting for him at the side.

'Send their Captain over. Follow the Kingfisher at a cable's distance. Keep their crew locked up so they can't give you any trouble.'

They shook hands and with an 'Aye, aye, sir,' he dropped down into the boat.

'Fend off, pull away,' Midshipman Highcliffe ordered.

The men pulled and within a couple of minutes they were hooking onto the Frenchman's chains. Ralph was first up, quickly followed by his men. He had learned French at school along with Latin and Greek.

'Who is the Captain?' he said.

He kicked an empty bucket into the centre of the deck.

'I am,' an angry looking man replied.

'Tell your men to place their knives and any other weapons in that bucket.'

'You British are nothing but pirates.'

'That may be, but if you don't order them, I will have you put in irons.'

He turned to his men. 'Do as he says.'

The men filed past the bucket and dropped in their knives.

'Search them, Baverstock.'

The men were patted down and another couple of clasp knives added to the collection.

'Take these men down and secure them in the cable tier.' Ralph ordered. 'Captain, please go down into the boat. You are going to the Kingfisher.'

'I protest!' he cried.

Ralph drew his sword. 'Go down now.'

The Captain blustered but went down into the boat under protest. Ralph gave him an ironic bow as he was rowed across.

'Make sail,' he said, and the men got the sails pulling again. He wore ship to bring them around astern of the Kingfisher.

Needing two watches, Ralph simply divided the men in two. Simmonds was a bosun's mate, and he got the second watch. They would do watch and watch about, changing over every four hours.

Once he had them settled in astern of the Kingfisher, he inspected the ship. She was bigger than a lugger, but smaller than a caravel. He started by searching the Captain's cabin – now his – and found her papers. He sat at the desk to read them. She was called the Bonne Louise, registered in Brest and owned by a shipping company. She carried a cargo of hemp, spices and jenever. Alarm bells rang in his head, and he quickly left the cabin for the hold that the manifest stated held the alcohol. There were voices.

'You men, out of there now,' he shouted. He could smell the juniper used to flavour the spirit.

The off-watch men came out of the hold holding their leather jacks and looking sheepish.

'Get up on the main deck now.'

He followed them up and called the crew to assemble.

'The hold with the jenever is off limits. Any man found to be drunk or even smelling of jenever will be reported to the Captain and flogged. Baverstock you are now the starboard watch overseer. If the men disobey this order, you are responsible.' Baverstock was a redhead with a fiery temper but he was liked by the rest of the men. 'Finch you are the overseer for the larboard watch. If your men break the rules, you will be flogged too.'

He looked at the men with their jacks. 'Empty them over the side.'

The men reluctantly did as they were told.

'You will be issued your rum ration as usual. Now go below and get some rest; you will be on watch in two hours.'

Ralph finished his watch and went to his cabin. *This is bloody luxurious,* he thought as he laid his jacket over the back of the single chair, sat and pulled off his boots. The cabin wasn't large but compared to his dog box in the Kingfisher, it was extremely roomy. He had four hours until his next watch, so he sat at the desk and went through the drawers more thoroughly than he had before. He found a well-used pistol, loaded but not primed, papers, letters and a bunch of keys.

One of the keys caught his eye. It was much smaller than the rest and stood out because of it. He began searching the cabin for a small lock that it would fit. The Captain had a large sea chest with a large lock, which contained some not so clean clothes. The drawers of the desk had locks but were again too big.

He sat in the desk chair and looked around – nothing. He felt the urge to pee. The cabin had its own head and he availed himself of the facility. As he stood and aimed his stream down the hole in the floor, he looked around. His gaze was casual and unfocused. Suddenly, his eye alighted on an oddly cut timber. *That's strange.* He finished peeing, then turned to look at it. It was definitely cut very differently to the other timbers. He took his knife and pried the board loose. Inside was a cavity with a small chest in it.

He put the chest on the desk and tried the key. It turned easily and he opened the lid. Inside was a document written in ornate script; he lifted it out and saw silver coins beneath it. He held his breath, half expecting it to be an illusion. Recovering his wits, he read the document. It was the bill of sale for the cargo of brandy they had taken to Amsterdam. The coin must be the profits. He sat and looked at it for a moment, then started counting. One hundred and fifty-two silver Dutch ducats. They were worth about two and a half British pounds each so he was looking at almost four hundred pounds. He had never seen so much money, only being paid six pounds a year as a junior lieutenant.

He was sorely tempted to pocket the cash but the prospect of a court martial tempered that. He needed to think this over.

The commissioning cruise continued for another three days, the Bonne Louise tagging along behind the Kingfisher. Ralph wrestled with his conscience and in the end convinced himself that a finder's fee was acceptable. He took fifteen ducats and secreted them in his bag after checking carefully that none of the paperwork gave the exact amount.

Captain Castle eventually decided that the Captain and crew of the Bonne Louise were an encumbrance and ordered them to be put into a boat a mile off the Northern French coast. Ralph heaved a sigh of relief. The only person who could expose him had been removed.

The ships docked, the Bonne Louise handed over to the prize court for disposal. The Kingfisher was made ready to sail again and they were visited two days later by the Admiral. He went below to talk to Castle who left the ship without a word of farewell immediately after. The Admiral spoke to the officers.

'Gentlemen, Captain Castle has fulfilled his mission on the Kingfisher and is on his way to take over a new third rate. The Kingfisher will proceed to Naples in two weeks' time in a convoy of merchant ships. Commander Kempthorne will join the ship later this week to take command.'

They all knew Kempthorne; he was the twenty-one-year-old son of Vice-Admiral Sir John Kempthorne and a renowned firebrand. He had a reputation as a fighting officer and the gossips had it that he had a way with the ladies as well.

The Admiral wasn't finished. 'I have received an excellent report on the ship's readiness and have every confidence you will fulfil the mission the King and I have given you. The prize and its cargo are expected to fetch a good price. You can expect to receive some well-deserved prize money before you leave.'

With that he wished them well and invited them to dinner on shore. None of them had any expectation of seeing a single penny before they left.

# Convoy

Commander Morgan Kempthorne arrived in a carriage with his family crest on the side and his luggage on the roof. He was tall at five feet ten inches and handsome, with dark wavy hair, a long straight nose and strong jaw. He had ice-blue eyes that pierced whoever he was paying attention to. He moved gracefully and was an accomplished swordsman who had duelled and won several times since turning sixteen.

He strode up the gangway and doffed his tricorn hat to the quarterdeck. He cast an eye over the side party then turned to Granger Felton.

Felton stepped forward. 'Granger Felton, First Lieutenant. Welcome aboard, Captain.' Despite being ranked commander, he was their new captain and would be referred to as such from then on.

'Delighted to meet you. I see you keep a neat ship.'

'Thank you, sir. May I introduce the other officers?'

They walked down the line and Kempthorne had a few words with the second and third. Then they got to Ralph.

'And you must be Mr Wrenn, my fourth.' Ralph's surprise that he knew his name must have shown. 'I had dinner with my father and

Admiral Mason. He mentioned you. If you give me the service he says you gave him, we will get along famously.'

'Thank you, sir, I will do my best.'

'Now, gentlemen,' Kempthorne said addressing them all, 'we will be leaving for the Downs as soon as we are provisioned and my babies are brought onboard.' He gestured to the dock as a pair of cavalry demi-culverin drawn by four horses each pulled up. 'Stow them on the forecastle.'

'We will be ready for the tide this afternoon. We only need to rewater, and the water hoys are waiting,' Felton reported supressing his curiosity.

'We have powder?'

'Yes, sir, a full load.'

'In that case we leave on this afternoon's tide to rendezvous with the convoy. I will be in my cabin; I want the ship's and your personal logs on my desk in the next half hour.'

The watering completed, they waited for the tide to peak. Felton brought them up to their anchor before the Captain appeared on deck.

'Anchor is up and down, sir,' Felton said.

'Set the jib, spanker and topsails,' Kempthorne said.

As the sails filled, he ordered, 'Raise anchor.'

The anchor broke free and the ship turned, gaining way.

'Rudder is biting,' the helmsman called.

The wind was from two points south of west which made sailing the river Medway easier. They soon rounded the bend at Saint Mary's Island and turned south of east to take Barlett Creek. From there they headed north by north-east to thread their way out between the sand bars to the Thames estuary and the English Channel.

The Downs was crowded with ships, and they had to search for their convoy. They spotted one of the ships, a caravel called the Swiftsure; the other ships were anchored close by.

They anchored and a boat was sent around the ships with a messenger to gather the captains together for a briefing. As they came aboard it became clear that Kempthorne was the youngest by far.

They met in the Captain's cabin. Ralph had the deck watch so could hear what was said through the skylight. Kempthorne introduced himself then a merchant captain spoke. 'This is a frigate? I didn't see any gunports.'

'We carry forty-six guns on two decks. They are hidden behind false bulkheads. We can clear for action as fast as a normal frigate.'

'Why?' asked another.

'Pirates run away when they see a fighting ship. We are designed to look like a merchantman to pull them in. By the time they realise their mistake it is too late.'

'Devious. Well, I for one wish you the best of luck. The Barbary pirates are a royal nuisance and need to be dealt with,' said a gravel-voiced individual.

'Now, if we can go over the order of sail,' Kempthorne said.

'We will stay together; don't you fret young man,' the same gravelly voice said.

'I have no doubt about that, but I was about to say that the Kingfisher will not be behaving like a navy escort and will take position in the middle of the convoy.'

'Will it now,' a west county voice said, 'and will you furl at night?'

'Absolutely.'

There was a pause while they absorbed that.

'Then I suggest you drop in third in line,' gravel voice said.

'Perfect, when do you plan to leave?' Kempthorne asked.

'Tomorrow morning.'

'Well, in that case, can I invite you all to dine with me tonight?'

The dinner was a roaring success. That is, all the captains got roaring drunk and had to be practically carried back to their ships. The start next morning was later than planned and largely managed by first mates and first lieutenants.

Ralph had the morning watch from four to eight and was asleep when the ship made way. He woke to a hull that was pitching over a long swell. He rose, washed, shaved and pulled on his uniform. He was eating his breakfast when Cecil Stockley, the third lieutenant, came down from his watch.

'It's starting to kick up out there. Waves have doubled in size during my watch,' he said.

'Really? Where are we?'

'A couple of miles off Hastings and heading as close to west as we can. The Captain says the merchantmen decided they wanted to give the Bay as wide a berth as possible and the wind has slewed. The master expects it to become more northerly as the day goes on.'

'Well, that will suit us, won't it?' Ralph said.

'While it lasts. He thinks we will see the wind swing back to the south-west once we are away from the storm.'

Ralph chuckled. The master was a renowned pessimist. 'Is Mr Felton on deck?'

'Aye, he is and he is giving Henry a hard time with sail evolutions.'

Ralph made his way to the deck and took up his position by the mainmast. The men that weren't attending sails were splicing or polishing. He looked at the sky and noted the line of cloud that stretched across the sky to their south. He knew a little about storms and knew they seemed to rotate. Why they did that he had no idea.

The ships were making a steady eight knots along the south coast of England and should be approaching Brighton. They would have to stay heading west into the Atlantic until they got well beyond the Scilly Isles to make the turn to clear Ushant and the Bay of Biscay if the wind was as the master predicted.

He kept the men busy and made sure the mids had their lessons. Just before noon he joined them with the master for the noon sighting. The quadrant was the instrument used and it had to be used carefully to get an accurate reading. Ralph had suffered a beating or two before he'd mastered it.

Noon came and the sun stayed hidden behind the clouds, so the lesson changed to one of calculating their position using dead reckoning. They were given a chart and asked to plot their course from the readings in the log. The log contained their heading, speed, and the time of course changes. The tides were available from an almanac as were the prevailing currents.

'I want to see your workings,' Ralph said. He felt someone behind him and turned to see the Captain watching with interest.

'Not so long ago we were doing that,' he said to Ralph. He wasn't wrong. The Captain was only two years older than Ralph. He had made lieutenant at eighteen and commander three years later because of his father.

The first mid came up with a solution. Ralph and the master looked at it.

'You have us in the Solent,' Ralph said. 'Do we look like we are in the Solent?'

'I don't know, sir. I've never been to the Solent,' Midshipman Barnes replied.

'So, in all your sea time you have never sailed from Southampton?'

'Oh yes, sir, I've sailed from Southampton.'

Ralph took him by the right ear and steered his head to the chart. 'See there, that is Southampton and this stretch of water that you have put us in is the Solent. Do it again.'

The second, young Teddington-Smythe, had them just north of Le Havre. He too had to repeat his efforts, but Ralph pointed out where he had missed a course change to help him.

Midshipman Highcliffe was just about on the money.

'Well done, Peter, now go over the others' calculations and show them where they are going wrong.'

Later, the Captain asked Ralph to join him on the quarterdeck.

'I was very pleased with the way you handled our young gentlemen,' he said.

'Thank you, sir.'

'Young Highcliffe has a sharp mind, don't you think?'

'He does, sir. He is ahead of the others in all things mathematical. His Latin and Greek are fair and his understanding of navigation is better than average I would say.'

'I understand you are keen on gunnery.'

'I enjoy the challenge of training the men to get the best out of them and artillery is a fascinating subject.'

'Hmm, indeed. I want you to devise a way we can test the readiness of all the gun crews. I want to cover both rate of fire and accuracy.' Ralph frowned. That was unusual as most navy ships just fired a broadside without aiming their guns at all. 'I have been giving some thought to the way we can fight those heathen pirates and I believe that targeted fire will be the only effective way.'

'Aye, aye, sir, I will give it some thought and make my suggestions in the morning.'

'Very good, carry on.'

Ralph spoke to the other lieutenants over dinner and tested his ideas on them. A lively discussion ensued where the pros and cons of each idea were examined. Ralph slept on the outcome, examining it again in the light of the morning before going to the Captain.

'I have an idea for training and testing the gun crews that is intended to replicate the way the pirates operate,' he said by way of introduction.

The Captain looked intrigued and gestured for him to continue.

'I will sail the cutter, towing a float with a flag on top, and mimic the lines and speed a pirate galley would approach the ship. The gun crews should shoot for the float and get within ten feet of it.'

'How long will the tow be?'

'We will have to experiment on how long it can be and still tow properly, but as long as possible.'

'I am pleased to hear you have thought this through.'

'I discussed it at length in the wardroom over dinner and took the comments and criticisms of the other officers into account.'

'That is very commendable, for now, but never lose sight of the fact that when you make captain you will have to make decisions on your own.'

'Aye, aye, sir. Thank you, sir.'

'Please proceed, I want to test the gunners as soon as possible.'

An hour later a crew boarded the boat while the Kingfisher maintained eight knots, which was exciting. Ralph soon had them under sail and beating past the Kingfisher with a large float on tow. A crewman gradually let out the cable to see how far they could have it behind and still have some modicum of control.

'That's about it, sir,' said Butcher. 'Any further and the rope will pull her over.'

'Tie her off,' Ralph said.

He waved a flag at the Kingfisher and the bulkheads rose. He started a run past her at about one and a half cables range, the float half a cable behind.

The first lower-deck gun fired. It missed by a wide margin. Flying well past. Ralph noted the distance. The second was closer but by the end of the run none had got near the ten feet he wanted.

He made a second run and this time the upper-deck guns fired. Two got close but the rest missed by a mile, many well behind the float. He made two more runs before the Captain signalled his return.

The Captain called all officers to a meeting in his cabin.

'Gentlemen, I want to inform you of my tactics for fighting pirates so you understand the need to improve our aimed gunnery.' He looked them each in the eye.

'Pirates attack en masse in a host of small galleys often armed with a single twenty-four-pound brass cannon in the bow. They rely on sheer weight of numbers to overwhelm any ship they take on. The exception to this is the Algerians who have some larger ship-rigged vessels with broadsides that could be problematic. None have our fire power but to be effective that firepower has to be directed.'

The carpenter had erected a chalkboard on an easel and the Captain turned to it. He drew the shape of a ship in the centre.

'The pirates will try and get alongside, while they believe we are a merchantman, to board and overwhelm what they think is a scant fifty crew. I predict that they will approach like this.' He drew two curving lines that came in from behind the Kingfisher and ended at her sides.

'Their slave driven galleys are more than fast enough to catch us when we sail like a merchantman. It will be up to the lower-deck guns to take out these craft before they can get along side. A simple broadside is not enough. These ships are fast, manoeuvrable and have a low freeboard. Aimed fire is the way to take them out with loads of small ball.' He was referring to loads of eight cricket ball sized iron spheres that the lower- deck guns could fire, turning them into enormous blunderbusses.

'Aye their hulls aren't thick and small ball will shatter them,' Felton said.

'Yes, and swivels firing down into them with cannister will thin out the crews. However, we can expect some to make it through and try and board through the lower ports and over the side. The gun crews will have to repel those boarders so extra weapons will be stored on the centreline along with a team of landsmen and soldiers who will reinforce crews who are being overwhelmed.'

'What about the upper-deck guns?' Twelvetrees asked as they were his responsibility.

'They will take on any ships that stand off waiting their turn to come alongside, but I believe that when they see our guns they will switch to trying to board over our bow and stern. We have my field pieces on the forecastle. The carriages allow them to shoot over the rail. We will rig tackles to control the recoil.

The Kingfisher was designed to have two demi-culverins as stern chasers. However, they have not been mounted and are stowed in the after hold. As soon as we make port, we will bring them up and mount them.'

'They will use up a lot of room in your cabin,' Felton said.

'I can live with that for the sake of the ship.' Kempthorne smiled.

Ralph was beginning to like his young Captain and his innovative approach to their mission. Aimed fire was unknown in the navy. The guns weren't accurate at any great range but his plan to use them as blunderbusses against specific targets within a couple of cables made absolute sense. In his opinion, the idea of having guns fore and aft in a frigate was brilliant.

'Sir, should we not exercise the men in close combat?' Cecil asked. 'I mean they will have to repel boarders at some point.'

'A very good point, Mister Stockley. Yes, we should. Mister Felton please arrange training sessions for the off-watch men. I am sure Mister Stockley will be happy to assist.

'Mister Wrenn, your idea for a towed target is a good one but I think you will be more valuable in directing and training the lower-deck gun crews.' He scanned the midshipmen who were standing together in the corner. 'Mister Barnes will take over the piloting of the target boat.'

The other two midshipmen sniggered; Barnes looked worried.

The Captain's steward brought glasses of red wine and when everybody, including the midshipmen, were served, the Captain proposed a toast.

'Gentlemen, to our endeavour. Confusion to the enemy.'

The men raised their glasses. 'Confusion to the enemy!' they called and emptied them to heel taps.

The next morning an extremely nervous midshipman boarded the cutter and set sail. His first pass was so fast that not a single gun fired.

'Slow down, damn you!' bellowed Felton through a speaking trumpet. The crew was highly amused.

The second pass was at the correct speed and Ralph had his gun captains fire. After they had missed or run out of time because they were trying to traverse their gun, Ralph called them together and explained.

'Look, the only adjustment to the gun you need make is in elevation. The rest is all about timing. Once you have the range set you need to anticipate how early to fire to drop your ball on the spot as the float passes it.'

The next pass after that was better. They all had the range, but their timing varied from good to appalling. Ralph did some trigonometry and worked out what angle the target should be at from the centre line of the gun when the gun fired. He then marked the edge of each gunport with chalk and had the gun captain stand in the correct place to use it.

It was better but not perfect as they all preferred to stand in a slightly different place and that changed the angle. He realised his basic idea was sound, but he had to come up with a consistent way of implementing it.

He relaxed in the afternoon by shooting some seagulls to supplement the wardroom stores. He had just bagged one that fell nicely onto the deck when he had an idea. He went to see the carpenter.

The next morning, he had a prototype ready to test and he fitted it to the gun barrel. He also had a notch filed in the breech of the gun at top dead centre. He explained it to the gun captains.

'You set your eye so you look through the notch at the peg on the front sight. You fire when the float reaches the peg. Rickford, you try it first.'

Rickford was usually the worst shot of them all.

He crouched behind the gun and lined his eye up as instructed. The cutter passed and a hundred yards behind came the float.

'Fire!' he said and jumped back out of the way. The linstock came down on the touchhole and the gun fired.

'Good! That was within twenty feet,' Ralph cried.

He made an adjustment to allow for the time the linstock took to drop and the primer to fire.

'Stanley, your turn.'

It was close enough and when the others tried it they were consistently close as well.

Sights for all the guns were made and attached. The improvement was such that the Captain came down to witness the next practice. He stood next to Ralph who left the men to it.

'You see, they are compensating for variations of the cutter's speed by watching the fall of shot of the previous gun,' Ralph said.

'I can see that. The last three guns are consistently closer than the earlier ones, but they are all hugely better than they were. Well done!'

# The Bay of Biscay

That evening they turned south to sail down to the Straits of Heracles. They were four hundred miles west of the Lizard in the Atlantic and twelve hours later a storm came in from the west.

Ralph had been asleep when the ship started to pitch violently. He woke suddenly. Water dripped through the joints in the decking onto his face. He jumped up and pulled on trousers, shoes and a shirt and struggled up to the deck.

The ship was under storm sails only. The deck was a river of water that deluged from the heavens. He was soaked to the skin in seconds.

'Mr Wrenn, you are inappropriately dressed,' Kempthorne shouted over the wind from inside a tarpaulin coat and hat. Ralph grabbed a stay and hung on.

'It's a little rough, sir.'

'Came in an hour ago and has been getting worse by the minute. All we can do is run before it.' There was a crack like the shot from a gun and rigging parted. 'Get that repaired or replaced immediately or we will lose a mast,' he shouted.

Ralph made his way hand over hand down a safety line and found some men on deck sheltering under the gunnel.

'You men come with me.' He led them to the mizzen and gave instructions.

'You, get up there and make this fast on the futtock shroud.' He handed the man the end of a rope.

'You, help him.'

The two started up the rat lines, hanging on for grim death. One slipped and his leg went through the line. He tried to catch hold but his hands slipped on the wet rope. His upper body fell and there was an audible crack as his leg broke. Ralph turned to the two men he had with him.

'When I get up there and that line is secured, make it fast where the broken line is made off and get it tensioned. Get more men, you will need them.'

He turned and started climbing. He reached the man who was dangling upside down and screaming in pain. He tried to lift his body so he could untangle him but it was hopeless; he was too heavy, and the ship was swaying so much he just couldn't do it. Then he felt the lines vibrate and two men appeared.

'We got him now, sir,' Barny Robshaw said. Ralph left them to it and continued up the mast to where Harry Smith III was struggling with the rope. (There being two longer serving Harry Smiths on board). The two of them pulled up enough slack to loop the rope through and splice it back on itself. It was thirty minutes of terrifying work with the mast swinging like a pendulum back and forth.

As soon as it was done, he shouted and waved to the deck and the rest of the men rove the line through a block and tackle to tension it. Ralph took a stay down hand over hand to the deck as they started to haul.

'Come on lads. One, two, three, HAUL. One, two, three, HAUL.'

The rope stretched and then settled. Ralph swung on it to test the tension.

'Make it fast that's tight enough.'

He looked around the deck. Through the rain he could see other officers in waterproof coats, leading teams of men. The ship was suffering and needed constant attention.

'Well done, Mr Wrenn. Now get below into some dry clothes and get your waterproofs on,' Kempthorne said.

Ralph didn't go straight to the wardroom but took a detour to the orlop deck. There were a half dozen men laid out.

'You look a trifle damp,' Weston, the surgeon, said looking at the pool of water forming at Ralph's feet.

'It's raining a bit. How are the men?'

'Hernia, crushed hand, broken collar bone, a bang on the head and a badly broken femur,' the surgeon said.

'What about the broken leg? Will he lose it?' Ralph said.

'I fear so if we cannot get it back into line. The thigh muscle makes it very hard to set the bone.'

'What does it take?'

'A lot of steady pull. More than my boys can provide.'

Ralph left, the problem running around in his head. He changed into dryish clothes and donned his tarpaulin coat and hat. The trip up to the deck was easier.

He reported to the quarterdeck and found both the Captain and first lieutenant.

'Aah, there you are,' the Captain said. 'We have entered the eye of the storm. A brief respite.'

'Permission to go below to assist the surgeon, sir,' Ralph said.

'You are not needed here at the moment, but why does he need help?'

'One of my men broke his thigh bone trying to replace that stay. It needs a steady force to set it and I have an idea how it could be done.'

'Do you bedamned. Well, you had better go and help. Perform a miracle!'

As he walked away, he heard the first say, 'Never heard of a broken thigh being saved at sea.'

'Invariably leads to the man losing his leg,' Kempthorne said.

Ralph snorted. He had no intention of letting that happen. He collected a pair of small blocks and a coil of messenger line, two men, a hammer and pair of ring bolts with spikes.

'I have an idea how we can pull his leg into place to set the bone,' he said to Weston.

'I'm willing to try anything to save a leg. What do we do?'

They moved the surgeon's table, sea chests with a door on top, so it was in line with a rib. He had the men drive in one ring bolt level with the tabletop and the other into the deck at the opposite end. The blocks were rove into a pulley system and one end attached to the ring bolt in the rib. The second block had a leather strap attached to it. They hoisted the victim up onto the table and lashed him around his upper body and under his arms to the ring bolt in the floor.

'Attach that strap to his ankle,' Ralph said.

The man was screaming in pain every time he was moved.

'Can't you render him unconscious?' Ralph said.

'Only with rum,' Weston said.

'I can do it,' one of the loblolly boys said and took the poor man in a neck hold. He increased pressure on the sides of his neck until he fell into a swoon.

'I was a wrestler. Now you need to be quick. He won't be out long.'

'Now or never,' Ralph said. 'Pull on that pulley block steadily.' The men pulled. The surgeon laid his hands on the break, feeling what the bones were doing. Ralph swore later he could hear them grate together.

'Keep going,' Weston said. Ralph latched onto the rope and helped. 'Keep the pull steady. Don't jerk it.'

'Hold it there!' Weston said as the bones aligned. He took four thick pieces of wood and splinted the thigh with them, wrapping the whole tightly in bandage. 'Now we just have to hope there isn't too much internal damage, and he doesn't get the rot.' He thought for a moment then said, 'Relax the pull a little.' They let go a little of the tension. 'Hold it there. Can you tie it off, so it stays like that?'

The whole crew had been put through the mill of the storm by the time it ended. Everyone and almost everything was wet. The men were tired, and they had been driven right into the Bay. Seven men were missing, presumed washed overboard and more were hurt. Hernias, strains and breaks being the main injuries. Ralph expected the crew to be dispirited, but he discovered that facing adversity together had somehow melded them into more of a team.

He puzzled over it, then realised something. The crew were looking out for each other; that was where their loyalty lay. They also respected and were loyal to their ship and Captain and, to his surprise, him. Saving Charlie Littleman's leg seemed to have raised his status in the men's eyes.

The rest of the merchant ships had been scattered and the good lord only knew where they were. The regular watch was sufficient to keep an eye out for them. A service was held for the lost men and one of the crew nicknamed 'The Preacher' gave a eulogy that was both uplifting and spiritual.

The Captain read from his Bible, Revelations Chapter 20,

*'And I saw an angel coming down out of heaven, having the key to the Abyss and holding in his hand a great chain.*

He started to read and when he got to the final part.

*The sea gave up the dead that were in it, and death and Hades gave up the dead that were in them, and each person was judged according to what he had done.*

The men sighed and nodded knowingly.

After that they spliced the mainbrace with an extra rum ration. The men appreciated the celebration of their mates' lives and the selling off of their belongings raised goodly amounts for their loved ones. Ralph bid on a particularly good piece of scrimshaw depicting whale hunting in the north on a walrus tusk. He paid two pennies for it, which was a lot, but he didn't mind as the man had a wife and two children.

Getting out of the Bay was almost as difficult as getting in. The wind had settled to a point south of west and they had to tack endlessly back and forth to make a mile of seaway. The men were working constantly, and tempers frayed.

'Stephen Goodyear, you are charged with disrespectful behaviour to an officer. To wit telling him to, 'Fucking well coil the damn rope himself if he didn't like the way you did it.' What do you have to say for yourself?' Kempthorne said as Goodyear was brought before Captain's Court.

'I be most humbly sorry for my words, Captain sir. They were spoken in a moment of madness I do believe,' Goodyear said, wringing his hat in his hands.

'Mr Stockley, this man is in your watch. What has been his character until now?'

'Apart from a tendency to save his nips and get drunk once in a while, Goodyear has been a steady hand, sir.'

'Has he. Well, I will not tolerate insubordination. I award you twenty lashes to be served immediately. Master at Arms, carry out the sentence.'

It was known the Captain didn't relish lashing the men and would only do it when he had no choice. Twenty lashes was a hard punishment especially as they had two bosun's mates, one left-handed and the other right, to deliver ten each. They had made the cats themselves along with their red velvet bags.

Goodyear was tied to a grate that was one of the covers to the aft hold; it had been lashed upright to the mizzen mast. He was stripped to the waist and a strip of leather placed between his teeth. The first mate shook out his cat, running his fingers through the tails to make sure they were not tangled. The Master at Arms gave the order to lay on and he counted the strokes. The mate applied them with force, knowing he could be sentenced to a dozen himself if he didn't. At ten the second mate stepped up and laid on from the other side. After twenty, Goodyear's back had a checker of welts and cuts. Blood flowed.

The surgeon checked him as he was cut down and he walked unaided to the orlop deck. He would be treated and back at work in the morning.

It took three days to tack out of the Bay, during which time four of the merchantmen rejoined them. Finally, they made enough sea room to turn south down the coast of Portugal. They had been at sea now for three weeks and were out of fresh food. The manger had been washed overboard in the storm with the loss of their goat and rabbits. Some of their fresh water was tainted as well.

'We will stop at Porto to replenish with fresh meat and water. Mr Wrenn, take care that the tainted barrels are emptied and scrubbed,' ordered the Captain.

Ralph selected a work party of landsmen and took them down to where the water was stowed. He had them draw off some water from each cask and he tasted it. A complete row was tainted.

*That's very odd,* he thought. The tainted casks made up the second tier of the stack. None above or below were affected. If they hadn't checked them, they could have got into real difficulty as the top tier would be used first, then the second tier and finally the bottom, leaving them short of water. As it was, they would have to bring up all of the top two tiers. Ralph decided to report what he had found to the Captain.

'You were right to come to me. This looks like a deliberate act of sabotage,' Kempthorne said.

'Once I get some of the middle tier out, I may be able to ascertain how they were tainted,' Ralph said.

For shelter, they anchored in the estuary of the river Porto. Ralph had all the casks brought up. He had the tainted casks broached and the lids removed. The first cask was inspected. The water was still clear and hadn't yet gone green. There were no clues apart from some flecks of something unidentifiable suspended in the water. Ralph asked the cook for a sheet of muslin cloth and had the cask's contents filtered through it.

The cook, intrigued by what was going on, followed him onto the main deck. He watched intently as the cask was emptied, then stepped forward.

'If I may, sir.'

He examined the tiny particles that had been caught in the cloth, picked one out and rubbed it between his fingers.

'This is meat. If I didn't know better I would say that someone has added salt from one of the beef barrels.'

'Let's check the next one and see if we can collect enough to be sure of that,' Ralph decided.

A crowd of sailors had gathered on deck to watch. As the cook's words spread, the cheerful banter exchanged with the team working the casks changed to angry muttering. Ralph noticed the change and urged his men to take care emptying the cask and not to miss the cloth.

'There is a shadow of bits now!' the cook exclaimed.

Ralph agreed and took the cloth from him. He was peering at it trying to see what it was when he felt a tap on the shoulder.

'Try this,' Henry Twelvetrees said and handed him a magnifying glass. Ralph looked through it and moved it back and forth until he got a clear image.

'What do you see?' Henry asked.

'Grey fibres, a few white ones that look fatty.' He continued to scan the cloth. 'Aha!'

'What?'

'A hair!'

'Who is missing a hair?' Henry asked the crowd.

'I be!' Jarhead Jones shouted, causing a burst of laughter – he was as bald as a coot.

'Be serious, Henry,' Ralph chided, grinning in spite of himself.

'What have you found, Mr Wrenn?' Kempthorne demanded when Ralph reported to him at the end of the day.

'The barrels were tainted by someone adding salt from the beef barrels to them. We filtered the water through muslin and found beef fibres. We also found a hair – about four inches long and light brown.'

'Interesting, what are your conclusions?'

Ralph had thought hard about it and said, 'Any of the crew could have gained access to both the beef and water barrels. The motive is unclear, but my guess is someone wanted to force us into port, probably to desert.'

'Pretty tenuous reasoning, Mr Wrenn.'

'More of a feeling, sir. I have wracked my brain trying to understand why someone would do this and endanger his mates.

'Have a boat with men you trust patrol around the ship tonight from an hour before dark. If you are correct, then our man should make a break for freedom at his earliest opportunity now his ruse has been discovered.'

'May I suggest we lessen the watch on deck, sir? Our man needs to make a move if we are to catch him.'

'My you are a canny one. Do so quietly. We don't want him smelling a rat.'

Ralph had a boat brought around two hours before dark to take him ashore. The ship was quiet, and the watch was reduced to just three men. The deck was cluttered with casks to be refilled which were in various states of preparation. The main brace was spliced, and the men were dismissed below for their evening meal. They joked that the boat crew were holed up in a tavern on shore, filling their bellies with exotic food and drinking themselves silly.

The reality was that the boat was pulled up behind the Swiftsure, waiting for dark to begin its patrol. Ralph had gone ashore and bought fresh bread, cheese and cured meats for the boat crew's evening meal. He also supplied a flagon of beer which the men passed around. It was a local light ale and pleasantly malty in taste. The men were happy; it was better than they got aboard.

Darkness fell. Clouds covered the sky. The boat slipped away from the Swiftsure to patrol between the Kingfisher and the shore. It moved slowly with rags wrapped around the oarlocks to prevent unnecessary noise. Ralph had a night glass which he trained on the ship. The image was upside down and back to front and he almost missed a movement at the bow.

'Someone is climbing into the chains.'

He lost sight of the figure as they moved into the shadows of the tumblehome.

'Make way, slowly,' he whispered.

The oarsmen dipped their oars in and pulled gently, moving the boat forward without a sound. A ripple in the otherwise calm water cast a reflection of the shore's lights. Ralph signalled the cox to steer an arc.

A break in the clouds allowed the faint light of the moon and revealed a hint of wake from something travelling towards the shore. Ralph centred them on it and they slowly came up to a man clinging to a small cask.

'Good evening, can we offer you a ride?' Ralph said as they slid up to him.

The man spun in the water and cried out when he saw the boat.

'I ain't going back!' he cried and let go of the barrel.

'Shit!' Ralph said as he disappeared under the surface. He tore off his coat and pulled off his shoes. He stood and unclipped his sword belt before diving over the side, slicing through the water cleanly.

He stroked to go deep, casting around for the deserter. It was as black as a witch's tit, and he despaired of ever finding him. Lack of air forced him to the surface.

'I saw bubbles over there!' Stan, the third oar shouted. Ralph stroked over to where he pointed and took a deep breath before rolling forward to dive down again. He went as deep as he could and was just about to turn back when his arm hit something. He turned in the water, agile as an otter, and grabbed whatever it was.

# Trial and Punishment

The quarterdeck of the Kingfisher was a solemn place. A table had been set up, behind which the Captain sat with the captains of the Swiftsure and Penny's pride either side of him. They were a tribunal that would decide the fate of the accused if he were found guilty. The deserter was held between two soldiers in front of them. The crew watched from the rigging and crowded the main deck.

'Jonathan York, you are charged with the deliberate sabotage of the ship's drinking water, and desertion. What do you have to say for yourself?'

York squared his shoulders. He was pale and obviously suffering the aftereffects of his near drowning the day before. Ralph had pulled him to the surface unconscious and the crew of the boat had manhandled him aboard.

They'd got him back to the ship where the surgeon had him face down and pressed on his back to force the water out of him. He used bellows to force air into his lungs and blow tobacco smoke up his arse – the recommended treatment for drowning. York had recovered consciousness and thrown up a prodigious amount of sea water. The surgeon had pronounced him fit to stand trial the next morning.

* * *

'Fuck you,' was all he said.

George Felton was prosecuting and he stepped forward. 'If I may, sir, I would like to call Cedric Hove as a witness.'

'Go ahead,' Kempthorne said.

Cedric came forward.

'Can you tell us about how York behaved while onboard the ship and what he said?'

'Aye, sir, I speak on behalf of his mess.'

'Very good, pray continue.'

'Well, sir, Yorky were never happy to be on the Kingfisher. He were in the navy because he was caught stealing fish from the ponds at Monkton Priory. The magistrate wanted to 'ang him but the monks asked for clemency.'

'So, he ended up in the navy instead?' Felton said.

'That be right, sir. You see, he never settled to a life at sea. He were always complaining about something, the food or the work.'

'Was he popular with his mess mates?'

'Naa, we was all fed up with his moaning.'

'Did he say anything that would lead you to believe he would do something to the ship?'

'No, sir, but the storm did frighten him something proper and he hid below decks rather than join his watch up top.'

'That wasn't noticed?' Felton barked, glaring at Midshipman Barnes whose division York was in. Barnes shrank away from the stare, his face turning white.

'Not that I know of, sir. Everyone was too busy to notice one man was missing.'

Felton turned to the bench. 'York had motive and opportunity; the means was available where he hid.'

'Do you have anything to say in response?' Kempthorne asked. York stayed silent. The three captains put their heads together and after a minute Kempthorne said, 'There being no defence put forward, we have no choice but to find York guilty on both charges. For the act of sabotage, he is sentenced to run the gauntlet; for the act of desertion he will hang.'

It was as quick and simple as that. The crew formed an avenue that ran up one side of the ship around the bow and back to the quarterdeck. Every man carried a rope end or a rattan cane. The mood was sombre and vengeful. They detested the idea that one of their own could put them all in mortal danger just because he didn't like being on the ship.

The principle of the gauntlet was simple. The accused walked at a pace set by an officer who walked backwards in front of him with a drawn sword. The sword point rested on the accused's chest. This was to stop him running through the avenue and avoiding any of the blows from his shipmates. The officer chosen for this duty was Midshipman Barnes.

Barnes stepped in front of York and raised his sword. Barnes' hand was shaking, his face white and pinched with fear. The Master at Arms called out, 'The prisoner may proceed.'

Barnes took a step back. York stayed where he was. The Master at Arms stepped behind him and slashed him across the shoulders with a cane

'If the prisoner fails to walk forward, I will lash him until he does!'

York stepped forward one step and then another. The first blow landed, delivered by a burly gunner. He staggered and another blow from a rope end slashed across his back. He staggered forward again and came up to the point of Barnes's sword. The men jeered.

'Slowly, Mr Barnes,' cautioned Felton. Barnes walked slower, tears running down his young face.

The punishment continued to the quarterdeck where York collapsed. A bucket of sea water was thrown over him. He staggered to his feet to the catcalls and jeering of the men. He collapsed again after a rope end hit him on the back of the head. This time he didn't get up.

'Is he alive?' Ralph asked before the Captain asked him.

The surgeon knelt beside him and checked his pulse. 'Barely.'

'Will he survive to the end?'

'I doubt it.'

'We will stop the gauntlet. I want him alive to hang in the morning,' Kempthorne said, and with that he left the quarterdeck.

'Get that offal off my deck. Mr Weston, I want him conscious for his hanging at six bells in the morning. Men dismissed,' Felton barked.

Ralph went to Barnes who was sobbing by the rail.

'Come with me.'

He led the boy down to the cockpit.

'You two get out,' he barked at Peter and Egbert.

The boys left post-haste, and when they were alone, he put his arm around the boy's shoulder.

'That was a rough duty for any man let alone a younger like you, Simon. Don't be ashamed of whatever you are feeling.

'It was my fault; I should have noticed he was missing during the storm,' he said, sobbing.

'Nobody was counting heads during the storm. We were all too busy surviving. His mates knew what he'd done, and they would have taken steps if he hadn't run. The lower deck has its own form of justice.

'Would they have killed him?'

'They certainly would have if they linked him to the water tainting, but punishment for that crime is the Captain's privilege.'

Simon sobbed a while longer, then calmed himself.

'He looked so… lost.'

'He knows he is a dead man walking; he has no hope and only pain and damnation to look forward to.'

'He will go to hell for his crimes?'

'The Lord will judge him and weigh the balance of his life.'

'Then I will pray for his soul.'

'You are a good lad. Keep doing what you have been doing and you will make a fine officer.'

'Thank you, sir.'

Ralph left him and found Felton leaning on the bulkhead outside the cockpit curtain. He beckoned for Ralph to follow him up onto the main deck.

'You heard?' Ralph said as they got to the top of the stairs.

'I did. I saw you take him down and I followed.'

'The mids are my responsibility.'

'So they are, but I wondered how you would handle him.'

'And?'

'You did the right thing. I acted in anger when I gave him the duty. It should have been you.'

'I was ready to perform it.'

'Of that I have no doubt.'

'How is York?' Ralph asked to change the subject.

'His mind has gone. He is babbling incoherently but he is alive and will hang on the morn.'

Ralph looked at Felton expecting something more; he wasn't disappointed.

'You will command the rope party and be responsible for getting the prisoner on deck.'

Ralph had a troubled night's sleep after he'd chosen and instructed the rope party. He dreamed of being hauled up the mast and dangling above the ship. He rotated slowly getting a wonderful view of Porto before a demon came to take his soul. He woke sweating and lay for a moment when there was a tap on the screen door.

'Mr Wren, sir. Tis almost dawn.'

'I'm awake.'

He dressed in his good uniform, buckled on his sword, stepped out of his dogbox, and made his way to the cable tier where York was being held. He met the surgeon outside of the door along with two soldiers.

'Morning, Wrenn,' the surgeon chirped happily.

'You're in good spirits considering the occasion.'

'Just looking forward to having the opportunity to dissect the cadaver.'

'Fresh meat must be rare,' Ralph said, sarcasm dripping from every syllable, but Weston didn't seem to notice. He turned his attention to the soldiers.

'Bring the prisoner out.'

The men turned, unbolted the door and entered. It was silent inside. For a moment Ralph thought that York had died overnight; then the men came out dragging him between them. He was conscious, but from the blankness of his eyes, not aware of what was going on.

Ralph led the way up to the main deck. The eastern horizon had a grey tinge to it. In its faint light he could see that the halter had been strung from the mainmast topsail yard and the mainsail yard had been swung around to allow a clear lift. The halter swung four feet from the deck. The four-man rope team were lined up and ready.

The Captain appeared, resplendent in his best uniform, the ostrich feathers in his hat band ruffling in the slight breeze. The crew were silent. The sun peeked over the horizon and sent a glorious golden light into the dawn sky. Ralph marvelled at its beauty that never changed despite what was going on in the small world of the ship.

As the light improved, he saw that the crews of the other ships were lining the sides to watch.

'Bring the condemned forward,' Kempthorne ordered.

A priest stepped forward and started giving the last rites.

*Where did he come from?* Ralph wondered. Hearing praying from beside him, he looked and looking around to see young Barnes, head down, hands clasped. The priest finished and Kempthorne stepped forward.

'Let the sentence be carried out!'

Ralph ordered the soldiers to position York in front of the halter. He slipped it over his head and tightened it so the knot was against the back of his neck. He took a hood from where he'd tucked it into his belt and made to put it over York's head.

'Isn't the sunrise beautiful,' York said.

Ralph almost dropped the hood in surprise but recovered his wits and started to pull the hood into place.

'Please don't,' York said, sounding quite calm.

'You don't want the hood?'

'I want to see the sun.'

Ralph hesitated before remembering it was regulation for the hood to be fitted – he had no choice. He stepped back. York was crying. 'Rope party, ready!' Ralph cried, surprised his voice was steady. 'Haul!'

The party took the strain then hauled York up – slowly. He kicked, and piss rained down followed by a stream of shit. The men jeered.

York, in his weakened state, only took eight and a half minutes to die. They left him where he was for another half hour until the word came to bring him down. His body was stripped, the clothes stuffed in a sack for disposal. The surgeon oversaw the cleaning of the body, then had it wrapped in a linen cloth and carried below. He hummed happily throughout the process. The deck was scrubbed and the ship returned to normal.

As a reward for the onerous duties, Ralph was given twelve hours shore leave. He had a condom made of finest pig's bladder and was determined to use it to relieve the tension that had built up inside him. But first, dinner. The ships would sail on the tide in the morning, and he wouldn't get another decently cooked meal until they arrived in Naples. He wandered into town and found the officers of the merchantmen gathered around a table in a taberna with others of their kind.

'Mr Wrenn, isn't it?' Allen of the Cynthia called.

'Yes, that's me,'

'We are about to order. Why don't you join us.'

Ralph couldn't think of a reason not to, so he pulled up a chair.

'Ever been to Portugal before?' another Captain asked, before introducing himself as Tom of the Hyacinth.

'No never.'

'Then I know just the thing to introduce you to Portuguese cooking.'

He ordered and a bowl arrived piled high with pork cubes, potatoes, clams, onions and, from the smell, garlic. The lot was flavoured with herbs and spices, and a sprinkling of pickled vegetables.

'It's good!' Ralph mumbled through a mouth full.

The wine was a red port that was beautifully dry.

A pair of guitars and a lute started to play a melancholic tune and a woman started to sing.

'By God that sounds miserable,' Ralph said.

Tom laughed., 'She is singing about a lost love. He went hunting and never came home. The Portuguese love a good fado song.'

'Don't they have any jolly music?'

'Never heard any.'

Ralph leaned towards him and asked quietly, 'Is there a place around here a gentleman can get some entertainment?'

'Of the willing female kind?'

'Yes.'

'Two streets back you will find the convent of the sacred virgin.'

'A convent?'

'Yes, in Portugal a lot of convents are actually high-class knocking shops. The King's mistress is a nun and he has several bastard children by nuns as well.'

Ralph could hardly believe it and suspected he was being teased. He sat back, a blank look on his face.

'You think I'm setting you up? I will come with you.'

Ralph reached for his purse to pay for his meal. Tom placed his hand over his and said, 'Save your money. Those girls are expensive.'

The port was conspicuously free of the usual girls looking for business. Pairs of soldiers dressed in shiny breastplates patrolled.

'The church doesn't want any competition, so they send out troops to keep the street girls away,' Tom explained as they walked along.

'It's hardly believable that nuns would behave so,' Ralph said as he struggled to come to terms with the idea.

'It's been going on here for years. A woman joins a convent. If she's good looking she will attract the attention of some wealthy bloke.

She's made for life as whatever happens the convent will look after her and any children she drops and the customer pays.'

'Doesn't sound very holy.'

'It's not, thank God.' Tom laughed.

They had reached the doors of a large building with a mural of the Virgin Mary above them. Ralph gave it a second look – the figure looked more like a portrait rather than the usual depictions. 'Who is that?'

'That my friend is the King's whore in all her glory,' Tom said and knocked on the door.

A small hatch opened and a rather pretty face peered out.

'Can I help you?' she asked in English.

'We are in need of some spiritual guidance,' Tom said and held up a pair of silver reais. He received a surprisingly wicked smile.

'You had better *come inside*.'

Through the door was a hall that led to another door. They passed through and found themselves in a lounge.

'Do you have any preference?'

'I like tall girls,' Ralph said.

She looked him up and down and walked to a side door which she stuck her head through, saying something in Portuguese. There was a giggle and a very attractive and shapely woman of about five feet nine stepped through and approached him. She wore a wimple and very little else except stockings and a smile. She held out her hand, rubbing her fingers together in the universal sign for money. Ralph pulled a silver sovereign out of his purse. She took it and weighed it in her hand, then held up two fingers; he gave her another without hesitation.

* * *

Ralph returned to the ship only a few minutes late. Leanor had been an absolute joy. He had delighted in her long legs, and she had demonstrated her flexibility. He started up the side, his head in the clouds.

'Mr Wrenn, you are barely on time,' Felton said, bringing him back to the present.

'Aye, sir, permission to come aboard?'

'Granted. Please attend to your duties. You will be taking the ship out of harbour in one hour.'

That was new. He had never taken the ship out of harbour before. He went below and got into his working uniform.

Fifteen minutes before they were due to sail Ralph was on deck. He checked that the on-duty watch was ready to set sail and that the crew for the capstan was ready with the bars installed. At ten minutes he said, 'Raise the preparatory.'

Felton was watching him casually from the main deck. Sensing his eyes on him, Ralph felt very alone and under pressure.

'Bring us up to the anchor.' His stomach flipped and he looked at the masthead pennant for the umpteenth time. The breeze was favourable and moderate.

The capstan clinked as the men put their backs into it. The nippers wrapped their lines around the messenger and anchor cable running back to the beginning when they got to the capstan.

Ralph watched but didn't let the activity transfix him.

'Anchor's up and down!'

'Avast hauling.'

'Ready spanker, top sails and jibs.'

Felton raised his eyebrows; his young protégé was going to make a bold manoeuvre.

'Signal the execute.' The signal flags dropped.

'Set sails.' The topmen and haulers went to work with a will.

'Haul anchor.' The capstan clinked and the ship heeled slightly as the wind caught the sails.

'Anchor free!'

'Bring her home and make her safe! Catch her helmsman!'

'Rudder's biting, sir'

'Steer due west.'

'Aye, aye, sir.'

The Kingfisher threw up a fine moustache of water from her bow as she accelerated out of the estuary. It was a fine display of seamanship spoiled only by a near miss with a fishing boat.

# The Straits

'What course, Master?' Ralph asked Hammett, their Cornish sailing master, as they reached a point three miles outside the Porto estuary.

'South by east. That will give us the sea room to make the run through the Straits,' Hammett replied with a strong accent that made his vowels long and t's non-existent.

Ralph gave the order to the helm and shouted orders to the sail handlers to be ready to come about. He would use the forecourse to help push the bow around and the mizzen against it to turn the stern in the opposite direction.

'Execute,' he bellowed, and the ship made a perfect turn.

'Well done, Mr Wrenn,' Kempthorne said from immediately behind him. Ralph jumped in surprise; he hadn't noticed the Captain come on deck and no one had warned him. He found out later the Captain had signalled the quarterdeck to stay silent so he couldn't blame the men.

'Thank you, sir,' he stuttered.

'Any fishing boats nearby?'

'No, sir.' Ralph blushed.

'When does your watch end?

'Another three hours, sir.'

'Very good. Try not to run anyone over.' Kempthorne grinned and went to talk to Felton before Ralph could reply.

The master sidled up to him. 'I think he approves of you. He doesn't tease many of the others.'

'Is that what he was doing?'

'Oh Arr, if you had done somatt wrong he woulda crucified yus.'

*Bloody hell, when he talks Cornish, I can hardly understand him,* Ralph thought.

The merchantmen had reformed around them, and he kept their speed to a leisurely eight knots. He was running his eye over the sails when a commotion broke out. There was a noticeable lack of other officers on deck, so he called to the midshipman on signal duty.

'What the hell is going on down there! Mr Barnes, go forward and see what's going on.'

Barnes left immediately and came back minutes later with two of the ship's boys in tow.

'These two were fighting, sir.'

'What are your names?'

'Jim, sSir.'

'Arnold, sSir'

'Why were you fighting?'

'He called me a pikey,' Arnold said.

'Why would he call you that?'

'I dunno.'

'Why did you call him a pikey, Jim?'

'Cus he looks like a gypo.'

'Have you ever seen a gypsy?'

'No, but I heard Sam telling a story about them and he looks just like what he said.'

Ralph sighed and called out for the Master at Arms. When he arrived, he said, 'You will both learn not to fight on this ship. A dozen strokes each and for starting the fight Jim will receive an extra half dozen. Master at Arms, introduce them to the gunner's daughter.' Moments later howls echoed around the ship as the punishment was served out by a pair of mates.

Twelvetrees came up to take the watch five minutes late.

'Heading south by east, speed ten knots. At this speed and heading we will be turning into the Straits in about twenty-eight hours. Wind is steady from the northwest; weather looks to stay fair,' Ralph reported as required.

'Thank you, Mr Wrenn. I have the watch.' Twelvetrees suddenly grinned. 'What was all the howling?'

'Nothing much, two of the boys were fighting and kissed the gunner's daughter as a reward.'

A soldier approached them. 'Mr Wrenn, the Captain requests your presence.'

'See you later,' he said and followed the man down to the Captain's cabin.

'You wanted to see me, sir?'

'I would like a report of the goings-on on your watch.'

Ralph recounted the incident as factually as he could.

'You didn't feel you needed to summon me to judge what punishment was appropriate?'

'I thought it better dealt with on the spot and too minor a matter to disturb you with, sir.'

The Captain looked at him thoughtfully.

'I see why the admirals have such a good opinion of you.'

Ralph was about to answer when there was a hail from the masthead lookout. Kempthorne ignored it and continued, 'I want us to continue practising aimed fire and I want the soldiers to practise repelling boarders at the bow and stern.'

There was a knock at the door and the soldier on guard shouted, 'Midshipman Teddington-Smythe, sir.'

'Enter.'

The snotty nosed youngster entered; he had another of his perpetual colds.

'What is it?' Kempthorne said.

'Mr Twelvetrees compliments, sir. He said to tell you that there are two strange ships that have turned towards the convoy.'

'That's all he said?' The boy nodded. 'Mr Wrenn, please accompany this boy to the deck and get a proper report.'

'Aye, aye, sir.' Ralph stood, touched his forelock, and ushered the boy out.

'Did I do wrong, sir?'

'Not if you told the Captain everything Mr Twelvetrees told you to.'

'I did, sir. Word for word.'

'Mr Twelvetrees, the Captain wants more information,' Ralph said as they reached the quarterdeck.

'That's all the lookout reported.'

'Mind if I go up and have a look?'

'Be my guest.'

Ralph grabbed a glass from the rack and headed up the mainmast. The lookout was sitting on the top yard. Ralph passed him and went to the mast head. He made himself comfortable and secure, then swung the glass around.

He swept the horizon, noted the two ships, and made sure there were no others. Then he focused on them. They were just hull up.

*Two decked, sailing as close to the wind as they can. Obviously together. Now what flag are they flying? None? That's odd. Wait, the front one is raising a ... Portuguese flag? Not in a month of Sundays are they Portuguese ships. Their rigging is pure Catalonian, and they are sailing a course to get to windward of us.* He waited another ten minutes, by which time they had closed to around four miles. He took another look and headed to the deck by the fastest route, reporting to the Captain.

'Lieutenant Wrenn, sir!' the sentry announced.

'Enter!'

'What have you to report, Mr Wrenn?' Kempthorne demanded as soon as he was through the door. Felton was sitting beside the Captain's desk and he looked at him expectantly.

'Two race-built galleons of Catalan design from their rigging. Forty guns each. Manoeuvring to get the wind gauge on us. Flying Portuguese flags.'

'What do you think they are?'

'My guess is privateers.'

The Captain gave Felton a wolf-like grin. 'Looks like we will give the gun crews some real practice. I want the ship to go to quarters, but the visible crew must be that of a merchantman. Let's draw them in. Load the starboard battery with round shot.'

As the ship went to quarters, Ralph took his station on the lower deck. He loaded his starboard guns. The two ship's boys he had caned were among his powder monkeys. They avoided eye contact.

*Wish I knew what was happening up top*! He could hear the creaking of the rigging and the footsteps of the men as they went about their duties. He checked his watch, a present from his father, and saw it had been almost thirty minutes since they went to quarters.

'Raise our colours!' Felton roared.

'Ports open, run out!'

The men hanging onto the ropes that swung the false bulkhead up heaved and daylight flooded in through the gunports. Ralph could see a ship almost alongside. The guns rumbled forward.

'FIRE!'

The big thirty-two pounders roared in unison, shaking the ship. Flames and smoke shot out of the barrels, propelling the balls across the water. His gun captains had aimed their guns rather than just firing blind, but that would not be possible for the second broadside if the smoke didn't clear.

He tried to see what effect they had had but it was like looking into the smog in London on a still, damp day. The crews were busy reloading and he knew he had but a minute. The breeze stuttered and a gap appeared. Their target had been hit at least half a dozen times close to the waterline. Flame erupted from her side. She was firing back.

The hull moaned as it was hit but nothing came through on the lower gun deck. The guns ran out again.

'FIRE!'

The upper-deck guns fired just after.

'CEASE FIRE! She has struck.'

Midshipman Barnes came down the stairs from the upper deck, stopping four steps up. 'Captain's compliments, be ready to take on the second ship, starboard side again.' He started up, then stopped. 'I almost forgot. He said to tell you "Good shooting".'

Ralph grinned at him then called, 'Lower the bulkhead! Reload.'

The bulkhead needed to seal the ports as he anticipated the ship would manoeuvre and there was a danger she would heel enough to put the ports under sea level. A six-degree heel would put the ports just three feet above sea level. Any more than that, with open ports, they could sink. It had happened to King Henry's flagship, the Mary Rose, a hundred or so years before and Ralph had no intention of letting it happen on his watch.

The deck canted as the ship turned. More sail had been set and she was showing her true speed. Barnes appeared again.

'The second ship has broken off and is running; we are giving chase. Mr Felton asks you to report to the quarterdeck.'

Ralph followed Barnes up.

'Mr Wrenn, good shooting,' Felton said as he made the quarter deck.

'Thank you, sir,' he said, looking around. 'Where is Mr Twelvetrees?'

'Wounded, you are acting third. Mr Highcliffe will take over your duties as acting fourth.'

'Aye, aye, sir. Is he badly hurt?'

'He will recover. A splinter took him through the left hand when a ball hit the rail.'

His new duties would be to look after the upper-deck battery but first he found Highcliffe.

'Do not forget to close the bulkhead when we are manoeuvring and trust the gun captains. They know what they are doing.'

'Aye, aye, sir.'

'Now go and let them know you are taking over.'

Ralph turned his attention to the upper deck. There was a pool of blood near the mainmast.

'You, get that cleaned up,' he told a waister. He didn't want anyone slipping on it in the heat of battle. Cecil Stockley, now acting second, patted him on the back as he passed by on his way to supervise the chasers. Two brass demi-culverins fired nine-pound balls and were mounted on field carriages with big wheels which allowed them to fire over the rail on the forecastle. Gun tackles had been added to the axles to control recoil. Ralph was curious how they would work.

He didn't have to wait long. They were a quarter mile behind the privateer and well within range. Stockley took the gun crews from the first two guns in Ralph's battery. They had obviously done this before as they smoothly loaded the guns, then ran them forward. Aiming was easier than the ship's guns as they just moved the trail from side to side then chocked it in position. Elevation was by a screw rather than wedges.

The guns fired. A chunk of rail flew out of the stern of their target. The guns rolled back until stopped by the tackles.

'One to the starboard team,' Felton said from behind him. 'Are you a gambling man, Mr Wrenn?'

'What did you have in mind?'

'A wager on which gun brings down the first spar. Shall we say a shilling?'

'I will take that. I say the larboard gun.'

'Excellent. As I think the starboard.'

The guns barked again, and they could see the balls fly away from them. This time the starboard gun punched a hole in the spanker of the rearmost mizzen. The larboard ball clipped the forward mizzen just below the crosstrees taking a visible chunk out of it.

'They have the range now,' Felton said.

The range had crept up to a cable and a half by the time the guns fired again.

'Oh! Good shot!' Ralph crowed as the larboard gun hit the main square in the futtock shrouds, sending stays tumbling. The starboard hit the transom and the ball careened along the deck, scattering men like skittles. The wind chose that moment to gust and with a crack like a cannon shot their main topmast came down.

Felton held out a shilling. 'Won fair and square. Now attend to your guns. We will be coming up on her starboard side.'

'Lower larboard battery! Load with round shot. Upper deck load with chain,' Felton bellowed through his speaking trumpet as they drew alongside. 'Clew up the mains!'

The chase gunners had returned to their guns in the main battery and were busy preparing their regular guns. Loading with chain meant that they would go for the ship's rigging.

'Chocks out maximum elevation,' Ralph ordered.

They pulled alongside and the privateer fired at almost the same time as the Kingfisher. Balls hit the Kingfisher's rail and flew across the deck. Men screamed as they were hit but the overall effect was minimal.

The same could not be said about the Kingfisher's more powerful broadside. The thirty-six-pound balls of her lower battery hammered straight through the privateer galleon's hull and out the other side. The nine-pound upper-deck gun's chain ripped through their rigging. Their mainmast wobbled.

The privateer struck and spilled the wind from her sails. A huge cheer went up from the Kingfisher's.

'Mr Stockley, take a boarding party across,' Kempthorne said. 'I want to know her condition and what she is carrying; send her Captain and papers here to me.'

Cecil took a squad of soldiers and twenty sailors. Ralph patted him on the shoulder as he prepared to go down into the boat.

'Well done, Captain.' He grinned.

The prize's Captain and all the papers from his desk were sent over and the two ships made their way back to the convoy which had surrounded the other privateer. A boarding party was sent across under Ralph's command. He boarded with a cocked pistol in his hand.

'Who is the Captain?' There was no response, only blank looks.

He tried again. 'El capitan?' he said, exhausting his knowledge of Spanish.

A man stepped forward. Ralph looked him up and down; he was dressed like the rest of the crew. Ralph shook his head and shot him in the chest. He had no time for this pathetic attempt at deception. He took a loaded pistol from the sailor closest to him.

'El capitan?'

'Si, soy es.' A much better dressed man said, stepping out from behind the men.

'You I can believe. Bring him along while I search his cabin. Search the rest for weapons. Any trouble, shoot the perpetrator without warning. The rest will get the idea.'

The cabin was stylishly furnished and tidy. The desk drawers were locked.

'Keys?' he asked the Captain and made a motion of unlocking something. The Captain looked straight back at him. Ralph sighed then raised his pistol, pointing it at his knee. He raised his eyebrows in question.

The Captain reached inside the back of his doublet and produced a ring with half a dozen keys on.

'Thank you.'

The soldiers were grinning; this would make a great tale back on the ship. Ralph tried several keys before finding the right one for the top lefthand drawer. He had noticed that the Captain was left-handed, so it made sense to start there. He found a packet of letters and a scroll with an ornate seal.

There was also a very nice pistol. Brass inlaid butt and stock, about twelve inches overall, seventy calibres, seven-inch barrel. He weighed it and clipped it to his belt.

The rest of the drawers gave up more papers, a knife and a pouch of coins. He gave the papers to the soldiers along with a couple of coins each.

'Take him over to the Kingfisher. I will send over a report shortly.'

When both captains were present, their papers were brought forward for examination.

'Does anybody read and speak Spanish?' Kempthorne called.

'I do, sir,' Midshipman Smythe squeaked.

'You do? And how is that, Mr Smythe.'

'My nurse, sir. She was Spanish.'

'Was she now. What do these papers say?'

The boy examined the scrolls with ornate seals first.

'These are letters from the King giving them the right to attack Spain's enemies.'

'So, privateers not pirates,' Kempthorne concluded.

'These are private letters to one of their wives.'

He then examined a leatherbound book.

'This is their log. This voyage they have taken two ships. They sent them to somewhere called Gibraltar.'

Kempthorne wasn't amused. He had been looking forward to some booty. The reports from his lieutenants didn't help his mood. 'Empty holds?' He paced up and down. 'Move everyone from that ship onto that ship.' He pointed to the one Ralph had taken which was the worst of the two. 'Burn the other after taking everything of value. Mr Wrenn is to sail the ship to Gibraltar and put the crews ashore before burning her and returning to the convoy.'

'He wants me to do what?' Ralph said, when he was handed his orders. 'This thing is falling apart!'

That and the fact that even with both prize crews they were outnumbered five to one. And if he did manage to reach Gibraltar, how was he supposed to get two prize crews and soldiers back to the Kingfisher? His orders were quite open in that regard, and on top of all that the convoy would not slow for them.

Ralph barked a series of orders. 'Right, I want all their powder shifted to the Captain's cabin. Fuses to be run from there up to the quarterdeck. One man to be stood beside them with a tub of slow match at all times. Turn those two cannons to point down the deck and load with langridge. They are to be manned at all times. All prisoners to be confined to the foredeck, a squad of soldiers to be lined up in front of the quarterdeck with loaded muskets. If those dagos want to get home alive, they will behave themselves.'

They sailed as close to the Kingfisher as they could. Ralph was below with one of the mates plugging the holes his thirty-six pounders had made close to the waterline. He did it himself through a perverse sense of 'he broke it so he should fix it'.

'Next time I will sink the bloody thing,' he moaned as he swung the mallet to drive home another plug. The mate just grinned.

The ship managed to stay afloat for another thirty hours, and they reached the Straits only a mile or so behind the rest of the convoy.

Ralph was irritated with the whole affair. Irritated he didn't sink the damn ship in the first place, irritated that its mainmast was no more than a stub – it had snapped and gone over the side the first time they put pressure on it – and irritated that the convoy didn't stop to let them get back aboard.

As they approached Gibraltar, he spotted a rather pretty Dutch galiote anchored behind the Petite Pointe d'Europe in a shallow bay. He decided on a rash action.

'Reduce sail, steer for that ship,' he said to the helmsman.

The ship was making barely a knot. He looked over the side. He could see the bottom some three fathoms down. He needed to get rid of the prisoners now.

'Bring the boats around. Get as many prisoners as possible into them that you can. They can row to shore.'

The Spaniards were forced into the boats, overcrowding them. They started to the shore before they sank. Twenty or so were left behind. Ralph looked at them; he was tempted to shoot them but decided they deserved a chance.

'Boarders ready,' he said as they came up to the galiote. A couple of crewmen were frantically waving them away. There was a crunch as the ship came alongside. The boarders leaped across, surprising the small watch crew that were aboard.

Ralph and two men stayed with the ship that was making minimum headway. He hauled the tiller over, separating the ships, then tied it off. It was heading directly for the shore. He lit the fuses to the powder in the Captain's cabin and when they had burned below the level of the deck he shouted, 'Over the side!'

The two crew left the cannon that they were using to cover the prisoners and jumped. Ralph was close behind them. He had chosen them because they could swim, a rarity amongst sailors. The now unrestrained Spaniards ran to the stern to try to extinguish the fuses. When they realised that wasn't possible, they threw themselves over the side. They didn't have far to go, as with a grinding crunch the hull ran up on the rocks.

Ralph was hauled up to the deck of the galiote. 'Get the anchor up and man those oars.' The ship had sixteen pairs of oars with benches, as well as two masts. There was a drum at the stern by the tiller. Ralph stood by it in case he needed to keep the stroke.

'Back starboard oars and for'ard larboard.' The crew got themselves sorted quickly and the boat spun in its own length. 'Avast. All oars make way.'

The men took the stroke from the rearmost oarsmen who looked at each other to keep synchronised.

'Excuse me, sir,' Bosun Fred Fredriksson said.

'What is it?' Ralph said. He was concentrating on getting them out past the rocks on the western end of the bay.

'What should we do with the Dutchies? The prisoners?'

'Throw them overboard,' he snapped, having had enough of prisoners.

There was a loud explosion. The rear end of the galleon turned to matchwood and the rest caught fire. Planks and other debris rained down around them.

'Get them over; they will find plenty to hold on to,' Ralph shouted. Shouts and screams came from forward followed by splashes, leaving them free of encumbrance.

They rounded the point and entered the Straits.

'Raise the main sail!'

The galiote had square main and top sails along with a gaff rigged mizzen. Ralph wanted to get the men off the oars as soon as possible as they weren't used to rowing and were tiring quickly.

The sail was hoisted and angled to catch the wind that was on their starboard quarter as soon as they turned south. As soon as it was pulling, he shouted, 'Ship oars, make all sail.' They accelerated. 'She sails like a witch!' he crowed as they heeled over. 'Cast the log.'

'Ten knots and a fathom.'

'Beautiful.'

# An Unexpected Guest

Ralph and the crew were enjoying sailing the Femke as the galiote was called. She carried a lot of sail for a ship her size and the crew from the galleon were more than enough to handle her handsomely. The convoy had a three-hour head start and as they would only catch them at a rate of around one and a half to two miles an hour, it would take at least until the next day.

'What provisions are on board?' Ralph asked.

'Cheese, bread, a load of fresh, a freshly killed goat, the usual dried stuff and salt meat,' Gill Farrow, his acting first mate, said.

'Not bad, it's time I checked the Captain's cabin. If one of the crew can cook, get them to prepare an evening meal.'

The cabin was furnished in heavy Dutch furniture. There was a tantalus with full bottles on the dresser along with wine glasses. The desk was locked so he used a dagger to prise the drawers open.

*Papers in Dutch. Hmm this looks like a manifest. I wonder what buskruit is?* he read. He found a small key and tried it in the tantalus. It fitted and he poured himself a glass of brandy.

The door opened.

'Brought you some food skipper,' Gill said and placed a trencher with cheese, bread and ham on it. There were two bowls of pickles. One of little silver onions, the other of sauerkraut.

'I checked the cargo.'

Ralph looked at him – something in his tone had caught his attention.

'And?'

'Gunpowder, about twenty tons. Musket, and cannon grade as far as I can tell.'

A bell rang in Ralph's head.

'Bugger. That's what *buskruit* means.'

'Skipper?'

'I found the manifest.' He went to the desk and pulled it out. 'See here? It says buskruit and next to it 27. Which I am guessing means twenty-seven tons. The question is who were they selling it to?'

The Captain's log was on the desk, and he picked it up.

Gill looked over his shoulder.

'None of us speak Dutch.'

After Ralph had eaten his dinner, he went back on deck to take over the watch. Bill had divided the men into two watches so they could run five four-hour and two two-hour dog watches during the day. He and Gill would share the navigational duties, him with the starboard watch and Gill with the larboard.

Four bells had been struck and they were cruising along under reduced sail. He looked up at the red ensign flying from the mizzen. The ship had a locker full of flags from all nations. He was just thinking how peaceful this watch was when the air was rent apart by a shrill scream.

'What the fuck?'

There was a commotion from forward and he went to see what the hell was causing it when he met one of their soldiers coming the other way.

'Captain, sir!'

'What is causing that racket?'

'Stowaway, sir. Female.'

'Well don't just stand there, man. Get her up on deck!'

The soldier turned and went below where there was a stream of invective in at least two languages being delivered in an angry, shrill voice.

A minute later Gill came aft, dragging a woman behind him.

'Stan, take the watch. Gill bring her down to my cabin where we can get a look at her.'

Once in the cabin he lit an extra lamp. The woman had long wavy, unkempt fair hair that hung over her face. She wore a dress with petticoats like a serving girl in a tavern. She was shapely without being buxom. Her feet were bare and dainty.

'Now, my lovely, let me see your face.'

She raised her head and looked at him through her hair, then shook her head back and ran her hands through it. The face that was revealed was pretty but marred by fear and anger.

'You speak English?'

'Yes.'

'What is your name?'

'Maaike.'

'You are Dutch? Please sit down. I won't hurt you.'

She looked at Gill warily as he was still ready to grab her if she bolted and rubbed her arm.

'Gill, I can manage this. Go and get your rest and station a soldier at the door.'

Once he'd left, she edged over to a chair and perched on the edge of it.

'Why are you on my ship?'

'It's not your ship. It's my father's.'

'It's mine now.'

'Who are you?'

'Ralph Wrenn, Lieutenant in King Charles' Navy.

'We are at war.'

'Yes. Unfortunately, we are.'

'Am I a prisoner?'

'You are not a combatant. So, let's call you a guest.'

'Phttt, that's the same thing.'

'Where did you learn to speak English?'

'My mother is English. I speak Spanish and Portuguese as well.'

She was relaxing as they talked, and Ralph made no move to touch her.

'Where was your father going to sell the gunpowder?'

She didn't answer, just looked at him defiantly.

'Do you want to be reunited with him?'

A flicker of fear crossed her eyes. Ralph looked at his watch to cover that he had noticed.

'Get some rest. You can use the bed in there.' He pointed to the sleeping cabin that was curtained off. 'I will be on watch for the next hour or so.'

He went to the door, turned and smiled at her before leaving.

Maaike sat still for a few moments before getting up and searching the desk. Once she had thoroughly searched it she turned her attention to the dresser. Finding nothing in the cupboards and drawers she ran her fingers along the underside of the top. She found what she was looking for and pressed a hidden stud. A secret drawer slid out. Inside were papers. She removed them and scanned them with a smile. They were proof that Frans van Gerwin was supplying weapons and powder to the Barbary pirates on behalf of the Dutch Government. She took them and tucked them into her bodice. Her government would be able to use the information to get better terms with their Dutch neighbours or leak the information to the British to improve their relations with them.

She had only been partly honest with the handsome English lieutenant. Her mother was English, but her father wasn't van Gerwin. He was a member of the Spanish court of Habsburg in Southern Brabant. He was also the Habsburg's spy master and a Habsburg through his mother's side.

She had come aboard the Femke in Gibraltar, posing as a servant girl who the Captain had met in a bar and sent to the ship for a good time on his return. The Captain would never return to expose her as a fake as he was lying under a midden heap with his throat cut. The over amorous bastard had tried to take her in the alley behind the tavern. She had cut his throat with his own blade.

She had been unlucky that the English had stolen the ship before she had a chance to find the papers and make her escape. Having hidden in the cable locker when they had boarded, she was quite comfortable until discovered by a sailor doing his checks.

She sat on the bed and thought. Now she had the proof, how was she going to get home with it?

Ralph finished his watch and handed over to Gill. It was midnight and he was tired. He went into his cabin. The girl was asleep on the bed, so he laid down on the transom bench and dozed off.

He awoke three hours later to see her sat in the chair with one of his pistols.

'Good morning,' he said and sat up.

'Hardly, it's still dark,' she responded with a smile.

'What are you going to do with that?'

'Make you take me to a Spanish port.'

'Really, why do you want to go there?'

'That is none of your concern.'

'It is. You are my guest, and I am concerned for your safety.'

She laughed. 'You are my prisoner now.'

'I am afraid not. Nor are you the former Captain's daughter. You see the Dutch are even more superstitious than we are when it comes to having women aboard ships. The crew wouldn't have stood for it.'

He stood and walked forward until the barrel of the gun was just a foot from his groin. He started to reach for it when she pulled the trigger.

CLICK

'I blew out the priming before coming down last night. Nice to know you would have shot me though. I know where we stand now.'

'Now you are going to tell me what you were really doing on this ship and who you really are.' He reached out, took the gun with his left hand, and cupped her chin with his right. 'You are not going anywhere until you do. We will be at sea for at least six months and the men get – hungry.'

'You would not!'

'Would I have a choice?'

'You are no gentleman!'

'Never said I was.' He smiled and left her again.

* * *

Food was brought to her. Breakfast was bread and ham; lunch was a rich goat stew flavoured with herbs and thickened with dumplings. She had the feel of the ship now and had worked out that Wrenn worked four hours on and four off.

She jumped as a cannon fired. The ship changed direction and the sound of feet echoed down from above. There was a change in the feel of the ship, and she saw a merchant ship out of the transom window. It was British from the flag and she saw another passing behind them.

The ship slowed and the stern of a ship appeared beside them. She opened the transom window and stuck her head out. She could see enough of it to note it was a large merchantman. There seemed to be a shouted conversation going on between the two ships.

The convoy had come into view just before the midday meal and Ralph had piled on all canvas to catch them up. To avoid any misunderstandings, he had the men fire one of their six-pound cannon and sent up a signal that spelled Wrenn.

They moved along the convoy until they came alongside the Kingfisher.

'Close up to hailing distance,' he ordered. 'Match her speed!'

'Mr Wrenn. So nice to see you! Have you brought me a prize?' Kempthorne called.

'Aye sir. Twenty-seven tons of powder,.' Ralph shouted back then grinned when he saw the men step back from the side. The Captain wasn't so easily intimidated.

'Where was that heading before you purloined it?'

'That is what we are trying to find out; we have a prisoner, but she is not cooperating.'

'She?'

Felton appeared at the side. He looked happy. Kempthorne passed him something which he took and pocketed.

'Well stay on the, the – what is it called?'

'The Femke, sir.'

'Femke, and persuade your guest it will be in her best interest to cooperate. Bring her on deck so we can get a look at her.'

'Bring Miss Maaike to the quarterdeck,' he instructed a hand.

Maaike appeared on deck. She had tied her hair back into a ponytail.

'Am I to be paraded like some kind of prize cow?' she demanded angrily. She tossed her head and put her hands on her hips.

'A spitfire, by the looks. You have until Naples. Take position at the rear of the convoy.'

'You are going to be my guest for a while now, and you better hope that no one tries to attack us as we are sitting on a twenty-seven-ton bomb,' Ralph told Maaike.

'Is there any chance of that?'

'Oh, every chance as we are well within range of the pirate bases.'

'But,' she blurted out, then caught herself.

'The pirates don't care if you are English, Dutch, Spanish or anything else as long as you are not Muslim. They are only interested in slaves, and young pretty women end up in their harems. You better hope we blow up if they attack us.'

'Won't you protect me?'

'No, you are an enemy, unfortunately. I have to look after my men first. I may even trade you if it will save us.'

'You would not!'

'Oh, I would in an instant if it would save the life of just one of my men.' He looked around the horizon. 'It seems clear and safe at the moment; you can stay up here until dinner.'

'Why, thank you,' Maaike said, sarcastically.

'You are most welcome,' Ralph replied and gave her a courtly bow.

Maaike paced the deck like a caged cat. She had been given the run of the ship but even if she managed to get her hands on a weapon, she had nowhere to go. That arrogant, smug, over polite asshole ignored her fury and just walked his quarterdeck. Considering her options, she started to think how she could get him on her side. She could seduce him, but that somehow didn't seem right given her Catholic upbringing. She had the papers. Would it do any harm to let him know the destination of the powder?

When she went to bed that night, he slept on the bench as usual. She could hear his breathing, strong and steady. She eventually fell asleep and dreamed.

In the morning when she woke and remembered the dream, the memory both warmed her and disturbed her. She lay listening to the sound of the sea and the voices of the men as they went about the business of running the ship. A bowl of water for her to wash with had been placed in the salon. She hadn't washed for days so she stripped, after putting a chair in front of the door, and gave herself a sponge bath.

Her clothes were filthy, so she looked through a chest in the sleeping area. It had the Dutchman's personal belongings in it and at the bottom was a package wrapped in a cloth and tied with a ribbon. She took it out and undid the bows. Inside was a long red Spanish dress with lace around the deep round neckline, long flowing sleeves, brocade under the bust and down the centreline. A present for his wife or daughter perhaps.

She put it on and laced up the bodice. She wished she had a mirror or a polished metal surface she could see herself in. It felt good and fitted well. There were shoes in the chest, but she ignored them. She tied her hair up with the ribbon and left the cabin.

The quarterdeck was serene until she appeared.

'Bugger, look at 'er!' a voice exclaimed.

Other exclamations confirmed she looked good in the dress. Lieutenant Wrenn looked at her goggle-eyed for a moment before regaining his composure. She smiled inwardly while keeping an aloof expression.

'Milady,' he greeted her.

*That's a first,* she rejoiced, before pulling herself up. Handsome as he was, he was still her captor.

'Lieutenant Wrenn, good morning.'

'Where did you get the dress?'

'The Captain's chest; he probably bought it for his wife or daughter.'

'Probably for his mistress.' Wrenn laughed.

'Maybe,' she agreed. She fluttered her eyelashes at him. He looked confused at the change in her behaviour. 'How far is it to Naples?'

'Around twelve hundred miles from our current position.'

'That is a long way. How long will it take?'

'Anything from two weeks to a month depending on the weather, currents and wind.'

She looked out at the sea. She noted abstractly that Seagulls were following them. She made her mind up.

'The powder was destined for Algeria.'

Ralph seemed surprised and a little confused.

'Why the change of mind?'

'We are both in danger and need to cooperate.'

'Spoken like a soldier, or an agent.'

'Well, I am no soldier.'

Ralph didn't state the obvious. Instead, he asked, 'Will you dine with me this evening?'

'Why, Lieutenant, I would be delighted to.'

# Skirmish

A week into the voyage and Ralph was frustrated. Maaike was attentive, flirty even, and was obviously attracted to him, but he had yet to bed her. Her scent seemed to follow him everywhere. His dreams were becoming increasingly erotic, and he was sure she knew exactly what she was doing to him.

The convoy had reached a point that was somewhere between Algiers and Palma, and they were on high alert for an attack by pirates. Ralph had reported the intelligence that the powder was destined for Algeria. The Captain had noted it for his report to London but had otherwise said nothing.

Now they were facing adverse winds and making very little progress at all. The convoy was tacking back and forth, sailing fifteen miles for every mile of progress made. It didn't improve his mood.

'Gun crews exercise your guns.'

The exercise, carried out in dumb show due to their cargo, proved they could fire a broadside every minute or so. The men were used to working much bigger guns, of course, and the little six pounders were much easier to run out and reload.

'Kingfisher is signalling, "strange sail on the horizon".'

'Can you see anything?' Ralph hailed the lookout.

'No, sir.'

It was annoying; he was longing for a fight to relieve his frustration. Thinking about how he would fight his ship, he had an idea. He walked to the nearest stack of balls. They were rusty and some were cracked. *Badly cast,* he thought and picked one up.

'Get me a hammer,' he said to the nearest crewman.

The hammer arrived. He placed the ball on top of a bollard and gave it a sharp hit. It broke in two. He fit the pieces together and turned them in his hands. Gill noticed what he was doing and joined him.

'Balls are all shit. Hardly any are true,' Gill said.

'True balls are good against ships that are heavily built but they go straight through lighter ones. The pirates have lightly built ships and rely on numbers to overwhelm their victims. We would use small ball in the lower-deck guns on the Kingfisher. Apart from loading our guns with scrap there is only ball on this ship.'

'What are you thinking?'

'Break these balls up in to as many chunks as we can.'

'That will ruin the barrels.'

'Maybe, but they will be scrapped as soon as we get to Naples anyway when she is sold off.'

Gill grinned. 'We will massacre the bastards.'

The crew went to work with a will once the reason was explained and very soon, instead of nice, neat stacks of balls, there were piles of fragments.

'How many do we put in a load?' a gunner asked.

Ralph hadn't thought of that, assuming that they would just load a broken ball per shot, but it was hard to judge that when picking up a pile.

'Put them in bags,' Maaike said, who had been watching with interest.

'I beg your pardon?' Ralph said, coming out of his reverie.

'Put the fragments in bags sewn from light cloth. Weigh the bag against a whole ball.' She smiled.

He paused in thought and then grinned. 'It will make loading faster as well. Where do we get the bags?'

'We can sew them up. I noticed that there was a pile of cloth in the hold when I was hiding.'

'Pursers slops! Of course.'

He found some men who could sew and put them to work with Maaike.

'New signal from the Kingfisher. "Enemy in sight".'

'Get the ship to quarters, Gill,' Ralph ordered.

'They're ready. Been ready since you started smashing up balls.'

Ralph looked around. The guns were manned, the deck sanded and wetted, weapons stacked on the centreline.

'Perfect.'

'What about her?' Gill asked nodding to Maaike.

Ralph went to her. 'There is going to be a battle. You should go below, as low as you can below the waterline.'

'I will stay in your cabin. Can I have a pistol to defend myself?'

Ralph looked into her eyes; they really were beautiful. He saw determination but no fear. 'Here, take this one; it is loaded and primed and has a new flint.'

He handed her the privateer's pistol he had taken. She had to hold it in both hands.

* * *

'Sails to the south!' the lookout called.

'How many?'

'Only a dozen or so.'

'Clown,' Ralph muttered.

The crew had found a sharpening wheel and one was busy putting an edge on the weapons. Ralph checked his sword and dagger.

'Put an edge on those if you please.'

'Aye, skipper.'

The sound of the steel on stone set his teeth on edge. However, a blunt blade was just a club so he had to live with it.

An hour later they could see the ships approaching from the deck – a mix of galleys of various sizes all carrying a lot of men.

'Driven by slaves, no doubt,' Gill said.

'Of a certainty we will have to fight both sides,' Ralph replied.

Two of the smaller galleys broke off and headed towards them. It was full of men who were screaming war cries and waving their swords

'They think we will be easy prey,' Ralph said before calling out, 'Gunners be ready. Wait until I give the order and make every shot count. Aim for the upper part of their hulls so you kill as many as possible before they get along side. Remember your training!'

He paced.

The galleys separated.

'They are going to try and sandwich us. Ready all guns.'

He waited until they started their runs and were only fifty yards away.

'Run out and fire as you bear!'

He watched as the guns ran out and trained around by men with jack staffs.

BANG, the first gun fired.

The effect was shocking. The ball fragments spread like Ralph expected and tore a large hole in the galleys side just above the forward oar. Screams echoed across the water as men were mown down. They literally looked to be dragged below the level of the rail then a mist of blood and body parts flew up.

The rest of the guns fired in sequence.

The side of the galley was a mess but there were still a lot of men aboard able to fight. The first gun fired again when they were almost alongside which really surprised the pirates – guns never reloaded that fast. Their oars were pulled in as the pirates prepared to board. Ralph fired his pistol at the first man to climb on the rail, knocking him back onto the deck.

'Ready grenades!' he shouted. They had found several crates in the hold along with the powder. The men had one each and lit them with slow match. The deadly little balls arced over the water into the approaching ship.

More men were killed instantly and the screams of the wounded were horrible. Many were cut off abruptly; they were killing their own!

The ships came together and the. The gun crews grabbed their weapons. The soldiers stepped forward, pikes at the ready.

Screaming men in long shirts and turbans leaped across the ever-narrowing gap and grapnels flew, binding the ships together.

The soldiers dealt with the first few but then the ships were pulled tight together and a wave came over the side. It was hand-to-hand do or die.

Ralph waited to see where the majority were coming across. He glanced at the larboard side and saw the second galley was in trouble. The larboard gunners had blown a large hole in her bow, and she was sinking. They were raking her with the shattered ball, killing men by the dozen. The survivors would drown as the ship was going down fast.

'Larboard guns, repel boarders!' he shouted and launched himself into the thick of the fight.

He found himself facing a man with a curved sword. It arced horizontally towards his chest.

Ralph parried with his dagger and kicked him in the gut. As he doubled over, he brought his sword down on his neck. A second came in from the side and he turned to take him just as a pike thrust took the man in the side.

He had no time to thank the soldier as he had to parry another sword thrust with his sword. He followed up by punching the Arab in the face with the guard and stabbing him in the gut with his dagger.

He had time to step back and assess the situation. The fight was now man to man and of roughly even numbers. His soldiers were making the difference with their cuirasses and pikes. Their disciplined fighting was taking a high toll.

There was a shot, then a scream from aft.

'Maaike!'

He raced to the steps and took them two at a time, bursting through the cabin door without opening it.

Somehow a small boat had got behind them and tied up at the stern. It had only contained four men and Maaike had shot the first one through the transom window. The other three had her pinned in a corner.

Maaika threw the empty gun at the next man who came through the shattered transom window. He batted it aside and advanced with a grin. She screamed as loud as she could and threw the first thing that came to hand. It was the tantalus which missed the man but hit the next one coming in. Brandy showered him. He snarled and came up beside his mate. A third lined up on the other side.

She grabbed a candlestick and took guard. Her attackers advanced together.

The door literally burst open followed by Ralph who was across the cabin in two strides.

He thrust with his sword; it entered the centre pirate at the base of the neck and came out his mouth. Blood sprayed Maaike and she swung a candlestick. It hit the right-hand man, who had been distracted by the spray of blood, square on the ear.

Ralph let go of his sword which was stuck between the pirate's teeth. The pirate to his left turned as he was struck by Maaike. He punched him full on the nose.

'Ralph! Look out!'

He spun, but the pirate got there first. His sword bit into Ralph's side. He grabbed it near the hilt and pulled the man closer. His dagger punched forward, killing the man. He stood and watched him go, then turned to Maaike.

'Are you alright?' he said but he didn't hear her answer as everything suddenly went dark.

Ralph came to in his cot. The first thing he noticed was her scent. Not a perfume, but a womanly, clean, pleasant smell he found almost unbearably attractive. He turned his head. She was sitting on the chair asleep. He looked at her in the early light coming in the broken transom window. She was lovely.

He tried to move.

Mistake!

Pain seared across his side.

He must have groaned because her eyes snapped open.

'You're awake,' she said. 'Stay still or you will pull out the stitches.'

He lay gasping, trying not to breath too deeply.

'Stitches? Who put them in?'

'I did, no one else seemed competent. You needed quite a few.'

'How many?'

'Around thirty, and a whole bottle of gin to clean the wound.' She changed the subject suddenly. 'Are you hungry?'

'I am and thirsty.'

She got up and left saying, 'I'll be back in a moment.'

He lay there and suddenly had a thought. He lifted the sheet. He was naked except for a linen bandage around his lower chest. He groaned; she had seen him naked as a baby.

The door opened and Gill walked in.

'She said you were awake. How do you feel?'

'Fucking awful.'

'Not surprising. That Arab nearly did for you. Lucky for you our guest knows something about treating wounds. She stopped the bleeding with a hot iron and then stitched you up as neat as you like.'

'Gin?'

'Oh, yes.' Gill laughed. 'She insisted we bring her a bottle of gin. Apparently in Holland they use it to clean wounds as well as to drink.'

The door opened again; someone had apparently mended it, and Maaike came in carrying a tray with a bowl of soup and some bread.

'Eat this. You need to build up your blood.'

'You did lose quite a bit. Took us ages to get the cabin clean.' Gill smirked.

* * *

The next three days were hell – a very pleasant hell as Maaike insisted on nursing him. But hell all the same as he hated being confined and frustrated that she was so close and yet he couldn't touch her. On day three she helped him sit up and she unwrapped the bandages. Her close proximity and scent had an instant effect on his lower regions.

She didn't notice it to start with as she was too busy checking his wound but then, as she was tying the clean bandage in place, her hand brushed it.

She froze. He blushed. She didn't move away. Her face was inches from his.

'You seem to be recovering well,' she said, breathily.

'Well enough,' he said.

She took a deep breath, steeling herself.

'Then you can get up and resume your duties.' She stood and left the room.

'AAARRRRRGGGGHHHH!' he groaned.

# Naples

By the time the convoy reached Naples, Ralph was largely recovered. Maaike said the stitches could come out after a dozen days and he couldn't wait as they were beginning to itch.

The Femke was tied up off the powder dock which was at the end of the Molo Grande. The rest of the convoy was tucked away closer to shore in its lee.

'When will we be able to go ashore?' Maaike asked.

'We have to spend a week in quarantine first. They had plague here in '50 and no ships can dock until they have quarantined for a week.'

'Oh.'

'So keen to leave my company?'

'I would like to get back to my family.'

'Not before you take the stitches out.'

'I will do that tomorrow; you have healed well.'

Naples was ruled by the Spanish Habsburgs, the same ones that ruled South Brabant where Maaike came from. The Viceroy was Francisco de Benavidas, her uncle, and she could expect aid and assistance. She had to admit that she was very fond of Ralph, and he had a manly attraction that she was finding hard to resist. But she was afraid the attraction would turn into something much more serious if she allowed him into her bed. She giggled at the memory of his reaction to her presence. He was very well endowed.

The powder could not be offloaded until quarantine was over, so Ralph took Maaike across to the Kingfisher by boat to meet the Captain.

'Mr Wrenn, good to see you. Have you recovered from your wound?'

'The stitches come out tomorrow, sir,' Ralph said as they shook hands.

'Taken out by your nurse no doubt.' Kempthorne smiled and held out his hand to Maaike.

'Captain Kempthorne, this is Maaike –' he suddenly realised he'd never asked her surname.

Maaike stepped in and saved him, 'Maaike de Benavidas.'

'A Spaniard?'

'Only half, my mother is English.'

'Well, we will endeavour to get you ashore as soon as possible. Now I must deprive you of Mr Wrenn's company while he gives me his report. Please stay aboard and enjoy my ship and do please join us for dinner this evening.'

Ralph followed the Captain to his cabin and, once Kempthorne was seated, he presented him with his written report and a bag of coins.

'My report, sir.'

'Excellent, I think we will keep the Femke for the time being. She may be useful for scouting.' He paused thoughtfully, turning the report over in his hands but not opening it. 'Who do you think Miss de Benavidas is?'

'I suspect she is an agent for the Habsburgs.'

'Have you bedded her yet?'

That was a very direct question and Ralph blushed.

'Come now, Ralph, your reputation precedes you.'

'No, she is an expert at avoiding that,' Ralph replied honestly and a little resentfully.

'Keeping you on a string.'

Ralph hadn't thought of that, and his temper threatened to flare. Kempthorne held up his hand to restrain any potential outburst.

'Put her ashore at the first opportunity. I am sure she will go straight to the royal palace. Have someone follow her.'

'Aye, aye, sir.'

'If she stays, you will keep her company while we are in port and report what she says and does.'

Ralph just nodded at that. He wasn't sure whether he was pleased or annoyed at the thought.

Kempthorne rose and went to the door. Call the surgeon please. He arrived three minutes later.

'Mr Wrenn was wounded and I want you to check it.'

'Let me see it,' Weston said.

Ralph stripped to the waist and stood in front of him while he sat. Weston leaned forward.

'Let me see now, raise your arm. Hmm, very neat stitches, no infection at all.' He sat back. 'How did she treat it?'

*Does everyone know Maaike has treated my wound?*

'Apparently she washed it out with gin after using a hot iron to stop the bleeding.'

'You were unconscious at the time?'

'Yes.'

'Did she treat all of the wounded?'

'Apparently so.'

'How many cases of rot did you have?'

'None. Why?'

'That, my boy, is unheard of.' Weston frowned. 'In England she would be burned as a witch.'

Ralph was alarmed. 'You think she used magic?'

'No, I think she just knows what she is doing. I have heard that the use of a strong spirit to wash wounds helps prevent the rot, but until now I've never seen it.'

Ralph sighed inwardly with relief.

'Go and fetch her. I would like to get to know this wonderous woman,' Kempthorne said.

Dinner was the best the Captain's cook could provide. They had slaughtered a chicken and had some freshly caught fish. The chicken was roasted and presented whole at the table with potatoes (the last of the Captain's private store), carrots and pickled cabbage. The second course was the fish, a large bass caught by the cook that very morning. It was fried and served with butter and caper sauce with freshly baked bread on the side. Dessert was nuts and dried fruit. To wash it down they drank a dry Madeira with the chicken, sack (a sweet white) with the fish and a semi-sweet ruby port with the dessert.

By the end they were all a little tipsy.

'You could stay here on the Kingfisher if you want,' Kempthorne offered Maaike. 'You would be much more comfortable.'

'I am quite comfortable where I am, thank you.' She smiled and glanced at Ralph.

'Well then, Mr Wrenn, you had better take your young lady home,' Kempthorne laughed.

* * *

The next morning Maaike found Ralph supervising some repairs to the rigging.

'Come, I will remove the stitches,' she said.

He followed her down into his cabin.'

'Take off your shirt.'

She had a small pair of scissors. 'This might tickle.' She cut the first stitch and pulled the catgut out. She was right, it did tickle unless it was stuck. She reached the last one and looked up. He was looking down at her, longing in his eyes. His arms slipped around her, not holding so much as caressing.

'Ralph…' she started to say when he dipped his head and kissed her. The objection evaporated and she kissed him back with passion. They broke apart, breathless.

'Oh my,' she said and then spoke a stream of Spanish. 'Chica estúpida ¿por qué lo dejaste?'

He looked at her amused and kissed her again.'

'We still have four more days of quarantine; what will we do to fill the time,' he said.

'I am a Catholic.'

'Ah.'

'My father would kill you.'

'Probably.'

He suddenly perked up. 'I have a condom.'

She stepped back, a dangerous look in her eyes,

'¿Sí? y ¿en cuántas chicas has usado eso?' she snapped and followed it up with a stream of Spanish mixed with Dutch and English.

Ralph beat a tactical retreat. On deck the crew went about their business with grins.

* * *

By the time the quarantine was lifted, relations had almost returned to normal. The powder was sold and offloaded. Maaike allowed Ralph to escort her to shore. They landed on the Molo Piccolo and walked a short distance to a very grand building. There were guards at the door.

'What is this place,' Ralph said.

'The home of my relatives.'

'Aah, but this is the royal palace.'

'That's right, my uncle two times removed lives here.'

'Two times…' He hesitated.

'Removed,' she finished for him.

They approached the door and she spoke to the guard in Spanish. He looked blank. She put her hands on her hips and spoke in Italian. The guard saluted and stood aside. She led them both into the portico where they were met by an official.

'We have to wait here.' she said as the official made his way sedately up a grand staircase.

'At least it is cool,' Ralph said. It was the end of summer and outside it was very hot. He examined the walls. There were frescoes everywhere depicting hunting scenes, battles and something dark and religious.

'Eclectic tastes,' he said.

'That is because they were painted by three different artists,' a tall very elegant man said as he came down the stairs. 'Battistello Caracciolo painted Tobias and the angel. I never liked it. The others are by Il Cosci and Belisario Corenzio.'

'Uncle Francisco,' Maaike said and curtsied.

*Francisco?* A connection clicked in his head. Ralph realised he was in the presence of the Viceroy and made a deep regal bow.

'Maaike, how is your father? Still maintaining the family business?'

'He is well, Uncle. The business is why I am here,' she said obliquely casting a swift glance at Ralph.

'We will talk of that in private. Who is your escort?'

'This is Lieutenant Ralph Wrenn of the British Navy. He is commander of the Femke.'

'Lieutenant, welcome. Thank you for escorting my niece.' He clapped his hands and a servant appeared.

'This man will take you to a waiting room where you can get some refreshment while waiting for Maaike.'

'As you wish, Your Excellency.'

Maaike walked with the Viceroy up the stairs. Ralph followed the footman to a richly decorated anteroom where he was brought sweets and wine. He amused himself by studying the pictures in detail. He was deeply contemplating one that showed two women cutting some fellow's head off when Maaike returned.

'That was painted by a woman, Artemisia Gentileschi; it shows Judith beheading Holofernes,' she said.

'You know a lot about art?'

Not really, my father has a copy in Brussels but that is the original.'

'It is very dramatic, full of intensity and violence. I almost feel sorry for him.'

'You shouldn't. He was an Assyrian general and was about to destroy her home. She got him drunk and – well, you can see the result.'

'She paints like a man.'

'She was influenced by Caravaggio in her early years, but her version of this is even more vibrant than his.'

Ralph turned to her and put his hands on her waist. 'I suppose you will be staying here?'

She grinned at him. 'No I will take rooms in the city. The palace is too stuffy for me.' It was a partial truth.

Ralph was delighted; this made fulfilling his Captain's wishes easy and, hopefully, pleasurable.

They walked. Naples was a city of wide boulevards and open streets. Even though it had been the most populated city in Europe before the plague, it was now less crowded and seemed to be in decline.

'Do you know where to find rooms?' Ralph asked as they strolled along hand in hand.

'The chamberlain said that I should ask on the Piazza del Olmo.'

They asked directions and found the piazza not far from where they were. It was surrounded by tall baroque-style houses made of stone. Maaike made her way to one on the north side.

*She knew which one to go for,* he noted.

The large arched double door had a large iron knocker in the shape of a ram's head. She banged three times. The door opened and an old woman stepped out.

'Si?'

'Capisco che hai alcune stanze da affittare?'

'Chi te l'ha detto?'

'Il segretario d'el Virrey.'

Ralph noted she was speaking Italian and mentally added that to his report. He had an inkling of what was being said as he knew Latin and he knew that Virrey was Viceroy.

The old woman indicated that they should follow her and she led them into a cool lobby with a grand staircase leading up to the upper floors. They climbed the stairs slowly, staying behind.

'Do you think she will make it?' Ralph asked, causing Maaike to giggle.

The old woman was slow but relentless and they reached the second floor. They walked along a landing and she pulled a large key from her apron pocket.

'Did she know we were coming?' Ralph asked suspiciously.

'Not that I know. Why?' Maaike answered, the picture of innocence.

Ralph didn't answer as his breath was taken by the view of the room that was revealed. They entered a sumptuous reception room, furnished with gilded furniture that was ornately carved with cherubs and flowers. A méridienne-style chaise longue dominated the centre of the room. As they walked through to the doors at the other end, Ralph picked up a trace of perfume.

The next room was an intimate dining room with a small dining table and just two chairs. Finally, they came to the bedroom.

'Bugger me!' he exclaimed as he looked at deep-red velvet wall coverings with paintings of the erotic variety and a huge four-poster bed.

When he got his wits back the old lady was leaving and Maaike had the key in her hand.

'You took them?'

'Yes, they are perfect.'

Ralph was decidedly uncomfortable.

'They look like an upper-class whore house.'

'Oh, really, and how do you know that?

'Err, what I meant was what an upper-class whore house would look like if…' He stopped digging; the hole was deep enough to bury him already.

'There's no kitchen,' he said to change the subject.

'The servants bring up food.'

'Servants?'

'Yes, servants. The house has servants, and they serve these rooms as well.

'Who had them before?'

'My uncle's courtesan.'

Ralph was incredulous. 'He gave you the rooms he used for his mistress?'

'Courtesan.' She had that dangerous glint in her eyes.

'There's a difference?'

'You wouldn't understand.' He was suddenly and sharply aware that she was of a much higher class then him.

'Why? Because I'm not aristocracy?' he said quietly.

Maaike suddenly seemed to realise what his problem was.

'Oh, my love, neither am I really. The Viceroy is my uncle.'

'But you are still aristocracy. I'm just the son of a landed gentleman.'

'Does that matter?' she said putting her arms around his neck. Her eyes burned into him. He held her and lowered his lips to hers. When they came up for breath she said, 'Did you bring your condom?'

'Fuck! No, I left it in my cabin.'

'Oh,' she said and pulled away.

'I didn't think we would… I don't suppose.' He looked at her expression. 'No, I don't suppose we could.'

# Scouting

Ralph ran back to the dock to be met by a midshipman from the Kingfisher who had just stepped ashore.

'Mr Wrenn,' Teddington-Smythe greeted him. 'The Captain wishes to see you.'

'Now?'

'Yes, sir. It's most fortuitous that I found you here as I am under instruction to find you and bring you to the Kingfisher immediately.'

*Bugger, shit, fuck, damn and blast…* Ralph fumed internally but he plastered on his working face and said, 'Then you had better lead on young man.'

The boat took him directly to the Kingfisher and he was announced at the Captain's door.

'Mr Wrenn, I have a job for you,' Kempthorne said as soon as he had presented himself.

'Sir,' he said, trying not to sound resentful. A touch must have leaked through as he got a sharp look from the Captain.

'Having a good time ashore?'

'I found out that the Viceroy of Naples is Maaike's uncle. I met him when she visited him.'

'Is he really? That is interesting.'

'Yes, and he has installed her in an apartment in town formerly used by his consort.'

'She won't be going anywhere then,' Kempthorne said, pulling a chart from his rack.

'I have a mission for you.' He ran a finger along the North African coast. 'I want you to run a patrol from Tunis to Algiers to look in the ports and estimate the pirate numbers. Try not to get into a fight. We are re-arming the Femke with British demi-culverins which will give you better range and punch.'

'May I ask where they will come from?'

'The merchants have a stockpile of them. They are charging us an exorbitant amount for them and the ball. The powder you have already. Or do you need more?'

'We topped up our magazine before we sold the cargo.'

'That is what I expected. Get over to the gun wharf, exchange your guns and load with ball and chain. I want you out to sea on tomorrow's tide.' He looked at Ralph and smiled. 'And yes, you can spend the night with your paramour. Tell her what you are doing but add that you are going to visit the Sultan of El-Djazair to try and renegotiate the treaty.'

'False information to verify that she is an agent?'

'No, I am convinced she is. This is to make the Viceroy think we are trying diplomacy.'

'Oh, I see.' Ralph knew it was an outright fabrication and decided he did not need to know why.

'I doubt you do but tell her anyway and make it convincing.'

'Aye, aye sir!'

* * *

They rowed the Femke to the gun dock and spent the rest of the day swapping their eight ruined 6-pound cannon for eight 9-pound demi-culverin. He drove the men hard to get it done by dark and did a private deal with the dock master for some extra stores. As soon as they were safely anchored in their original position, he went ashore – not forgetting his condom.

He knocked at the door of the house and was let in by the old lady, who didn't say a word. He climbed the stairs to Maaike's rooms and knocked on the door.

'What kept you?' she said frostily as she opened the door wide enough to talk without letting him in.

'My Captain, he is sending me on a mission, and we had to prepare the Femke to sail on the tide in the morning.'

'Oh' – she opened the door wide – 'you had better come in.'

She was dressed in a pale-blue robe that was held together with a ribbon around her middle.

'How long will you be gone?'

'About three weeks.'

'But,' she started to say when he took her in his arms.

'We have tonight,' he said. Her arms reached around his neck. They kissed, a little uncertain at first but their kisses soon became more passionate.

'Did you?' she panted.

'Yes,' he replied and pulled the bow on the ribbon.

The robe slipped to the floor. They kissed as he carried her naked body to the bedroom. He placed her down gently on the bed and threw off his clothes. She pulled him onto the bed giggling as he held up the condom.

She sobered suddenly as he kissed her. 'Be gentle, it's my first time.'

* * *

He left the house before first light, kissing her gently on the forehead before he left. She murmured something and smiled. His ship was waiting.

He whistled and a boat came out of the dark; it was one of the Femke's, coxed by Gill.

'Are we ready to sail?'

'Aye, sir, as soon as there's light to see by.'

'Good, get us aboard; then tie this boat behind for towing. Are the men ready to row?'

'Aye, sir, they don't like it but they will put their backs into it.'

'It will toughen them up. They may have to row for their lives during this trip.'

Once aboard he consulted with the sailing master who pointed out they had two choices with the prevailing winds – south through the Straits of Messina, down to Bengasi then follow the coast East to Tripoli. Then up to Tunis. A trip of around fourteen hundred miles before they even started their patrol and with the added disadvantage that they would be going against the current for the leg along the Tripoli coast.

The alternative was to go north, follow the coast up to the Bay of Genoa, then west by south-west along the northern Mediterranean coast close to Marseille. Then south by south-west to the southern tip of the bay of Valencia. The last leg would take them south-east to Algiers. Eleven hundred miles with the current behind them all the way. Disadvantage, the storms the northern Mediterranean suffered in the autumn and winter.

'It's a choice between the devil and the deep blue sea,' the master said.

'What would you choose?' Ralph asked.

'To stay in port.'

Ralph gave him a hard look.

The master sighed and said, 'I would go north., It takes us along our patrol in the right direction to get back here.'

'Despite the risk of storms?'

'There are bays we can shelter in if it gets too bad.'

'North it is then.'

'I can see a grey goose at a mile,' the lookout called. It was officially dawn.

'Up anchor, prepare the oars.'

The windlass creaked and the anchor cable was drawn in. It came free of the bottom, and they started to drift.

'Make way starboard oars, hold larboard.'

The ship turned until they were parallel with the sea wall.

'Give way together.'

The Femke cut a neat wash out beyond the Molo Grande, then turned west to get out of the Bay of Naples.

'Raise the mainsails and spanker. Belay rowing, oars in.'

They were under sail and making ten knots. The Femke sailed well with the wind on her quarters, even with a dirty bottom.

'If we could careen her and burn off her bottom, I think we could get another knot out of her,' Ralph surmised.

There was a good knot of current pushing them along, so they were making twelve and a half land miles an hour. If they could keep that up day and night, they could make three hundred miles a day.

'Four days to get on patrol, say seven days to finish it and two days to get back to Naples. Thirteen days, call it two weeks.' Ralph wiped his brow as he finished measuring on the chart.

'In a hurry to get back?' the master asked. 'On a promise?'

'None of your business.' Ralph grinned.

'Sex will drag you further than the wind can blow you.'

'That is probably true.'

Ralph turned his attention to the ship and its surroundings. They were proceeding in a generally north-westerly direction following the coast towards Rome which they would pass in the dark. The horizon was clear in every direction, the wind steady from west by south-west.

He ate supper and went to bed. Two hours later he woke with a start. The ship was pitching and rolling in an uncomfortable fashion. He quickly dressed and went on deck.

'Wind has picked up and swung more to the south,' Gill reported.

'Are we making more speed?'

'God no. All this bucking is slowing us down. We are making eight knots.'

Things didn't improve when the sun rose; in fact, it looked to be getting worse. There was an arc of black cloud coming in from the south and it was catching them up.

By the end of the day, they were off Corsica and the sea had grown from rough to mountainous.

'Is there a place on the Corsican coast we can shelter?' Ralph shouted over the wind to the master.

'Nothing on the west coast until we get to Basti.'

Ralph looked around; he could see only a few tens of yards and they really had no idea where they were.

'How do we know when we get there?'

The master looked to the heavens and shrugged. 'Your guess is as good as mine.'

‘What hazards are in this area?’

‘There’s islands and rocky shoals. That’s why we try and follow the Corsican coast to avoid running into them.’

‘We can’t keep running with this sea,’ Ralph shouted.

‘We have no choice. We can’t let it get on our beam or we will go over.’

Ralph knew it was true. They just had to survive the pounding. The wind was gusting, and he feared for their masts. He had the meanest of storm sails set and that was as tight as a drum.

He stayed on deck throughout the night and the following day. The storm started to abate as the sun began to set.

‘You need to rest,’ Gill said as he came on deck. He had grabbed a couple of hours sleep at Ralph’s insistence.

‘Not until we know where we are. The clouds are breaking up and we should be able to take a reading from the stars.’

‘Where is the master?’

‘Sleeping.’

Gill shook his head; there was no arguing with Ralph in this mood.

An hour after dark the clouds parted to show them the polar star. Ralph took a reading with an astrolabe and the master checked it. They agreed and worked out their position.

‘We are somewhere off la Spezia; we need to turn west,’ the master declared.

The wind was blowing directly from the west. Making progress would be difficult. But if they continued north they would run into the coast and a lee shore.

‘Maybe we should head for la Spezia,’ Gill said.

‘If we do that and this wind doesn’t change, we could be stuck in port for a month. No, we will just have to tack.’

And tack they did, making a sea mile of progress for every ten miles they sailed. By the morning they had travelled a whole eight miles. Ralph was grumpy when he woke and even grumpier when he read the log. Then the wind dropped completely.

'Man the oars!' he shouted and the watch took to the benches.

This was better than sailing. They were going with the current and the men were pulling well. He estimated they were making at least five knots. The men were getting used to rowing the ship now and their stamina had increased. They could row for a full watch if needed, even in the heat of the Mediterranean autumn.

They came in sight of land and asked a fisherman where they were.

'Imperia, where the hell is that?' the master said.

He examined the chart along where they thought they were with a magnifying glass. Failing to find it he moved west then east.

'Ahh, there it is. The current must be stronger than we thought. Another four hours rowing, and we will be off the coast of France.'

The second watch was two hours old when a puff of wind rippled the water. It was followed by another and then, like an old man coughing and wheezing as he got out of bed, a steady south-westerly breeze developed.

'Make sail! Mains and tops, spanker, and jibs.'

They were soon cruising along at eight knots. Added to that was around a knot of current. Ralph luxuriated in the feeling of the sun on his face and the wind in his hair.

'Sail on the larboard bow,' cried the lookout, disturbing his peace.

'Bugger,' he said and grabbed a glass. 'I'm going up for a look.'

He could see that it was a large French merchantman from the cut of its sails, which were brown with age.

'Probably heading to Nice,' he said, using a stay to get to the deck.

* * *

As per their orders, they avoided contact with potential enemies and concentrated on reaching Algiers. When they arrived at the bay, they found it full of craft of many types. Feluccas, dhows, galleys and galiotes, even a carrack or two. It was a large crescent-shaped bay about nine miles wide and five deep. Algiers was tucked away in the western corner.

They entered slowly, flying the Dutch flag, making note of which ships were armed and which were likely pirates, working their way closer to the town. Lookouts noted where any fortifications were, and the master sketched furiously. The town was walled, moated and heavily fortified. A hook-shaped stone-built dock sat towards the northern end.

'There's a boat heading towards us. Some bloke in a dress is waving his arms,' a deck lookout said.

'They must think we are delivering the powder,' Gill said.

'Let's see what he has to say,' Ralph replied.

The boat got closer, the man on the single stern oar working like a maniac.

'Are you crazeee? Take it to dock over there!'

The man in a long robe shouted and pointed to a block house at the end of the dock.

'No powder near the palace!'

He flapped his hands at the oarsman who turned the boat around and headed back to shore.

There were a few roofs that showed above the wall. Two were obviously mosques as they had tall minarets standing above them. One further back had a gilded dome and was ostentatiously shouting power and wealth.

'Head for that dock as if we are going to moor up,' Ralph ordered.

They passed a large galley with ports for twelve guns a side. There was a ram mounted at the bow. It was anchored fore and aft and had a smaller sixteen-gun galley tied alongside.

'Those are European ships.' Gill pointed to a trio of caravels moored alongside each other a cable away.

Ralph scanned them with a glass. 'They have been modified. They have extra gun ports and, by the look of it, installed some nine-pounders.'

'I wonder if they reinforced her knees?' Gill said.

'If they haven't the recoil will rip them apart.'

'Look at the ports. They have just been sawn through. They haven't even fitted covers.' Gill took the glass and confirmed Ralph's observation.

'I would thrash our carpenter if he did such a shoddy job,' Ralph said.

They were closing with the dock and a few grinning Arabs appeared from the block house followed by a line of slaves. Slave masters used whips to keep them in line.

'Good God, they are almost all European!' Ralph said.

The two looked at each other. Dare they?

'If we kill all the guards quickly, we could rescue the slaves and be away before the Arabs know what's going on,' Gill said.

'Which is against our orders to not get into combat.' Ralph fumed. This was one frustrating trip.

'But we can't just leave them there!'

'We will have to, or we will be chased back to Naples and that is not what the Captain wants.

'Bear away, helm, we have seen enough.' He paused as a thought occurred to him. 'But they will chase us anyway if we do that because they will want their powder.'

'Avast that, take us to the dock. Gill, get a team together armed with knives and clubs. I want all the Arabs put out of action as soon as the slaves come aboard to unload us.'

They used the oars to put themselves alongside the dock and men jumped to tie them on. Except they didn't, they only looped the cables around the bollards and held them.

A gangplank was lowered, and Gill gestured for the slaves to come aboard. They were a pitiful bunch and shuffled up the gang plank. The slave master's whips cracked, and a slave cried out. When most were aboard, Gill shouted, 'NOW.' Men vaulted the side and attacked the slave masters and overseers, knocking them to the ground and tying them up.

'You! Get on board now!' Gill shouted at the last line of slaves.

Aware that they had a chance for freedom, they rushed the gangplank, causing a jam as they fought each other to get aboard. Gill laid about them with a rope end until he had restored a semblance of order. The last man came aboard. Several fell to the deck crying.

'Cast off!' The men ashore leaped back on the ship.

'Get those men below where they can't be seen!' Ralph shouted.

'Man the oars; get us out of here.'

They rowed away from the dock, making as direct a line out of the bay as they could. As soon as they had wind, they raised the sails. The problem was it was a levanter and blowing due west.

'We need to get further out! We need to pick up the mistral and easterly current,' the master said.

They reached the open sea and headed north-west to cross the wind and current. No one pursued them and they had the opportunity to feed and water the slaves.

Ralph walked amongst them. There were Spaniards, Genoans, Venetians, French, British and Irish. He stopped to talk to a Welshman.

'When were you taken?'

'They raided our village two year ago now. We was just simple fishermen, wasn't we. Stood no chance. Took everybody. Men, women, and children. I don't know what happened to my wife and kids.'

He heard similar stories from other men but then came across a sailor.

'They took our ship two months ago; she was one of those caravels.' They made us cut new gun ports and enlarge the old ones. Then they armed them with eighteen-pound culverins.'

'Is that all they did? They didn't strengthen the deck or knees?' Ralph asked.

'No and we didn't tell them they needed to either.'

'What do you think will happen when they fire the guns?'

'The first couple of shots will be alright, but the anchor points will pull up the planking and the knees will give way.'

An hour's sailing later there was a cry from the mainmast lookout. 'Sir, there be sails behind us on the horizon.'

'What is it?'

'Lateen sails at least two of them.'

'That'll be Abdula Mohamad, he was our owner,' said one of the slaves. 'He has the fastest dhows in Algeria. He's lost face. He will be looking to kill everybody because of it.'

'What is their armament?'

'A pair of twenty-four-pound cannon in the bow, but that is not how they fight. Each boat carries a hundred men. They will get alongside and swarm you.'

'We have fought them before and won.'

'How?'

'By fighting dirty.'

# A Dirty Fight

'How many of you men can shoot?' Ralph called to the thirty odd former slaves that sat around on the deck. Several of the slaves translated it to the rest.

A dozen or so put their hands up.

'How many can throw a ball? You lot who can shoot put your hands down.'

Almost all of the rest raised their hands. One man sat looking confused.

'What is the matter with him?'

'He is deaf,' a boy told him.

Ralph went over and crouched in front of him. The man looked at him quizzically. Ralph mimed shooting; the man grinned when Ralph pointed to him and gave him a questioning look. He nodded and grinned showing he was missing teeth.

'Bring me one of our new weapons and its loading materials,' Ralph called. A sailor came and handed him a gun. It was a blunderbuss. Its fourteen-inch-long barrel had a one inch bore and flared out to two inches at the muzzle. It had a flintlock action and a brass bound stock. Ralph handed the man the gun, powder horn and bag with shot and wads.

'Go ahead try it,' he said.

The man pulled himself to his feet. He checked the flint, sparking it. He pulled the hammer to half cock, primed the pan and flipped the frizzen plate down to cover it. Then he placed the gun butt down on the deck before pouring a measure of powder down the barrel followed by a wad. The bag contained thirty calibre buckshot. He took a small handful and dropped them down the barrel followed by another wad. Instead of ramming the load, he tapped the butt firmly, twice on the deck, before bringing it to his shoulder and pulling the hammer to full cock.

He looked at Ralph who nodded. Aiming it out to sea, he leaned forward, right leg advanced, and pulled the trigger.

Woof, bang! The gun fired. Its recoil was ferocious, but he absorbed it and came to attention like a soldier with the gun held slanted across his chest.

'Well done!' Ralph applauded and slapped him on the back.

'You gunners will practise loading and firing in the way our friend here just demonstrated. If he corrects you do as he says; he is army and knows what he is doing.'

Ralph turned to the man who pointed to himself and said, 'Jed,' in a strange voice. 'Jed, train them,' he said as clearly as he could. Jed watched his lips and nodded.

Ralph grinned and patted his shoulder, then turned to the rest of the men. 'You all say you can throw a ball.' He walked across the deck to where he had placed a crate. He opened it and reached inside. He lifted out a dull metal sphere with a fuse sticking out the top.

'This is a grenade. Light this fuse and when it burns halfway down, toss it into the pirate's ship where it will explode, killing several of them.'

He picked up a burning slow match and blew on it before applying it to the fuse. He walked slowly to the side as it burned down. It burned down to halfway and he cast his eye over the men around him. Most looked concerned; some had backed away. He spun and threw it as hard as he could. It exploded in the air some forty feet away.

'You will all be given two. You light them from the slow match stored over water buckets on the centreline. When giving the command, 'GRENADES!' you will light the fuse, walk to the side and toss the grenade into any pirate boat that is alongside. Then you will go back to the centreline and get ready to do it again. Let's try it.'

He got them lined up down the centre line and had them mime carrying a grenade.

'Grenades!' he shouted.

They mimed lighting the fuse.

'STOP!' They stood looking confused.

'What did you do wrong?'

A boy stepped forward. 'They didn't blow on the match.'

'Correct! Start again.'

'Grenades!'

The line mimed picking up and blowing on a match, then applying it to a fuse. They walked forward to the side and tossed the imaginary grenade. Then most of them walked back to the centre line. All except one. The boy, who stood staring over the side.

Ralph walked up to him and put his arm around his shoulder. 'What are you looking at?' he asked quietly.

'I'm watching them die; they raped and killed my mother. She was pregnant at the time. They made me and my father watch.' The boy had tears running down his face.

'What happened to you father?'

'I don't know. I haven't seen him since then.'

'We will kill them all,' Ralph promised him.

The Femke prepared for a fight. The dhows were catching them fast, being better sailors with the wind on their quarters. Even with the wind on her stern the Femke wouldn't outrun them. Nets of musket balls were brought up on deck and hung on hooks between the guns. The former sailor walked over to Ralph and Gill. 'How will we fight?'

'The first round we fire is at fifty yards and is a ball with a net of these on top. The second round we fire is a pair of nets at twenty feet. Right down into their boats. After that it's up to you lot with the blunderbusses and grenades. What's left after that, we fight the old way,' Ralph said.

'We stand a chance then.'

'I bloody hope so.'

Ralph stretched the chase out for as long as he could to give the men time to train with the new tactics, but the inevitable came. The two dhows were no more than a quarter mile behind when they fired their cannon. The balls, all four of them, missed by yards, but the fire served to fire up the pirates, who climbed the sides and waved their weapons.

'Everybody ready?' Ralph bellowed and got a unified shout back. His sail handlers clued up the mains and the rate of closure increased dramatically as their speed suddenly dropped. That was designed to upset the pirate's timing as they came alongside quicker than they expected.

'Guns, FIRE AS YOU BEAR!'

The nine-pounders barked and as soon as they were still from the recoil the crews were reloading. For speed they didn't swab, taking the risk of a premature detonation.

Ralph watched as the dhows took the first rounds. All hits as far as he could see. The one on the starboard side was holed in half a dozen places. The larboard dhow hung back after the first broadside, which was not what Ralph wanted.

The starboard guns fired again. Half of their men were dead and the dhow was full of holes. Yet still they closed. They were almost alongside when he shouted, 'GRENADES.'

A couple of slaves stood too terrified to move. Most went through the drill. One couldn't get his fuse to light. The rest walked forward and tossed their grenades down into the ship as it got within a few feet. The blunderbuss men followed them. Even with the carnage they caused, there were still enough pirates left to cause them trouble and they started coming over the side. Now it was up to the starboard watch and their soldiers to repel them.

Ralph glanced around. The other dDhow was coming in. He didn't need to tell the gunners what to do, but he did need to tell the slaves. He ran down the line turning them around and making sure they had their grenades ready.

Behind him, the blunderbuss men were reloading.

Abdula Mohamed was captaining the second boat himself and saw some of the damage the Femke had done to the other ship. His own had been pierced with shot and he had seen men shredded. 'Allah, welcome their souls to paradise,' he said and touched his heart.

He waited until the crew of the first dhow was alongside and boarding before making his approach. The Dutch ship had slowed and was only making a couple of knots. He angled in to make contact closer to the stern to avoid their guns, then slid his hull along theirs under their guns.

'Guns! Maximum depression!' Ralph ordered each gun in turn as he ran down the line. The noise of the hand-to-hand fighting behind him made it impossible to shout orders and be heard.

The noise of the dhow scraping along the side was loud and pirates started coming over the side. Ten were on deck before the first gun fired. Ralph drew his sword and there was a bang from his right. The middle of the group was cut down. Jed had stepped up and fired into the middle of them. He dropped the empty blunderbuss and grabbed a boarding pike.

Side by side the two advanced and engaged the pirates. Just as Ralph crossed swords with the first, he heard a young voice shout, 'GRENADES.'

He and Jed killed the four remaining pirates then turned to help out in the general melee that was covering the deck.

Jed gripped his arm and pointed to a man in a red robe with a golden cord around his headdress. Ralph realised that it must be Abdula. A slave threw himself at him only to be brutally dispatched by the pirate's scimitar.

'Abdula, you scurvy dog!' Ralph shouted.

The man slowly turned to face him. With a jet-black goatee and moustache, dark eyes and a hooked nose he looked the part.

He raised his scimitar and advanced. Ralph drew his dagger and twirled his sword before slashing down with an overhead attack. The scimitar came up to parry, but then Abdula stopped, his eyes wide.

His mouth opened in a silent scream as the point of a boarding pike appeared from his chest.

Ralph expected to see Jed appear as the pirate folded to the deck but what he saw astonished him. It was the young boy with Jed standing behind him.

Abdula wasn't dead. He tried to struggle to his feet but only managed to get to his knees. Ralph gave the boy his dagger. He showed him where to place it and, as Abdula knelt on the deck, Ralph guided the boy's hand, pushing the dagger home, down through the shoulder into the lungs. Blood gushed out of Abdula's mouth as he drowned in his own blood.

The fight was over. They threw the dead and wounded pirates into their ships and set fire to them. Sharks gathered looking for an easy meal. They hadn't got away scot-free. Almost half of the slaves had perished along with seven of his crew. There were a dozen wounded, four mortally.

Ralph was bone tired. The adrenaline that had sustained him during the battle had worn off, but his first concern was his ship and crew. They had no prisoners. The pirates either jumped overboard or threw themselves on their own swords rather than be taken. Their wounded cut their wrists unless the slaves got to them first when they were hacked to pieces.

His ship was a charnel house and he wanted it clean before he rested. The deck was sluiced down to remove blood and body parts. Then he had the men holystone it to remove the stains and flog it with mops to dry it.

They found the mistral and turned for Tunis. The sun set and Ralph collapsed onto his cot. His last thought before he fell asleep was that the pillow still smelled of her.

He awoke refreshed an hour before dawn. He went on deck and

stretched, enjoying the morning air. The slaves were asleep on deck, and he moved through them to find the young boy. He was sitting practising tying a knot. Ralph sat beside him.

'Who showed you that?'

'Alex, the one who used to be a sailor.'

'That's a bowline. Do you know any others?'

'I can do a clove hitch, a reef knot and a round turn and two half hitches.'

'What's your name?' Ralph asked.

'Tim.'

'Well, Tim, you know almost all the knots that a sailor needs.'

'I want to be a sailor.'

'Can you read?'

'I was going to school before we came here.' He sniffed as the memory of his family returned. 'I can read and do my numbers.'

'I think you would make a fine sailor, even an officer.'

'How am I going to do that?'

'By joining my crew. I lost men during the fight, and I will offer to take on any of the men we freed who want to join.'

The sun poked its nose over the horizon and Ralph stood. 'Come with me.' He led Tim to the quarterdeck. 'This is where we run the ship from. The men call it officer country. It is the Captain's domain, especially the windward side. You do not approach him without permission. The man on the tiller is the helmsman.'

Ralph looked down and saw the intensity with which Tim was listening.

'If I take you on as a midshipman, it will set you on the road to being an officer someday. Would you want that? It will be hard work and you will need to learn a lot.'

'Does that mean I can kill pirates?'

'You will fight all of the King's enemies.'

'Then yes, I want it.'

Gill had come on deck and heard the last part of the conversation.

'Is he our new mid?'

'Aye, he will be entered into the books,' Ralph replied.

'What's yer name? Gill asked.

'Tim.'

'Is that Timothy?'

'Yes, Timothy Marchant.'

A search of the hold turned up some clothes which were distributed amongst those who signed on. After that, what was left was given to those that didn't.

'Alex will be your sea daddy and teach you how to reef, steer and splice. I will teach you mathematics, Latin and Greek. The master will teach you navigation.'

Tim stood taking in every word. He was dressed in new clothes and had been given a dirk as a symbol of his newfound rank.

They looked into the Bay of Bejaia, noted what ships were moored where and left before they could be approached. Ralph studiously avoided making contact with any ships now, aware he was in enough trouble. The next stop was Skikda which sat at the bottom of a huge bay that was unnamed on the chart. Apart from a few small dhows there was nothing there.

Tunis was the last stop.

'What can you see?' Ralph called up to the lookout.

There was a long pause and he was about to shout again when the lookout reported, 'There's half a dozen large galleys, a few feluccas, a dozen or so dhows and two carracks in the inner harbour.'

Ralph noted that on the slate used for the running log and was about to order a change of course when the lookout shouted, 'One of the feluccas is coming out and heading our way.'

'Steer north by east. Man the oars!'

The wind was light and from the north-west. Ralph set a fast stroke rate, wanting to get over the horizon and away from any pursuit. His course should take them close to Messina on the island of Sicily, and from there straight to Naples.

The closer they got to Messina the more the wind swung around to the south-west until it was close enough to a stern wind to pull in the oars and just go with sails.

# A Brief Reunion

They pulled into Naples to see the Kingfisher on the careening beach. Men were burning weed and barnacles off her bottom. A boat came out with a message from Captain Kempthorne for Ralph to report to him at a local osteria.

'Mr Marchant, you will accompany me. Bring the boat around and get it manned.'

'Aye, aye, sir.' Tim replied, quite the sailor.

'He's shaping up right proper,' Gill said as Ralph collected his written reports and put on his best coat.

'I just hope the Captain accepts him,' Ralph said.

'He will, he is always looking for good youngsters.'

The Captain had taken rooms in a seafront osteria. Ralph and Tim were shown to them by a servant girl.

'Mr Wrenn, welcome back, and who is this?'

'Thank you, sir. May I present Mr Timothy Marchant who I would like to put forward as a midshipman.'

'Would you now.'

'Aye, sir. He can read, write and is picking up navigation like he was born to it.'

'And where did you find this prodigy?'

'That, sir, is a long story. May he retire?'

'Mr Marchant, please be so kind as to go downstairs and introduce yourself to the other midshipmen. They are probably in the bar.'

Ralph supressed a grin; his boy had been accepted.

'You will of course be responsible for him and cover his expenses.' The urge to grin disappeared.

'Aye, sir, I will sponsor him,' Ralph said, grateful he had diverted some funds from a previous capture.

'Good, now tell me this long story.'

Ralph made his report. The Captain listened silently until he'd finished, then sat with his fingers steepled under his chin.

'Let me get this clear. You went into the Port of Algeria, against my orders, rescued slaves, also against my orders, and then had to fight two dhows full of pirates also against my orders. On top of that you lost half the slaves in the fight and seven of our men. Which you claim to have replaced with volunteers from the freed captives.'

'Aye, sir. When you put it like that you are quite correct.'

'I know I am, I'm a captain and we always are.'

'Aye, sir.'

The Captain looked at him for what felt like an age; finally, he opened his report. He examined the sketches and the detailed description of the ports of Algiers and Tunis.

'On the other hand, you have brought a very detailed account of Algiers, what ships are in harbour and their fortifications. Added to that, statements from the slaves giving us some inside information into the activities of at least one of the pirate captains. You also reduced their number by around a hundred men and two ships.'

Ralph said nothing.

'I think the scales are evenly balanced. You have gotten away with it this time, young man. Now go and see to those captives who did not volunteer. They have to be sent home somehow.'

*I see. I freed them, so I get to nurse them,* Ralph thought but he kept his expression strictly neutral as he about-faced and left.

Once the door closed, Kempthorne chuckled, and Felton came in from the dining room.

'If that had been any other officer on this ship, I would have said he was telling a fairy tale,' the first lieutenant said, grinning as he picked up the report from the desk.

'Yes, by God, he is a fighting officer with initiative as well.'

'Do we leave him in charge of the Femke?'

'For the time being; I have another task for him but first let him have a couple of nights in port.'

'With his Spanish girl? He's a lucky git as well.'

'You're just jealous. Mind you she is a tasty morsel if ever I saw one.'

Ralph found Tim with Barnes and Smythe. They were sitting at a table with beers in front of them. He joined them.

'How has your education been progressing in my absence?' he asked.

'Mr Twelvetrees has been teaching us, sir.'

'Has he recovered from his wound?'

'He lost his hand, sir. It got the rot, and he now has a hook instead. He is back on duty though.'

That pushed Ralph back to fourth lieutenant and Highcliffe back to midshipman.

'Mr Marchant, you will stay with me on the Femke until I re-join the Kingfisher. Remain with these two reprobates for now and the three of you stay out of trouble. Be back on the Femke by nine o'clock this evening.'

'Where will you be, sir?' Barnes asked with a mischievous grin.

'That, young man, is none of your business,' Ralph replied and feigned a swipe at his ear as he got up to leave. He held out a small pouch of coins to Tim. 'Get yourself some new clothes; Highcliffe knows what you need, and I will hold him responsible if you don't get the right items or poor quality. I will be back aboard on the morrow and will want to see what my money was spent on.'

With that he left.

'Where is he going?' Tim asked the grinning mids.

'Don't you know? He's got a princess tucked away in the town. He visits her with his condiom.'

'Condiom?'

'Don't you know anything? They's to stop the girl getting a bun in the oven.'

'She be a real beauty and deadly. I heard she's a spy,' Smythe chirped conspiratorially.

'I'd love to see her,' Tim said.

'Come on then,' Barnes said, 'we can follow him.'

Ralph walked to the piazza and knocked at the door. The old woman answered and shook her head, denying him entrance.

'Is she not here?' he asked, in broken Italian.

The old woman shrugged and closed the door.

'She was saying that I am not at home,' Maaike said from behind him.

'What? How long have you been there?'

'Long enough. Have you had breakfast?'

'Will you cook me one?'

'No, you can buy me one.'

They walked together to a café that was part of a bakery and sat at a table on the street. Maaike ordered sfogliatelle and zeppole served with freshly squeezed orange juice. The sweet pastries were still warm and delicious.

'How was your mission?' she asked.

'I'm afraid I exceeded my orders and am now in trouble.'

'How?'

He told her an exaggerated tale and made her laugh with his embellished version of rescuing the captives.

'You didn't get to talk to the Sultan?'

'That was my other failure. I sacrificed the chance to meet him for the rescue.'

'What flag were you flying during all of this?'

The question surprised him, and he had to think. 'Dutch, we were flying the Dutch flag; I completely forgot to change it.'

'Then they will believe the Dutch have double crossed them?'

Ralph's eyebrows shot up in realisation. 'Why I believe they will.'

Maaike smiled then frowned as she looked across the street. 'Are you expecting company?'

'No, why?' Ralph answered. 'Let me guess. Three young midshipmen.'

'Yes, sat at the osteria two doors down pretending not to be watching us.'

'They are supposed to be shopping for clothes for my new mid, but the temptation to see you must have been too much.'

She grinned devilishly. 'Well then, let's give them something to chat about.'

She stood, moved around the table and sat on his lap. She gave him a smouldering look and planted a lingering kiss on his lips. She pulled back, her eyes full of promise, then stood and walked across the road to the boys who looked at her sheepishly.

'I think you will find that the gentleman's tailor is two streets over in that direction. We are going to my rooms where we will spend the afternoon making love.' She smiled before returning to Ralph.

'What did you say to them?'

'That we would spend the afternoon making love.'

'That will be all around the ship by the time I return. However, first I need to organise some transport for the freed captives.'

She pouted before saying brightly, 'Uncle can help with that.'

They walked to the palace and were ushered inside without hesitation this time. A footman showed them to an anteroom. 'The Viceroy is in conference. I will fetch you when he is free.'

They drank water flavoured with lemons from the Amalfi coast and chilled with ice brought from the Alps. *That must cost a fortune!* Ralph thought. An hour later the footman reappeared.

'The Viceroy will see you now,' he said, and led them to the throne room. Ralph bowed and Maaike curtsied.

'Please make yourselves comfortable,' the Viceroy said. They sat together on a settee that appeared to have been brought in just for them. 'What do you two youngsters want from me today?'

'Uncle, Ralph has rescued some slaves from Algiers, and he needs to get them home.'

'How did you come by these people?'

Ralph wasn't about to give a full report to someone his Captain clearly treated with suspicion, so he gave an abbreviated version of the one he had given Maaike earlier.

'Your desire to help the captives is laudable; how many need transport?'

'There are three Spaniards, a Greek, two English and a Sicilian. The English I can place on a British merchantman, but I have no connections to Spanish or Greek ships.'

'Ships of all nations visit here. As a gesture of good will towards the British, I will fund their passage.' He pulled a bellpull that hung beside the throne. A clerk appeared, his hands stained with ink, and the Viceroy talked to him in Spanish. The man set up his table, wrote three notes and passed them to the Viceroy.

'Give these to the captives. They are promissory notes to the captain that takes them, that we will cover the cost of their passage.'

*Very generous considering four of them are your people,* Ralph thought but he kept a smile on his face as he took them.

They spent a few more minutes chatting, then were dismissed.

Ralph wanted to get the notes to the captives himself so he headed towards the osteria they were staying in at his expense. He handed them the notes, which they were all fawningly grateful for. That left the British captive whose name was Simon Westbury.

Ralph led Maaike and Simon to another taverna where British captains traditionally met up. He spotted Captain Allen of the Cynthia and approached him.

'Mr Wrenn, nice to see you. Who is this delectable beauty?' he said with a leer, ignoring Simon completely.

'Maaike de Benavidas, niece of the Viceroy of Naples.'

The leer faded.

'My pleasure, madam.' He turned back to Ralph. 'What can I do for you?'

'Do you know of any ships going to England in the near future?'

'The Lady of Poole is leaving tomorrow I believe. Why?'

'Simon here was a slave who we freed from the Algerians. I want to purchase passage for him to England.'

Allen looked Simon up and down, noting the visible scars from his slave shackles.

'Where are you from?'

'Looe in Cornwall. They raided our village.'

'How long were you a slave?'

'Must be close to ten years now.'

'Good God,' Allen said and stood. 'Come, let us away to get you home.'

He took them to a dock where a carrack was finishing loading. He hailed the Captain from the side.

'Ahoy, John. Have you a moment?'

'Allen! Come aboard!'

They walked up the gangplank and were taken down to his cabin where he served them wine.

'So, you need this fellow taken back to England. He can work his passage,' John said.

'I can pay for it,' Ralph insisted.

'No need for that, sir, you done enough with getting me free. I be 'appy to work my way 'ome,' Simon said.

'We will drop you off at Looe; it's on our way,' John said, clapping Simon on the back.

Ralph sighed. 'Alright if that's what you want to do.'

'He can start now unless he has some things to collect,' John said.

'No, all I 'ave is on me back. What about the osteria?'

'I'll take care of that,' Ralph said.

Simon turned and shook his hand. 'Thankee, sir. If I were younger, I would have signed up on yer ship but all I wants is to go 'ome.'

'I understand, Simon. Fairwinds and I hope you find your family when you get there.'

Back in Maaike's apartments he lay looking at the ceiling. They had made love and she had been to order lunch from the servants.

'What is the English expression? A sixpence for your thoughts?'

'A penny for them. I'm not that costly.'

'What were you thinking about?'

'That I have been lucky so far, and that I have pushed my luck hard.'

'That is the tradition of the English sailor, no?'

'To act with dash and zeal. Yes, it is, but I took it too far.'

'It is what makes you who you are.'

'Maybe, but does it make me my own worst enemy?'

She loosened her robe and climbed on the bed beside him, determined to take his mind off what bothered him.

They woke the next morning to knocking at the door.

'Mr Wrenn, sir. It's Tim Marchant. The Captain wants to see you.'

Ralph groaned and sat up. Maaike sighed. She'd thought she would have him for another day.

The knocking came again. 'I heard, Mr Marchant!' Ralph said. 'Damn and blast, he told me I would have two days ashore,' he said more quietly.

He dressed and she helped tie the laces on his shirt. Her nipples brushed his chest.

'Are you sure you want to go?'

'Get thee behind me, witch.' He laughed.

He buckled on his sword belt then grabbed her, kissing her on the lips. 'I will see you later.'

'Now, Mr Marchant, what is so urgent that you disturb my shore leave.'

Tim didn't answer; he was standing with his mouth open and eyes wide. A semi-naked Maaike was fully visible through the open door. Ralph shook his head and closed it. He clipped the boy's ear.

'Pay attention. What does the Captain want me for?'

'He has a mission for us.' Tim said, rubbing his ear.

'Well, let's not keep him waiting. Lead on!'

Kempthorne was in his rooms and as Ralph entered he caught a glimpse through the half open door of the comely barmaid sprawled naked on his bed.

'Mr Wrenn, I trust you slept well.'

'On and off, sir,' Ralph said with a completely straight face.

'Good, I have a mission for you. Those two carracks you spotted in Tunis harbour had no flags?'

'No, sir, we think they were prizes.'

'I want them either burned or brought back here.'

'Sir?' Ralph said, wondering how his crew could manage the latter.'

'You will choose an extra thirty crew and twenty soldiers from the Kingfisher. It will be crowded on the Femke but it will give you the hands to cut at least one of them out.'

'Thank you, sir.'

'Take Mr Highcliffe with you; he needs the experience.'

Ralph took that as his dismissal and turned to leave. As he closed the door, he saw the Captain advancing on his bedroom undoing his breeches as he went.

* * *

Highcliffe was waiting below with Tim.

'Where are the crew of the Kingfisher staying while she is being cleaned?' asked Ralph.

'All over, sir. Mainly osterias and brothels.'

Ralph sat and came up with a list of names of the crew he wanted. He handed it to Highcliffe. 'Find those men and tell them to report to the Femke immediately.'

He turned to Tim and looked him up and down. His new uniform looked clean and well brushed.

'I want you to find Sergeant McDonald. Tell him I want him and a platoon of his soldiers on the Femke by sundown.'

Ralph went to a ship's chandlers. He walked around the store until he found what he wanted, lamp oil. He bought twenty demijohns and had them taken by handcart to the dock. He whistled to the Femke and they sent a boat over.

'Get that oil stowed in the hold on top of half a dozen barrels of powder, then get the ship ready to take on an extra fifty men.'

'What's afoot?' Gill asked.

'We have a mission.'

'Already?'

'The Captain is a busy man.' Ralph smirked.

'So I'm told.' Gill smirked back. Apparently, everyone knew about the barmaid.

'Get the ship ready to sail.'

'Aye, aye, sir!'

The search for the sergeant took Tim to places he would never have normally gone to. He found two soldiers in an osteria who told him that the sergeant was in a brothel just off the waterfront. He approached the building curiously. He had heard about brothels of course but had never experienced entering one.

He approached the door tentatively. It was covered by a curtain. He looked for something to knock on and, finding nothing, he pulled the curtain aside and stuck his head inside. It was very dim and as his eyes adjusted, he saw shapes moving; he recognised they were people doing all manner of things.

He saw a man with tattoos like many of their soldiers. He was busy with a girl who was on her hands and knees in front of him. His hairy backside pounding away like, well he didn't know what. The man grunted and the girl collapsed face down.

'Sergeant McDonald?' Tim said tentatively.

'What do you want?' the sergeant said in a Scottish brogue.

'Mr Wrenn's compliments and you are to report to the Femke with a platoon of men by sundown.

'Am I? Nightfall you say? Well, I've worn this one out, and I don't fancy any of the others.'

He dressed.

'Come on then, let's go find my boys.'

The sergeant was a huge bear of a man. Tim noted that he was at least six feet tall, much taller than most of the men he knew. His chest was like a barrel and made up of slabs of muscle. His arms were like most men's thighs, his thighs like a bull.

The girl cast Tim a grateful look and winced as she rolled to sit up. Another girl came and put an arm around her. She didn't weep but she looked like she wanted to.

They exited the brothel into the late afternoon sunshine. McDonald led him to a series of bars and cheaper brothels collecting men as he went. They marched to the warehouse where the Kingfisher's stores and the men's personal goods were kept and retrieved their weapons and armour.

Peter Highcliffe had a harder job, having to find thirty named men on his own. He had a bit of luck and found a dozen having a rowdy party in a bar not far from the beach the Kingfisher was careened on. Getting them to go to the Femke was harder and he threatened several with a flogging if they didn't obey. That didn't work so he went to another bar where a group of bosun's mates were having a, not so quiet, drink. They were only mildly drunk, and he managed to convince them that he was acting under Captain Kempthorne's orders. One of their names was on the list to the great amusement of his fellows.

The four mates were more than a match for the delinquents in the bar. Davy Cooper, called out names and the other three got them lined up. They now had twelve including the mate. Questioning the men got them several potential locations for the rest.

'It be just like the press,' one man complained.

'If I'd pressed you, you would have a lump on your head from my stick.' Cooper snarled at him.

The next stop was a brothel and a team led by Cooper entered. There was a shout, and a sailor came out backwards, arms flailing, landing in a heap. Three more men followed, one with his trousers around his ankles. Whores laughed and threw insults from the upstairs windows. One hung out, showing her breasts and jiggling her assets making young Peter blush. A tour of the seafront bars found the rest who came relatively quietly.

# Fire Ship

The next morning overmanned and stocked with flammables, the Femke left the Bay of Naples. This time they turned south past the island of Capri and followed the coast. A day and a half later they came to the Messina Strait. Not trusting the wind, Ralph took to the oars. As he had so many men and they needed work, he changed rowers every two hours.

The Bay of Tripoli lay two hundred- and eighty-five-miles due south once they reached the island of Capopassero with its distinctive fort. The fort, built just ninety years before, was well armed and manned by the Neopolitan army to combat the ever-present threat of the Barbary pirates. Ralph thought it a waste of time.

The wind wasn't a rank muzzler but too fine on the bow for the galiote to sail against. Ralph had sufficient men to put them two to an oar and still run two watches. He put the mids on each watch to manage the stroke. The added beef had them cutting through the water at eight knots which was excellent progress. They would be rowing four on four off for thirty-two hours.

After sixteen hours, a storm came up and the men got a break as the best they could do was sit tight and ride it out. It was impossible to row as the ship pitched and rolled. The wind swung from south to east to north in six hours. The good thing was with the wind from a point or two east of north they could sail south. The bad thing was they had no idea where they were. The sky was obscured by cloud and there was no way they could take a sun or star shot.

'Land Ho!'

'Where away?'

'Off the starboard bow.'

Ralph went to the chart where the master was already poring over it.

'Any idea where that could be?' Ralph asked.

'Well, as we were blown north and west my guess is Malta. Wherever it is we need to keep heading south.'

They passed a French caravel and hailed them.

'Well, that answers that. Malta it is,' Ralph said.

'Is that what he said? I couldn't understand a word of it.' Gill snorted.

'The skipper was probably from Marseille; they have a strong dialect, but he said it was Malte which is what the French call Malta.' Ralph laughed.

'I didn't know you spoke French.'

'I can get by, but that's about all. My Italian is better having been taught Latin.'

Two hours later the crew were back on the oars. A day later they were off the coast of North Africa near to Sharqi Island. The current had carried them further west than they had anticipated.

'We will work our way along the coast until we reach this headland where we will wait so we can time our attack on Tunis to be at false dawn,' Ralph told his assembled officers crowded around a chart.

'Good idea,' the master said. 'Which ship of the two will we take?'

'Both if they are still there,' Ralph said.

'But we don't have the men to take both carracks and sail the Femke.'

'He isn't taking the Femke back. Are you skipper?' Gill said who was attending even though he wasn't officially an officer.

'You know me too well, Gill. No, she will sacrifice herself so we can get the other two ships away,' Ralph replied.

Gill looked at the master who seemed baffled. 'That's what all the lamp oil is for. To turn this into a fire ship,' he said.

The master was aghast. 'Burn her?'

Ralph looked at him. 'Prithee, what is worth more? A carrack and a galiote or two carracks?'

'Two carracks, especially if they are fitted out as men o' war.'

'Exactly,' Ralph said, ending the discussion.

'The last time we were here, the two carracks were moored alongside each other, here in Tunis inner harbour,' Ralph explained to the gathered men. He had sketched a map of the bay and the inner harbour on a slate and pointed to the spot with his dividers.

'If they are still there, we will pull alongside them and, except for me and my chosen men, we will board, capture, and prepare both ships to sail. Mr Highcliffe will command one with Gill as his second.' Ralph looked at the beaming mid. 'Listen to Gill, Mr Highcliffe. He has vastly more experience than you.' He turned to Tim. 'Mr Marchant, you will be my second. Mr Highcliffe has the lists of who will be on which ship. Take everything with you along with all the stores from the Femke. We cannot assume the carracks are in any way ready for sea.'

He looked around the assembled faces. There were no questions and no expressions of doubt.

'Good, while you are doing that, me and my men will sail the Femke into the largest collection of ships in the harbour and set her afire. We will have grapnels hanging from the yards and the guns loaded. She should create enough confusion that we can sail our prizes out without interference. Mr Highcliffe, you are not to wait for us but get under sail as soon as you can. Mr Marchant, you will have the second ship ready to sail the moment I set foot on deck.'

'How will you get back to us, skipper?' one of the mates asked.

'I'm touched you care about me,' he jested, eliciting a laugh. 'We will tow the ship's boat and just before the Femke goes up, we will take to it and row back to the carracks. You can all help get the Femke ready.'

The men worked enthusiastically, piling combustible materials into the hold and on deck, attaching grapnels to snag in another ship's rigging to hold her in a death grip and attaching bindings that would hold the tiller when Ralph and the men abandoned her.

It was fifty-five miles, give or take a couple, to the harbour from where they were anchored. They set sail at two bells in the middle watch and turned the corner into the gulf of Tunis at four bells. Right on schedule. After that they had to row. The sky was clear, the Milky Way visible as a smear of stars across the sky.

The wind was very light and from the west. The men put their backs into it and as the first grey light of false dawn stained the eastern horizon, they saw the entrance to the inner harbour. The carracks were where they had seen them before.

Ralph took the helm and pushed the tiller over to steer for the entrance. It was guarded by a fort, but no one showed on the battlements. They passed through, *so far so good.* The harbour was quiet with only the odd fishing boat coming in from a night's fishing. Ralph gave commands sotto voice which were passed to the crew through the mids. The oars dipped and rose slowly to minimise splash. He steered for the ships.

'Oars in.'

The Femke's momentum carried them the last thirty yards and they came alongside.

'Boarders away.'

The men swarmed up the carrack's side, passing sacks and crates up in an organised yet hurried fashion. As soon as they were done, Ralph's men pushed the Femke away into the current. He could hear muffled thuds and grunts as they drifted on the tide past the ships as any crew were taken care of.

'Raise the fore course and spanker.'

With just the two sails set they made enough headway to steer with the slight onshore breeze. The sun peeked over the horizon illuminating the harbour and town. Tunis was fortified with a high wall that ran all the way around it. On the seaward side, merchants and shipwrights had buildings between the wall and the stone dock. Behind the wall, minarets were about all they could see from the deck. Their golden turrets glistened in the early sun.

There were a cluster of dhows and feluccas near the shore but more interesting was a line of four big armed galleys tied up stern on to the dock. He aimed for the gap between the middle two.

'Let go the grapnels.'

The hooks had been tied up so they didn't tangle with the carrack's rigging but now with a tug of a cord they swung free at the end of the yards. Ralph pulled a lanyard and the union jack unfolded on the mainmast.

The wind picked up a little. Ralph adjusted the tiller accordingly.

'Set her afire,' he ordered, and lanthorns were thrown down into the hold where the men had smashed several of the oil jars, igniting it with a whump.

They were a mere hundred yards away.

A head appeared at the bow of the middle galley on the right and looked at them curiously. Ralph waved. The man waved back but the curious look turned to one of alarm as flames and smoke started to come out of the Femke's hold. He started yelling the alarm.

'Bring the boat up,' Ralph ordered and looped the lashings over the tiller. The men pulled it up to the stern and two slid over the rail to man the oars.

'Everybody in.' He did a final check on their heading and all the men were safely down in the boat. Flames were erupting from the hold now and running up the mainmast; they were leaving without a moment to spare. He dropped down into the boat and the men immediately pulled away.

The Femke continued on and moments later slid between the centre two galleys. Men frantically tried to fend her off. She was well ablaze now and that touched off her guns. Splinters flew as the double charged and shotted guns blasted through the hulls of the first two galleys and into the outer pair. Flames leaped across from one ship to the next and men started jumping over the side. All this to the sound of an Iman starting the call to prayer from one of the gilded minarets.

'Wait for it,' Ralph murmured.

Suddenly the Femke seemed to expand then burst as the powder they had stored deep in her hold under all the lamp oil exploded, sending a fireball high into the air. The shock wave pushed their boat along and ruffled Ralph's long hair.

The men were rowing like demons, and they got to their carrack as the other was heading out of the harbour under full sail. Ralph looked back. Not only were the galleys fully ablaze but, as burning timbers landed amongst other ships and the workshops along the wall, fires were erupting everywhere.

They boarded the ship.

'Make sail. Let's get out of here,' Ralph said.

By the time they were underway on the increasing breeze, Tunis harbour was a sea of flame.

'Bugger me, you set fire to the town an' all,' Tim said.

'Looks like it; they should be right angry now, so we need to make all speed.' The sails cracked as they caught the wind. The anchor cable cut to speed their way.

The carracks, like most square-rigged ships, sailed well before the wind and two hours later they could only see smoke behind them. Ralph had the lookouts keeping a watch for pursuit.

They caught up with the other prize. Highcliffe was grinning and waving from the stern. With the breeze on their quarter and the current behind them, Ralph was beginning to think they were home free.

'Sails astern, looks like a half dozen dhows.'

*Bugger*! 'What powder and ball do we have?' Ralph said and walked forward to check on the guns.

The guns were old but serviceable. Stone balls were stacked along the centreline.

'No powder on board, sir, magazine is empty,' Sammy Littleton reported.

Ralph felt a moment of panic, then got a hold of himself.

'Then all these guns are just extra weight. Throw them overboard and the balls.'

Gill saw what they were doing and had Highcliffe follow suit. They were in a foot race. Without the guns they made an extra half knot and Ralph went looking for more things to lose.

Spare spars, anything in the holds, anything that they could do without was jettisoned.

'Wet the sails,' Ralph said. Men filled buckets with sea water and passed them up to men on the yards. They doused the sails.

'What are we making?'

The log was run. 'Ten knots and a fathom, sir.'

That was about as fast as a carrack would go.

'Lookout. What can you see?' Ralph called.

'The lead ships are hull up.'

'How fast are they catching us?'

There was a pause as the lookout assessed them by eye. 'Hardly at all, maybe half a knot.'

'Now we must pray the wind stays on our stern.'

They came in sight of the western tip of Sicily. If they could make a port, they would be safe for the night, or they could carry on and try to make it to the Bay of Naples. Ralph had done the maths and estimated that the dhows were at that moment twenty miles behind and catching at a tad over half a mile an hour. That meant they would need forty hours to catch them. At this speed, they could be in Naples in half that.

They got about halfway. As the sun came up the next morning, the wind veered. Ralph was already on deck. He looked at the pennant which was streaming out to starboard. The wind was almost on their beam.

'Cast the log.'

'Six and a half knots!'

The dhows were far better sailors with this wind.

'Fuck! Lookout, how fast are they catching?'

'Faster, they are all hull up now, maybe two knots.'

'Damn, our safety margin is well gone.'

It would take their pursuers under five hours to catch them at this rate and Naples was still more than ten away.

They had no choice but to stretch out the chase for as long as they could and pray. The glass was turned every half hour and every turn was like the tick of doom. They could see the dhows from the deck now a scant six miles behind. Ralph took a series of sightings and calculated they were catching at just under two knots. They had three hours.

Every eye on the ship was on the dhows. They got close enough to see their crescent flags. Shortly after, they could see men in the rigging, the glint of the sun on steel. A puff of smoke as a gun fired at maximum range, the bang following seconds later. The splash of the shot fifty feet wide and astern.

The distance closed to half a mile. Another shot. Ralph's heart was in his mouth as it landed between the two ships. Surely, they were doomed.

As he stared towards them, heart racing, the dhows suddenly turned away.

'What the hell?' Ralph said.

'It's the Kingfisher!' a man shouted.

Ralph spun and saw the frigate, upper-deck ports open, guns run out, coming towards them under full sail and flying the Neapolitan flag. As she passed, Captain Kempthorne raised his hat. Ralph waved, his knees weak.

Back in the Bay of Naples, Ralph, Gill and the mids reported aboard the Kingfisher. Kempthorne met them on the quarterdeck.

'Mr Wren, welcome back.'

'Only thanks to you, sir. If you hadn't found us in time we would have been scuppered,' Ralph said.

'What would you have done if they had caught you?'

'Fought to the end and burned the ships with them on board.'

'Rather than be captured?'

'Capture means a bad death with the heathens. I would rather die on my own terms.'

There were many calls of 'here, here,' and 'absolutely' from the assembled officers.

'What happened to the Femke?'

'I used her as a fireship to cover the carrack's exit. She took many ships in the harbour with her including four large galleys. She flew the ensign as she went.'

'I will read your report later and sell your prizes. I have engaged an agent in anticipation.'

Kempthorne turned to Gill. 'You are made bosun as a reward for your sterling service to Mr Wrenn.'

Gill tugged his forelock and bowed.

'Sir, may I ask how you found us?'

Kempthorne grinned, making his face look boyish.

'Why it was pure chance. We were shaking the ship down after her clean and refit and heard the gunfire. When we saw two carracks running for their lives, we investigated. Then when we saw they were flying ensigns we knew it had to be you.'

'You were just in time, sir. The shift in the wind nearly did for us.'

'Please join me and the other officers for dinner at seven. Now go and reclaim your berth in the wardroom.'

# Accusations and Recriminations

Life returned to normal aboard the Kingfisher. 1689 was drawing to a close and winter in the Mediterranean was well and truly on them. Successive storms and a westerly wind kept them in port. Ralph picked up the mids education and his friendship with the hook-handed Twelvetrees grew.

The best part of being in port was that he got shore leave once a week and could spend it with Maaike. Just before the end of November on a crisp winter's day they decided to visit Mount Vesuvius.

The climb was steep, and the smell of sulphur was strong. The trail didn't go straight up but rather wound its way around the cone. The volcano was active, and smoke rose from the crater. Every now and then there would be a bang and a bright plume of lava would leap into the air.

It got warmer towards the top as well. He could feel it through his boots. He could also feel the tremors and rumblings of the monster beneath his feet. Swathes of solidified lava crossed the path and lay in fields in the valleys to the side of the cone. Nature was attempting to reclaim them – trees grew, and grasses struggled to get a hold.

The last major eruption had been in 1631 . The volcano had spewed out a huge cloud of pumice, and lava had flowed down the sides destroying a couple of villages. Naples had been untouched apart from the six inches of ash that had landed on it.

They reached the top, and as Ralph's head came above the crater rim it was assailed by a wave of heat. Not the heat of the sun, but the heat of molten rock. Hot enough, he felt, to melt steel. At least as hot as the blacksmiths forge he had worked at during the construction of the Kingfisher.

He looked down into the fires of hell, raging and bubbling red, white and orange. Gobbets of lava flew into the air as bubbles of gas popped. It was a sight he would never forget.

'It's frightening, isn't it?' Maaike said, holding on to his arm.

'Fascinating,' Ralph replied lost in the spectacle.

'Come on, we need to get down before dark and it looks like rain,' she said.

He knew she was right and looked up. He stared in surprise. It was raining but the drops were turning to steam before they hit the ground. It wasn't until they had walked someway down that they started to get wet.

They arrived at the bottom soaking wet and laughing. They ran to their carriage and jumped aboard. The driver set off for the city immediately.

They arrived at the house and were about to climb the steps to the door when an officer of the Neapolitan army and a squad of six soldiers marched up.

'Lieutenant Wren?' the officer asked.

'Yes?'

'You are under arrest and are to come with me.'

'On what charge?'

'You will find out when we get to the palace.'

'You cannot arrest him for no reason,' Maaike said. 'I will talk to my uncle, the Viceroy.'

'You can if you like but he is the one who ordered his arrest.'

Ralph looked at the soldiers; they were all well armed and alert. This had to be a mistake.

'I have done nothing wrong. Maaike, please get word to my Captain.'

He was marched to the palace. They entered through a side door, and he was given a few moments to shed his cloak and hat. His sword and knife were taken, and he was searched for any other weapons. A different officer came with a pair of soldiers in cuirasses carrying pikes. He escorted Ralph to a cell and locked him in.

The cell was ten feet to a side, so not too small. It was clean, with a rug on the floor. It had a bed with linen sheets, a chair, a small table against one wall with a lamp, wash basin and jug, and a second table with a single chair which he assumed was for eating at. The walls were bare stone and the ceiling about ten feet above him was slightly domed. There was a single barred window high up on one wall.

After an hour or so, the officer came in and asked if he'd eaten. He disappeared and ten minutes later a servant was let in with a tray of food. Under a cover was a plate with slow roasted lamb flavoured with marjoram in a rich gravy, roasted potatoes with rosemary and carrots. There was a small jug of wine and another of water.

When he had finished, the same servant came and took the tray away. He noticed there was a guard on the door. Nothing else happened; it was quiet, so he undressed and got into bed.

*Not what I had planned for tonight,* he thought and blew out the lamp.

* * *

He awoke at dawn the next day and washed himself down before dressing. His damp clothes had mostly dried out overnight so they weren't too uncomfortable. He was given breakfast, after which he sat for a while. Bored with that, he lay on the bed counting the stones in the ceiling and watching the sun traverse the wall through the window.

He was anticipating lunch when the door opened, and the officer stepped in.

'Come with me,' is all he said.

Curious to find out what was going on, Ralph followed, and a pair of soldiers fell in on either side of him. They climbed several sets of stairs and walked down several corridors until they came to an area that was familiar.

They entered the throne room. The Viceroy was sitting on his throne and beside him on a comfortable chair was a man in Arabic clothing. They spoke English.

'Is this the man?' the Arab said.

'We believe so, but first the formalities if you don't mind.'

He turned to Ralph.

'Mr Wrenn, this is Murat Reis, a citizen of the Ottoman Empire who has levelled a charge of piracy against you. He maintains that you entered Tunis harbour, stole two of his ships and set fire to another ten and several businesses. Do you admit or deny the charge.'

Ralph thought carefully. If he was handed over to the Ottoman, he could expect a fate worse than death. He was about to answer when the door opened and Captain Kempthorne entered.

'Mr Wrenn is under my command,' he said as he approached and gave the Viceroy a deep bow.

'Your intervention is suspiciously well timed,' Murat Reis said in a voice full of scorn.

'Not at all. I summoned him. If the boy is guilty then his commanding officer must also be guilty,' the Viceroy said.

'Mr Wrenn is a senior mate on the merchantman Kingfisher. He was acting on my orders.'

'You ordered him to attack Tunis?'

'I ordered him to retrieve two British carracks. Which he did.'

'They were my carracks as were two of the galleys and four dhows that he burned.'

'If they were your carracks, why did they still have their British registration papers and manifests in the Captain's desk?'

'Can you prove that?' the Viceroy said.

'Certainly' – Kempthorne pulled a sheaf of papers from his doublet – 'these are the papers we found in the ships.'

'We only have your word for that,' Murat snarled. 'You could have made them yourself.'

'Are you accusing me of forgery?' Kempthorne said quietly.

'I say you would do anything to protect your boy.'

'That sounds awfully like another accusation.' His hand went to the hilt of his sword.

'Gentlemen please, let's keep this civilised.'

Murat tried to change tack. 'We have a treaty with the British. You have no right to attack us.'

Before Kempthorne could answer that, the Viceroy held up his hand.

'Do you have proof that Mr Wrenn set fire to your ships?'

'Proof no, but you heard them admit to taking the carracks.' Murat spat out the words.

'Yes, he did, but he has proof that the ships were British.'

'They are fake or from other ships.'

'They might be, which is why I will have them sent by messenger to London to validate them,' the Viceroy said.

'That will take months!'

'Yes, especially at this time of year. Which brings me to the question of the burning of the ships. Mr Wrenn, did you set fire to Murat Reis's ships?'

Ralph heard Kempthorne mutter, 'Careful.'

Ralph paused, considering his options. He had set fire to the Femke but not directly the Ottoman ships.

'I did not; I set fire to our ship to stop it being used by the Barbary pirates. If she drifted into some other ships, that was not my doing.'

Murat leaped to his feet. 'You deliberately steered your ship into mine!'

'Unless you can provide someone who will swear that under oath there is no proof, and under our law, they would have to swear on a bible which I do not think your man would do,' the Viceroy said.

'No Muslim would ever swear on the book of the infidels.'

'Then at the moment it is your word against Mr Wrenn's.'

'We have a treaty with the British.'

'You had one,' Kempthorne said, 'but since you have regularly taken British ships and raided our towns for slaves, the King has deemed that to be null and void.'

*Bugger, but he looks smug,* Ralph thought.

Murat Reis was furious and exploded when the Viceroy announced that Ralph was free to go due to lack of any evidence. He left talking Arabic and spitting at Kempthorne's feet. The Viceroy was blandly straight faced until he left; then he grinned broadly.

'Well done, Ralph.' He laughed. 'You played that to perfection.'

'What?'

'You didn't expect me to give that pirate anything did you?'

'I...'

'Come, we will go back to the ship,' Kempthorne said.

On their way -out Ralph's weapons were returned. It was late afternoon.

'We missed lunch,' Kempthorne said. 'Are you hungry?'

'Starving if I might say so, sir.'

Kempthorne led him to an eating house and there, sitting at a table, was Maaike.

'You?'

'Uncle Francisco told me what they were going to do.'

'So, the whole meeting with Reis was pre-arranged?'

'Not entirely, we didn't know how you would react.'

'You could have let me in on it.'

'We were not sure you would react properly,' Kempthorne said, patting him on the shoulder.

When they had finished eating, the two men walked back towards the docks. Suddenly Ralph became aware that the road was empty ahead and behind them.

'Captain. Something's wrong.'

As soon as he'd spoken, four men dressed in robes and holding scimitars stepped out into the road ahead of them. A glance over his shoulder showed another three behind them.

'Reis's men no doubt,' Kempthorne said, drawing his sword and main-gauche. Ralph followed suit and moved behind Kempthorne to face the three behind them.

'Let them come,' Kempthorne said.

'A pistol would be useful right now,' Ralph said.

'Didn't bring one, sorry.' Kempthorne laughed.

The pirates moved closer, swords at the ready. Ralph studied his opponents. The one in the middle was a step ahead of his mates and was concentrating on Ralph. The one on his left was moving out to try to attack Ralph's flank. The third was alternately looking at Ralph and looking around as if afraid reinforcements would arrive any second.

Ralph let them get to two sword lengths before stepping forward with a stamp and a shout.

'HAH!' He knocked the leader's sword aside and kicked him in the gut. As he doubled, Ralph swung his dagger and smashed him in the side of the head with the guard. The leader staggered towards the flanking man. Ralph turned on his other, nervous, opponent. He parried a wild swing which put the man off balance. That gave him time to spin and shove the staggering leader into the flanker before turning just in time to parry another swing with his dagger. It was another uncontrolled wisd swing and left his opponent open. He thrust with his sword, which entered the man's throat just below his chin. He twisted and withdrew.

He spun around. The leader had recovered somewhat though blood trickled down his face. The two men advanced, moving apart to divide his defence. He watched them and waited. They started to circle him in opposite directions. He needed to take the initiative.

Ralph stepped back, then suddenly dived between them. The swish as they tried to slash him was loud. He rolled, sword slashing, and came to his feet. The flanker screamed, staggered and dropped to a knee as his right leg gave way. Ralph ignored him and pressed his attack on the leader. Sparks flew from their blades as they parried, cut and thrust.

Ralph stepped back and slipped on the blood from the nervous man. He dropped to a knee and barely got his sword and dagger up in time to block a vicious over hand. His arms quivered as the scimitar was pressed down.

He glanced down and saw a sandaled foot sticking out beneath the robe. He took the risk and pulled his dagger from the block and stabbed down. The man screamed and it went up an octave when Ralph twisted the blade.

The pressure left his sword arm and he brought it around in a slash that took the man across the gut. He staggered back, his intestines spilling out. He fell and landed on his arse cradling his guts in his arms.

Ralph turned to help his Captain and was surprised to see Twelvetrees had joined the fight. Two of the attackers were down and Twelvetrees was showing that he could use his hook effectively as a main-gauche. He trapped his opponent's blade in the hook, twisting it to hold the blade while he thrust his rapier through the man's chest. Blood spewed out of his mouth, and he fell.

A groan behind him, reminded him that two of his opponents were still alive. One was lying on his side gripping his ankle where Ralph's sword had severed his Achilles tendon. The other was sitting in a pool of his own blood holding his guts. Ralph looked at them thoughtfully.

'Nice little fight,' Twelvetrees said as he stepped up beside Ralph.

'Yes, good exercise,.' Ralph said. and decided. He stepped over behind the leader and cut his throat with his dagger.

'Are you going to finish this one?'

'No, I will leave him to the Viceroy.'

City guards finally started to arrive, and they called for men to clear away the offal. The sole survivor was dragged away. The British officers were allowed to return to their ship.

* * *

As the sun rose the next day there was a new addition to the waterfront. A gibbet had been raised. At noon, the sole survivor of the attack on Captain Kempthorne and Ralph was brought forward in chains and raised up onto the gibbet. His body was to be on public display for seven days after he died. It was a clear message to the pirates that such acts would not be tolerated in Naples.

# Christmas in Naples

December came and Maaike took Ralph to the Via San Gregorio Armeno, where artisans made nativity decorations.

'My family are from Spain, and we celebrate Christmas differently but here they celebrate from the conception to Epiphany and the main thing is to have a nativity scene in your house.'

'That's why we are here then, to get you one?'

'To get *us* one.'

She found the shop she was looking for. It had a table outside with complete scenes and baskets of figures. Ralph was surprised that they contained much more than the traditional scenes he was used to in England.

He examined one; it resembled a mountain with a Corinthian column at the top. On the peak were Mary, Joseph, the Three Kings and other main characters. An angel perched on top of the column. The next layer down depicted shepherds and farmers tending a variety of animals. Below them were scholars and philosophers and around the base was a depiction of a market complete with produce, stall holders and customers, a fishing boat and fisherman, and a tavern.

'Good Lord, the work that has gone into this is unbelievable,' he exclaimed.

The artisan came out to talk to Maaike and noticed Ralph's interest.

'He asks if you like it?'

'È meraviglioso, it is wonderful,' Ralph said.

'It is, isn't it,' she said.

'Quanto costa?' Ralph said.

'Dieci ducata.'

That was ten ducats, the equivalent of roughly five sovereigns.

'Troppo, ne pagherò cinque.' Ralph had offered five ducats before Maaike could say anything.

'Aah, mister, you are robbing me. I have a wife and eight children to keep. I couldn't sell it for less than eight.'

'I could go as high as six.'

'Will sir meet me in the middle at seven?'

Ralph held out his hand and the old man shook it.

Maaike looked at him in amazement. 'Where did you learn to barter like that?'

'I don't spend all my time on a ship you know. Anyway, you will have to pay him; I don't have that much.'

She reached into her purse and paid the man who asked where it should be delivered. He asked her to choose a figure of the infant Jesus which should be added on Christmas day and gave it to her as a gift.

Having made their purchase, they stopped at a market and bought bows of evergreen trees and dried flowers and herbs. They returned to the house to find the nativity scene had already been delivered to the approval of the old lady.

The afternoon was taken up with decorating the apartment and making love. That evening Maaike insisted they attend Mass. Ralph felt awkward attending a Catholic church as he was Anglican high church, but he sat through the service and was struck with the similarities rather than the differences. The incense and the body and blood of Christ. One major difference was the quality of the wine. The one used was a high-quality local wine.

*No wonder there is such a queue for it,* he thought.

Weather permitting, the ship would sail on training exercises where different configurations of sail and masts would be used. The ship would often go out in one guise and return in quite a different one.

Ralph had been given the role of Gunnery Officer, and he worked with the master gunner to ensure the gun crews were trained to be their best. This was not a normal position and he was sure that it wouldn't count on his record as, on the ship's book, he was still listed as fourth lieutenant.

He shared the Captain's view that the only way to train gunners was to actually fire the guns against targets. That led to a shortage of powder, and he found himself on a quest to source six tons. He took the gunner with him to the powder dock where he talked with the merchant who he had sold the contents of the Femke to.

'I am sorry; I only have a couple of tons of our locally made powder that is cannon grade.'

They took a sample and the gunner tested it.

'It ain't much good, burns slow as it's coarse, but it hasn't been sieved so not consistent.'

'Signior,' Ralph asked the merchant in his broken Italian, 'who makes the powder?'

'That is Leonardo de Sario. His works are outside the town of Arpino.'

'If you can take us to him. We can help him improve his powder. We will still buy it from you if he can supply enough.'

'I come with you.'

When they got to the powder mill it was closed for the Christmas period. The merchant took them to the owner's home which was, unsurprisingly, a safe distance away.

'Leonardo, it's Franco,' he called from outside the gate. A man of around thirty-five years came from an outbuilding.

'What do you want, Leonardo? It's the holiday.'

'These English gentlemen want six tons of powder.'

'Six tons at this time of year? The English are crazy.'

'I am English but not crazy,' Ralph said. 'We need sieved powder. Can you provide that?'

'I can, but then it's too expensive for my buyers.'

'We will pay a premium price for six tons of cannon grade, sieved powder.'

'You can have it at the end of January.' He turned and walked into the house.

'Well, that went well,' Ralph said, and the gunner laughed.

Back aboard the Kingfisher, Ralph was missing the roaring fire of Maaike's apartment. The temperature at sea level was not far above freezing and a wet snow was falling. He was on deck, having the harbour watch, and wrapped in a coat and a cloak. He stamped his feet trying to keep them warm.

'I thought it was supposed to stay warm here,' Twelvetrees said as he came up to relieve him.

'Every few years it gets cold enough for snow and this is one of them,' Ralph grumbled.

'Nothing happening I suppose.'

'Church bells ringing for Mass but, apart from that, quiet as a grave.'

'When you go below, look into the cockpit. I heard someone crying there.'

Ralph took his leave and went below. Heading to the wardroom first, he shed his cloak and heavy coat. It wasn't so cold below although it couldn't remotely be described as warm. He went to the cockpit where the mids should be sleeping. He could hear low voices.

'I just wish I was home. I've never spent Christmas away from my family,' Egbert said, sniffing.

'You are lucky. I can't remember Christmas. I was taken when I was five years old,' Tim replied.

'Don't they have Christmas in Arabia?'

'Nope, I don't think they celebrate anything to do with Jesus, but I did hear they think of him as some kind of prophet.'

'You have never had a Christmas present?'

'No, do they give them here?'

Ralph went back to the wardroom. Tim seemed to be helping Egbert come to terms with his sorrow, but all the same he decided that there must be something he could do for the youngsters. He went to talk to the Captain.

'Mr Wrenn what can I do for you?' Kempthorne said.

'If I may, sir. I was wondering if there is something we can do for the crew and the youngsters of the ship for Christmas?'

'A laudable ambition. It is easy to forget that we have children onboard. Did you have something in mind?'

'In Italy the children receive presents on the eighth of December and Christmas Eve. I was thinking that all the ships youngsters could receive a small gift from the officers as we are their surrogate parents.'

'I think we can go one better than that.' Kempthorne smiled.

For the next few days, supply boats traded back and forth between the shore and the Kingfisher. Mysterious crates and sacks were brought aboard.

Kempthorne held a church service on Christmas Eve with all the crew lined up on deck. The lusty singing of carols could be heard ashore. The officers and the duty watch worked for several hours before dawn and the ship was transformed.

It had stopped snowing and raining, and the morning was crisp, cold and still. The bosuns and their mates roused the ship after first light.

''ands off cocks and on with yer socks! Up and about or I'll cut yer down!'

'Bugger you, don't you know it's Christmas day!' was heard from more than one crewman.

'Stop whingeing and get dressed warm. It's nippy up there.'

The drumming of feet preceded the appearance of the men on the main deck and it was replaced with exclamations of wonder.

The mainmast was bedecked in boughs of evergreen fir, holly and ivy. Ribbons had been strung from the mizzen and foremasts. The smell of baking drifted across the deck from the galley which had a thick column of smoke rising from its chimney.

Tables lined the deck covered in fresh loaves of bread, plates of ham, cheese, preserves, olives, dates, salami and nduja. There were large bowls of fresh butter and jugs of fresh milk, orange juice, and small beers.

Kempthorne called them to order.

'Men, it is Christmas day and your officers have provisioned not only this breakfast but a proper Christmas meal for midday as well. We will have a service of thanksgiving at midday then the celebrations can begin. Now enjoy your breakfast.'

'Three cheers for the Captain and the officers!' shouted Highcliffe and the men responded with a roar, then got stuck in.

Ralph helped himself to some fresh bread slathered in butter and a couple of thick slices of ham. He put a half dozen of the fat green olives on the side of his plate and a large dollop of mustard. Then he joined the mids who were eating their way through plates heaped high.

'Don't forget you will be eating again,' he cautioned.

'What's them green fings?' a ship's boy asked.

'Olives, they are extremely tasty and good for you,' Ralph replied overlooking the lack of the sir. He held one out. 'Be careful; they have a pit in them.' The boy took it and put it in his mouth. 'Bleuugh! That's 'orrible!' he cried and spat the offending fruit over the side.

Highcliffe, having enough of his behaviour, leaned forward and said something to him. The boy looked at Ralph wide-eyed. 'I'm sorry, sir.'

'Mind your manners and you will have a good day,' Ralph cautioned with a smile.

Breakfast over and cleared away, the men settled down to make and mend. Many a happy burp was heard and a couple of resounding farts which caused much amusement.

At noon the men were called to midday service. More carols were sung accompanied by a couple of timbals, a fiddle and penny whistles.

Ralph had to do the reading which was from Matthew 1 and part of it went like this:

> So all the generations from Abraham to David are fourteen generations; and from David until the carrying away into Babylon are fourteen generations; and from the carrying away into Babylon unto Christ are fourteen generations.
>
> Now the birth of Jesus Christ was on this wise: When as his mother Mary was espoused to Joseph, before they came together, she was found with child of the Holy Ghost.
>
> Then Joseph her husband, being a just man, and not willing to make her a public example, was minded to put her away privily.
>
> But while he thought on these things, behold, the angel of the Lord appeared unto him in a dream, saying, Joseph, thou son of David, fear not to take unto thee Mary thy wife: for that which is conceived in her is of the Holy Ghost.
>
> And she shall bring forth a son, and thou shalt call his name Jesus: for he shall save his people from their sins.
>
> Now all this was done, that it might be fulfilled which was spoken of the Lord by the prophet, saying,
>
> Behold, a virgin shall be with child, and shall bring forth a son, and they shall call his name Emmanuel, which being interpreted is, God with us.
>
> Then Joseph being raised from sleep did as the angel of the Lord had bidden him, and took unto him his wife:
>
> And knew her not till she had brought forth her firstborn son: and he called his name Jesus.

Ralph got through the reading without any blunders until he closed with, 'and so it says in the book of God and blessed be the Father, the Son and the Holy toast.' Sniggers spread; he went bright red when he realised.

The Captain, showing immense self-control, carried on as if nothing had happened. Until, that is, he dismissed them for their Christmas lunch.

'Holy toast?' he said and walked away, shoulders shaking.

The officers would eat together that evening and only had a light lunch. Felton came to him. 'You will give the loyal toast this evening after dinner.' Twelvetrees sniggered from the other side of the deck. Felton didn't show any emotion or judgement or that he had heard. 'You are the youngest of the officers. The mids will not attend.'

The mids and the youngsters would have a party of their own supervised by Highcliffe. Every boy would get a new knife as a present, the mids, a dirk. The navy was eminently practical after all.

The officer's dinner was a sumptuous affair. Five courses – soup, fish, chicken, beef, dessert. Lots of fresh seasonal vegetables of which Naples had ample, a blessing from the volcano. Wines for every course, a dry white Greco from Tufo with the fish and soup, a superb Fiano from Avellino, complex and fruity, with the chicken, and a red Anglianico from Taurasi with the beef. They drank sweet port with the dessert.

Feeling quite tipsy, Ralph stood to give the loyal toast.

'Gentlemen I give you the King!'

To which they all replied, 'King Charles the second!'

'A song!' the Captain said.

Hammet, the sailing master, had a strong baritone voice and started them with The Bay of Biscay.

*Ye gentlemen of England who live home at your ease,*
*It's little do you think of the dangers of the seas;*
*When we receive our orders we are obliged to go*
*On the main to proud Spain where*
*the stormy winds do blow.*

*Was on the fourth of August from Spithead we set sail*
*With Ramely and Company blest with a pleasant gale;*
*We sailed along together in the Bay of Biscay,*
*Oh, Where a dreadful storm it did arise and*
*the stormy wind did blow.*

*The Ramely she left us, she could no longer stay*
*And by distress of weather from us she bore away;*
*When she arrived at Gibraltar they told the people so*
*How they thought we were all lost at the Bay of Biscay, Oh.*

*Kind heaven did protect her, it was not quite so bad,*
*First we lost our foremast, and then we lost our flag.*
*And then we lost our mainmast, one of our guns also*
*And the men, we lost ten on the Bay of Biscay, Oh.*

*When the mainmast started, it gave a dreadful stroke,*
*In our starboard quarter, a large hole did it broke.*
*Then the seas came battering in, our guns soon overflow*
*So boldly she plowed it on the Bay of Biscay, Oh.*

*The night being dark and dreary, at twelve o'clock that night*
*Our Captain in the forecastle he was killed then outright.*
*The ring upon his finger in pieces burst in two*
*There he laid until next day when we overboard him threw.*

*The storm it being abated, we rigged up jury mast*
*And steered it for Gibraltar, where we arrived at last*
*They said it was a dismal sight as ever they did know*
*We forced to drink wine and drowned all our woe.*

That was followed by more popular songs like Spanish maids and Greensleeves but the drunker they got the bawdier the songs got.

*I went into the chandler's shop some candles for to buy,*
*I looked around the chandler's shop but no one did I spy.*
*I was disappointed and some angry words I said,*
*Then I heard the sound of a (knock, knock, knock)*
*up above my head.*
*Then I heard the sound of a (knock, knock, knock)*
*up above my head.*

*Well I was slick and I was quick, and up the stairs I sped,*
*And much to my surprise I found the chandler's wife in bed;*
*And with her was another man of most gigantic size,*
*And they were having a (knock, knock, knock) right before my eyes.*
*And they were having a (knock, knock, knock) right before my eyes.*

*When the fun was over and done and the lady raised her head,*
*She was quite surprised to find me standing by the bed.*

*'If you will be discreet, my lad, if you would be so kind,*
*I'll let you come up for some (knock, knock, knock)*
*whenever you feel inclined.*
*I'll let you come up for some (knock, knock, knock)*
*whenever you feel inclined*

The next morning Ralph woke to a massive headache and a mouth that 'tasted like a rat shat in it.' He staggered into the wardroom to find all the other officers were suffering as well.

'Damn, that was a fine night,' Twelvetrees said. 'Can't seem to remember getting into my cot, though I must have done as that is where I woke up.'

He looked at Ralph.

'What are you doing here?'

Ralph looked at him in surprise.

'What?'

'I thought you were spending Boxing Day with your woman and her uncle.'

'Fuck!'

Ralph quickly washed and dressed appropriately; he had completely forgotten in his misery of his headache. He bullied a boats crew to take him ashore, then walked quickly to the house.

'You are late, and you look awful,' Maaike said.

'We had dinner with the Captain,' he said by way of explanation.

'Well, Uncle will be waiting,' she snapped and led the way.

It was close to nine when they entered the palace and were guided to the private apartments. Francisco and his wife, Francisca Josefa, with sixteen of their eighteen children were waiting for them. Francisco took one look at Ralph and smiled.

'To be young again. Are you able to eat?'

'I am, sir.'

'While we are in our private rooms you can call us Francisco and Francisca. I don't expect you will be able to remember all our children's names.'

Ralph knew this was a huge privilege. He took his seat to the right of Francisco. They ate, breaking their fast quietly. After, Francisco asked Ralph to walk with him.

'Have to talk to you about the future,' Francisco said.

A cold shudder ran down Ralph's spine.

'Maaike is not only my niece, but her father is also a high-ranking official in the court in Brabant.'

'She mentioned that.'

'Her future husband will be chosen by her father.'

'I see.'

'She will be returning to Brabant in the New Year.'

Ralph's gut clenched.

'Does she know?'

'Not yet, I will give her the letter from her father tomorrow. There is no need to taint this day of celebration.'

*Why did you tell me then!*

'Thank you for that,' Ralph said.

'She will need your support; do not make it hard for her,' Francisco said.

'I knew it would end when we sailed. I just never imagined it would end like this.' His pain showed in his eyes.

'I understand how you feel; life is often difficult for those of us in the aristocracy. There is a price for the privilege of ruling as there is a price for the privilege of command.'

They returned to the family. The younger children were playing a game of blind man's bluff with Maaike blindfolded and chasing them. Ralph plastered on a smile and joined in.

The day dragged by, his headache overshadowed by the ache in his chest. It ended eventually when the children went to bed and they left the palace to walk to the house. It was as they passed the basilica that the attack came. Four Arabs came out of the shadows, blades glinting in the moonlight.

Ralph drew his sword. 'Maaike run, it's me they want.'

'I'm not leaving you.'

*Shit.* 'You have to.'

He could say no more as the first two attacked while the other two circled. It was no time for elegant sword play.

He stamped and shouted, 'HA!' slashing at the nearest man. His rapier hissed as it cut the air and sparks flew off the edge as it was parried. He followed through with a shoulder barge knocking the man off his feet.

He ducked a swing from the second, spun in the crouch and slashed him across the front of the thigh. The man, whose face was covered by the end of his turban, staggered back.

Maaike screamed and there was a clash of blades from behind him. He spun and just got his sword up in time to block a vicious slash from the first man. Maaike had a long blade in her hand and was fending off the other two attackers.

Ralph focused on his opponent, who was favouring his left leg. Ralph circled anticlockwise forcing him onto his injured right leg.

Ralph stepped forward on his left foot and slashed at his right side forcing him to parry, then kicked him in the right knee. A backhand slash across the throat finished him. The second man lunged at him hoping to catch him off balance, but Ralph was ready for him and he ran straight into his blade.

Ralph tried to free his blade, but it was stuck. Maaike screamed again.

Ralph pulled his sailor's knife and charged the two men attacking her. He crashed into the first, hitting him in the chest as he had been taught while playing Campyon. They both went down and wrestled on the ground. Ralph's short-bladed knife was an advantage now and he stabbed him repeatedly in the side. The man finally succumbed after what felt like an interminable struggle and Ralph stabbed him one last time in the neck to finish him.

Realising it was ominously quiet, he turned to see the fourth man lying on the ground in a pool of blood, Maaike's long blade sticking out of his abdomen. Maaike stood, her hands on her stomach, looking at him wide-eyed. He stepped forward and saw blood seep from between her fingers.

'The doctor says she will be fine. The wound is deep but did not damage anything vital. She will have to stay here until she has recovered,' Francisco said.

'Can I see her?' Ralph pleaded.

'Later, she is sleeping. I want you to tell me exactly what happened.'

Ralph took a deep breath and recounted the fight.

'We recovered the bodies. We think they are Murat Reis's men,' Francisco said when he'd finished.

'What will you do about him?'

'Apart from barring all Arabian ships from entering the Bay, there is not a lot I can do. It is up to you and the Kingfisher to finish this at sea.'

Ralph knew this was true. The Neapolitan Navy was made up of smaller ships, mainly galleys, which were designed to protect the coast. A regular green water navy in real terms. He knew another thing, if he ever came across Murat Reis he would kill him without hesitation.

# A New Year

Maaike was bored. Her stomach itched where the stitches were pulling, and she would have a scar to mar her perfect skin. She was confined to bed and a nurse was in attendance twenty-four hours a day. She had read a book and was trying to do some needlepoint, but she was fundamentally unsuited to sitting still, let alone lying in bed.

She fidgeted. The nurse immediately looked up from her knitting and glared at her. She went back to her needlework muttering obscenities under her breath and jabbing the needle in harder than needed.

She remembered the fight. To begin with, the two men who had attacked her had been more interested in capturing her than killing her. Ralph had arrived just in time. She had been tiring and the men were beginning to move in. Unfortunately, after Ralph took out one, the second decided she would have to die. He had attacked with real intent for the first time and in desperation she had tried to get inside his swing. He was fast enough to slash her across the stomach, but she had kept up her charge forward and stabbed him upwards under the ribs.

Ralph had picked her up and carried her to the palace where her uncle's physician had been pulled from his bed. He had given her something which made her very woozy and stitched her up. Apparently, she had giggled throughout it and had made some inappropriate comments about Ralph. To make matters worse she had been recalled to Brabant. She didn't want to go but she couldn't disobey her father. She would be leaving as soon as she was deemed fit and the weather permitted. It was not the parting with Ralph that she had planned.

There was a knock on the door and Ralph put his head through.

'Are you indecent?' He grinned.

'For you anytime.' She grinned back.

The nurse stood and threatened him with her knitting sticks, speaking rapidly in Italian.

'The doctor said it would be alright,' Ralph said in Italian, holding his hands up.

'For fifteen minutes only and no bad behaviour,' she said and plonked herself down again.

'Wouldn't dream of it.' Ralph grinned.

'Liar,' Maaike whispered as he sat on the chair next to her bed.

'How are you healing?'

'It's itching.'

'That's a good sign. It will itch until they take out the stitches.'

'I will have a scar.' She pouted.

'I will kiss all the way along it,' he said, his heart in his eyes.

Maaike reached out and took his hand.

'You may not get the chance. My father has ordered me to go home.' Tears welled up in her eyes.

'I know, your uncle told me, but the weather is bad and there is no way any ship can leave the bay.' He held her gaze for a minute. Then he smiled. 'I have some good news. The doctor says he will take out the stitches the day after tomorrow. Then he will allow you to get out of bed.'

'I missed the new year celebration.'

'You didn't miss much. The town was alive with drunks and the fireworks were only slightly spectacular.'

'I heard the fireworks.'

'I stayed on the ship. It has a great view of the harbour and town.'

'Hmph, rub it in,' she said, pouting again, then glanced at the nurse who was dozing. She kissed him quickly on the lips, her eyes filled with tears.

'I am going to miss you so much.'

'I will miss you too.'

'After you get back to England, will you be able to come to Brabant?'

'Would I be welcome?'

'Of course you will.'

'I didn't mean by you. Would your father welcome me?'

'Oh, I see. No probably not.'

The stitches came out, an uncomfortable procedure as the doctor had used a special type of stitch that not only went through the skin but down into her muscles to prevent there being a void under her skin. Once Maaike was alone, she examined herself in a mirror. There was a fine pink scar with dots every half inch either side of it running for six inches across her stomach. Her stomach felt pinched.

*I hope that fades.* She ran her fingers over it. Feeling it, she could imagine Ralph kissing it and…

She put the thought firmly out of her head, got dressed and walked slowly to her uncle and aunt's apartment.

'Hello, my dear. You are looking much better,' her aunt said. 'Sit here with me.'

Maaike did as she was told, sitting back into the cushions.

'When can I return to my apartment?'

Her aunt looked at her knowingly. 'So you can liaise with Ralph?'

'Phht, not with my stomach muscles feeling like they do. The doctor said it would be weeks before the muscles heal properly and not to do anything strenuous.' She looked thoughtful for a moment. 'But it would be nice to be held by him.'

'I am sure it would, but he can do that here where you can be cared for.'

The tone of her aunt's voice told her that she would brook no argument. Then she surprised Maaike by saying, 'I have an apartment prepared for you here. You have a hand maid, a cook, a maid of all works and a butler.'

'Thank you. Why a butler?'

'He is a former guard and is there to protect you as much as serve you.'

Maaike made to protest but her aunt held up her hand.

'Until you are fully recovered, I insist. I will not answer to your father for your death.'

In the meantime, Ralph was busy on the Kingfisher. The ship needed constant maintenance and Kempthorne wanted her appearance changed before they finally set sail. The rake of her masts was changed to a more French angle – top masts removed. Her name was changed to the Annabelle. He was deliberately keeping busy to take his mind off Maaike, but it didn't really work. He would find himself paused in mid-action gazing at the town.

'Mr Wrenn, a message has been delivered for you,' Tim said, bringing Ralph out of his reverie and back to the present. Ralph took it and recognised Maaike's handwriting. He opened it.

*Dearest Ralph.*

*I have had the stitches removed and am mobile again. My aunt insists that I stay in the palace where they can care for me and she has provided me with my own apartment. Please, if your Captain will allow, come and visit me.*

*I miss you so much my love*

*Maaike*

'Is the messenger still here, Tim?'

'Yes, sir. He is waiting for your reply.'

'Please take over from me here. I need to speak to the Captain.'

The Captain saw him immediately.

'What can I do for you, Mr Wrenn?'

'Sir, may I go ashore for three hours this evening? Maaike has had her stitches out and I would like to see her if possible.'

'I am not sure it is safe for you to go. You have been attacked twice now and I do not need to lose a competent officer at this time.'

'She is staying at the palace. Her aunt insists she stays there for her recovery and, once she is well, they will ship her back to Brabant.'

'I see. What are your plans?'

'Plans? My plans?'

'Yes, your plans for you and the young lady.'

'Sir, I am a sailor and an officer first and foremost. She is the daughter of a member of the royal family and her father would never allow our relationship to continue, especially as I am not a Catholic or of the blood.'

'So, you have no plans?'

'No, sir. I accept that this pleasant interlude is almost over.' Kempthorne could see the hurt in his eyes.

'You are growing up fast, Ralph; you are not the young man who I met when I came aboard this ship. The navy is a harsh mistress, especially in affairs of the heart. You can go ashore after your watch is over. Be back by midnight.'

'Thank you, sir.'

'Make the most of this opportunity as we will sail as soon as the weather allows, and I want your attention on your duties.'

His reply was simply, *I am coming.*

As Ralph approached the palace, a line from the Shakespeare play Romeo and Juliet came to mind. *Parting is such sweet sorrow.* He nodded to the guard who in turn nodded him through. A page escorted him to the private apartments where Maaike waited for him.

He found her reclining on a sofa. Her colour had returned, and she looked comfortable. He knelt beside her and took her in his arms, careful not to hurt her.

'I was afraid you wouldn't be allowed to come,' she said.

'The Captain took pity on me.'

'Are you ready to sail?'

'We are, and as soon as the weather allows, we will go to sea.'

'Then this is the last…' She broke off with a sob.

He lifted her chin and gazed into her eyes.

'Shhh, do not weep. I want to remember you smiling.'

'It is hard, my heart…'

'Mine is as well. But we are both slaves to duty. You to your family and me to the navy.'

'Are you expecting to fight?'

'I hope so. It is why we came.'

She hugged him. 'Please stay safe.'

They sat together, enjoying each other's company until the clock struck eleven. Maaike reached behind a pillow and produced a box.

'I want you to have this to remember me by,' she said as she handed it to him. Inside was a beautifully engraved gold pocket watch. On the back in a cartouche were R and M entwined. He flipped it open; inside was engraved, 'para siempre'.

'It means "forever".' She smiled. 'I will never forget you.'

Ralph removed his signet ring. 'I have not been able to buy anything special, but this has never left my hand since I was fourteen. I want you to have it.'

It was too big for her slender fingers, so she threaded it on her neck chain, so it hung between her breasts.

Her sobs echoed in his ears as he left.

# Preparation for Battle

Ralph and Dusty Miller, the gunner, were inspecting the guns on the lower deck. The gunports were open and light flooded in from the early morning sun. The gunner had a small hammer which he used to tap the gun barrels to check for cracks.

'What exactly are you listening for?' Ralph asked, as Dusty tapped his way down the barrel of the first gun.

'It should sound the same everywhere I tap. If there is any honeycombing or a crack, it will sound different.'

'Do all guns sound the same?'

'Each has its own voice.'

Ralph was intrigued. He used wax and a bandana around his ears to protect them when the guns fired and knew that Dusty did the same. 'They sound almost musical.' Dusty was a renowned musician on the ship playing the taille. It was rumoured he had travelled to Paris to buy one from the famous Hotteterre family of instrument makers.

'Aye, it is.' He tapped the length of the barrel and the trunnions. 'This one is good.'

They moved down the starboard battery and then onto the larboard.

Dusty suddenly concentrated on a spot on the breech of the number six gun.

'Hear that?' He tapped again.

'Sounds dull.'

'Exactly.' He tapped the end of the barrel. The sound was definitely brighter. He tapped the suspect spot again. 'We have here what is known as a problem.'

'How do we find out what, and how bad it is?' Ralph asked.

'That is the hard part.' Dusty looked around and spotted a boy. 'You! Go fetch Adam Farley.' Farley was the captain for that gun.

Farley arrived post-haste; no one kept the gunner waiting. He touched his forelock to Ralph.

'Have you noticed anything different about this gun lately?' Ralph said.

'I haven't that I can think of,' Farley replied.

'What about your crew?' Dusty said.

'Now you mention it, Dewi was complaining that his swab were catching on something.'

'Get the boys and run this gun inboard,' Dusty said. He excused himself and went to the magazine to fetch something. He returned as the gun crew were hauling the gun back.

'I want the muzzle in the sun.'

The crew heaved on jack staffs to put the barrel into the patch of sun coming in through the port. Dusty took a piece of highly polished brass and reflected the sunlight to shine down the barrel. He peered into the six-inch diameter muzzle, adjusting the mirror to examine as much of the eleven feet as he could. He hummed and hawed as he did it.

'Aah, that be it.'

'What do you see?' Ralph said.

'There is a flake hanging about nine foot down. That probably means there is honeycombing.'

The problem with honeycombing was it weakened the iron and the barrel could explode when the charge was fired. The result would be catastrophic in the confines of the gun deck with shrapnel flying around killing or wounding not only that gun's crew but the crews of the adjacent guns.

Ralph made a note on the slate he carried. 'Let's do the rest and then we can move on to the upper deck.'

'We have one demi-cannon that has a honeycombed breech. It's the number six gun on the larboard side of the lower deck,' Ralph reported to Felton.

'What is the gunner's recommendation?'

'He thinks we should replace it, sir.'

The Captain came on deck and walked over to them. He had noticed their concerned looks.

'Problem?'

'A honeycombed gun, sir.' Felton said.

'Is it bad?'

'About a foot in front of the breech, sir. The Gunner thinks it should be replaced,' Ralph said.

'Worst place. But easier said than done.'

'I think we should find out if we can get a replacement before we lift it out,' Felton said.

'I have to check with the merchant when our powder will be available. I can ask about a gun when I see him,' Ralph said.

'Do that and report back to me,' Felton said.

* * *

Ralph met Franco, the powder merchant.

'Good day, Franco. Any word from Antonio?'

'Yes, he says he will deliver the first two tons at the end of the week.'

'Excellent. I have another request.'

'Yes?'

'I need to find a replacement demi-cannon.'

'A demi-cannon? That is not so easy. You only want the barrel I suppose.'

'Yes. We have one that has honeycombing in the breech.'

'Can that be offered as salvage?'

'Against the cost of a new one. Yes.'

Franco grinned. He enjoyed dealing with Ralph who was smart and honest.

'Come, we need to talk with Masolini, the gun merchant. He is an awkward man. He considers himself superior to everyone because he is a fencing master.'

They walked towards town. Ralph glanced at the Kingfisher as they left the powder dock. A glint told him that someone was watching. Two of his boat crew stepped up beside him as they walked past the place the boat was moored. They carried cutlasses and pistols.

'Your Captain is worried for your safety,' Franco said.

'Yes, Murat Reis has put a price on my head.'

'Pfft, that pirate. No one here will try and claim it.'

'There are Arab galleys here; their crew will. I have been attacked twice.'

'Yes, I heard that Miss Maaike was hurt last time. It is bad, she is a nice girl.'

They came to a warehouse with a sign depicting crossed swords. Inside it was a fighting man's heaven. Racks of rapiers, cutlasses, and small swords, pistols of different lengths and calibres, daggers and dirks, punch knives and stilettos festooned the entry room. A tall, elegant man stepped forward to greet them.

'Signore Masolini, this is Signore Wrenn from the British Navy. He is in need of a demi-canon, and I thought you might be able to help,' Franco said.

'You can pay cash?' Masolini said.

Ralph was taken aback by the abruptness of the question and lack of polite greeting.

'Yes, I can.' The Captain had a large fighting fund. He looked at Masolini's sword. It had a fancy guard and intricate basket hilt which was unusual as most had a knuckle bow, quillons, and side rings around the ricasso. 'That is an unusual sword. I have not seen a rapier with a basket hilt before.'

'It is a sword of my own creation,' Masolini said, standing even straighter.

'May I see it?'

Franco coughed to hide a grin. Ralph was working Masolini perfectly.

The sword was drawn with a flourish, spun and handed to Ralph, hilt first, across Masolini's forearm.

He took the sword and examined the hilt which was wire wrapped rather than covered in shagreen like his. The basket hilt was well designed and didn't impede the wrist. He tested the balance point. It was five inches in front of the ricasso. The blade was made of fine steel and perfect. In fact, it looked unused. Ralph handed it back.

'A fine weapon,' he said.

Masolini sheathed it with a flourish and looked at Ralph's workman-like sword. 'May I?'

'Certainly, it is nowhere near as grand as yours,' Ralph said, handing his sword over hilt first.

A similar examination ensued.

'A good sword, English by Wilkinson. The balance point is only four inches from the ricasso. You prefer the thrust?'

'On ship in hand-to-hand fighting there is less chance to slash and there is the chance of tangling in the rigging with a long blade.'

'Indeed, a shorter blade would be better.' He turned to a rack of small swords and ran his hand down until he came to a particular specimen. He lifted it off its pegs and offered it to Ralph.

'Try this.'

Ralph tested the hilt which was wrapped in wire and fitted his hand well. It had a knuckle and a shell guard. He looked at the blade. It was twenty-eight inches long, rhomboid in shape, like his rapier, with one sharp edge for most of its length but double edged for the last nine inches to the point.

'This is an unusual blade.' He was right, most modern small swords were for thrusting only and had much lighter blades.

'You know your swords. This is an old blade which I have re-hilted. It dates from 1590. The steel is from Toledo in Spain. The balance point is further forward than the new ones to aid slashing.'

Ralph swung it and did a short shadow fencing exercise. It felt like an extension of his arm.

'It is a lovely sword. It would work very well in close combat,' he said and handed it back.

Masolini nodded and put it back on the rack.

'Come with me.'

He led them from the room into the warehouse where there was an array of field pieces of all types.

'I have one demi-canon which is on a field carriage. I do not think you want the carriage.'

Ralph noted that Masolini didn't ask questions but made statements as if he was all knowing.

'No, we don't.' Ralph replied, despite the lack of a question.

The gun was in a corner and had a layer of dust covering it. It was made of brass and from the state of the barrel, unused. Ralph took a cord from his pocket and measured the bore against a pair of knots tied at the bore of his guns. It was close enough. He checked the priming hole and trunnions, then took Dusty's little hammer from his pocket and tapped the length of the barrel.

'It is a sound piece. What do you want for it?'

'A thousand ducats.' That was five hundred sovereigns, a small fortune.

'That is extortionate for a gun that has been sitting here for a long time,' Ralph said and made his point bybut wiping his finger through the dust on the barrel. 'I can offer five hundred.'

'That is not enough, I can come down a little to nine-hundred and fifty.'

*Two can play at that game.* 'That is no move at all. I can offer five hundred and fifty.'

'How am I to make a profit on that? Eight hundred.'

*That's better.* 'Let us meet in the middle at six hundred and fifty.'

'Seven hundred.'

'Six hundred and fifty and you can have the old cannon as salvage.'

'Agreed.'

'I will send a crew to collect it. They will return the old barrel.'

They walked back into the store. A page from the palace whom Ralph recognised from Fransisco's apartments was waiting. He handed Masolini a letter and bowed to Ralph. Masolini's eyebrows arched in surprise as the youth turned and left his establishment without a word. He pulled a knife after examining the seal, which elicited another look of surprise. He read the letter, coughed, swallowed and coughed again.

'I am instructed by the Viceroy to allow you to choose two personal weapons at his expense. There is no limit placed on the value.'

His whole demeanour towards Ralph changed in that instant.

'Now why would Uncle Francisco do that?' Ralph said quite deliberately. Apparently Masolini spoke some English.

'You are the nephew of the Viceroy?' His voice went up half an octave at the end.

'No, it was a figure of speech.' Ralph grinned knowing he had caught him out. He stepped over to the rack of small swords and picked up the one Masolini had shown him earlier. He hefted it again and then picked up a fancier one for comparison. He definitely preferred the first one.

'I'll take this with a sheath.' He ignored the disappointed look on Masolini's face and moved over to the pistols. He spotted an absolutely beautiful sixty calibre flintlock. He picked it up and turned it over in his hands. It had a zebrano wood full stock with brass trigger guard, escutcheon, and furniture. An iron action and cock that was robust enough to survive at sea and a nine-inch-long round barrel.

'Does this come with all its accoutrements?'

'It comes in a rosewood case with everything you need.'

'Can a belt clip be fitted?'

'My armourer can do that while you wait.'

A sheath was chosen, plain to match the sword, and the pistol modified and presented in its case.

Franco and Ralph left to find the same page waiting outside for them. He bowed and handed Ralph two letters.

'One is from Lady Maaike.' He grinned and left.

'Thank you,' Ralph said.

The two walked away from the warehouse and as soon as they were around the corner and out of sight, Franco burst out laughing, holding Ralph's arm.

'What's so funny?' Ralph asked, chuckling despite himself.

'That was priceless! Masolini thought he could swindle you on the price but you bargained like a gypsy. Then he gets that letter and realised that you are connected to the palace. His face!'

'It was a picture wasn't it!' Ralph spluttered and joined in the laughter.

Ralph had time to read the letters before the gun arrived. He read the one from the Viceroy first. It basically said that the weapons were a farewell present from him and his family. It was signed simply with an F. The second letter from Maaike was spotted with tears and told him she would be going to Rome by carriage as there was a Habsburg ship there that would take her home. She was leaving that very afternoon.

He sighed; it was already late and there was no way he could get away as the gun was due at any time.

Just as dark was closing in, his crew brought it on its field carriage to the dock where the Kingfisher was moored. The barrel was detached and lifted, then lowered to the lower gun deck where it was dropped onto its new carriage. The old barrel was lifted out, fitted to the field carriage, and pulled by twenty strong men back to the warehouse.

He went below. The new brass cannon stood out from its iron brothers, but it was the right bore and completed their battery. The gun crew had already named it 'Miss Mikey'. Ralph smiled at their attempt at Maaike's name and left it at that.

* * *

Other preparations revolved around tactics for repelling boarders, mounting swivel guns between each of the main-deck guns, the use of grenades, and cooperation between the soldiers and sailors as a coordinated unit. The idea was to kill as many as possible in their own boats before they could scale the sides, then create a wall of steel to push them into the sea if they succeeded in gaining the deck.

The Captain also decided that the stern was a particularly vulnerable area and lined the stern rail with swivels as well. Ralph bought up every swivel gun in Naples and the adjacent ports to meet the Captain's demands. The magazine was enlarged to take more powder and more of the hold was dedicated to the storage of projectiles.

The logic was that if they were to get into a fight it would be in the Mediterranean. They would carry only two months supplies as they could make it to a friendly port to resupply without too much trouble. Therefore, they could fill the hold with ammunition and gun spares. Other spares were replacement spars, sails, rigging, glass for the transom windows, timber for repairs, iron stock and charcoal for the blacksmith's brazier.

The Kingfisher sat a little low in the water once it was all stowed away.

'We will have to take care of the lower deck ports with this load,' Kempthorne said. 'I want them reinforced and the tackles renewed.'

Ralph got the job, of course, as the officer with the most knowledge of her construction. He rounded up the carpenter and smith and set about coming up with a plan.

'Double up the tackles to make sure they stay shut?' he said.

'With respect, that is doing it the hard way,' Frank Smith, the blacksmith, said. 'I can forge extra bolts that can be fitted there, there,

there and there on each bulkhead to lock them shut. A quick tap with a mallet will release them and allow you to lower or raise them.'

'That will certainly be stronger. Do we need to reinforce the bulkheads themselves?'

Finnegan the carpenter examined them, then stood back and scratched his head.

'With the bolts they will be stiffer when they are shut. Do they flex much when they are opened?'

Ralph ordered the men to raise it.

'It flexes a little and a brace fixed between here and here will take that out without making them overly heavy,' Finnegan said.

'Do that then,' Ralph said.

When the work was completed, and the tackles replaced, the Captain visited to inspect them.

'Good work, how fast can you get them down?'

'We would release most of the bolts in anticipation before the order to run out was given,' Ralph said and signalled the crew. Men moved forward with mallets and knocked the bolts back.

'Run out!' the Captain ordered.

The crew knocked back the two remaining bolts then hauled on the tackles and raised the bulkhead into the firing position. The guns were run out.

'Under thirty seconds. Not bad. See if you can get it down to twenty,' he said.

'Aye, aye, sir,' Ralph said.

'The only way we can get these beasts run out in anything close to twenty seconds is to put extra men on the tackles. The soldiers will have to help,' Ralph said, later.

Mock groans greeted that pronouncement from the gun crews who considered the soldiers to be clumsy.

'They will tread on our toes!' a voice quipped from the dark.

'Then you better make sure you teach them to dance,' Ralph called back making the men laugh.

Training started straight away. The soldiers would only be needed for the initial running out but that didn't change the level of training they received. At the end of the day, he had the exercise down to twenty-three seconds. He reported to the Captain.

'We can do the initial run out in twenty-three seconds, sir.'

'I am surprised. That is very fast. How did you do it?'

'I added two soldiers to each tackle. At that stage of a fight, they aren't doing anything other than stand around and their added muscle makes all the difference.'

'If they were to help during the initial stages of an engagement, would that increase our rate of fire?'

'It would speed things up as running out is one of the longest tasks. It may knock up to seven seconds off.'

'But on the other hand, they would be fatigued when their turn came to fight. I will give this some thought.'

Ralph was dismissed.

# Setting the Trap

The fact that the Kingfisher was setting sail disguised as the Annabelle was the worst kept secret in Naples. They had been very careful to exercise the false bulkheads out of sight of other ships but the changes to her appearance were done in plain sight. The lookouts noted that as soon as the weather started to clear enough to sail, a galley left the port and rowed rapidly south.

There were still Arabs in port as two galleys remained. They assumed that they were spies. A small convoy was assembled and rumours that they would be carrying a valuable passenger were circulated. The Captain arranged with the Viceroy that a carriage would travel from the palace to the dock to deliver what appeared to be the Viceroy's niece to the ship. Maaike had already left for Rome in secret so the passenger that would be delivered was a page dressed as her, who would leave the ship in men's clothes before they sailed.

The galleys changed their moorings to be further out in the bay. It was obvious to everyone they were watching for signs the convoy was about to sail. An hour before they sailed, the carriage arrived and a cloaked figure hurried up the gangway attended by several attendants and guards. Several large and obviously heavy trunks were brought aboard. The attendants and guards left.

Ralph made a show of meeting the cloaked figure and helping her down belowdecks. As soon as they were out of sight, the page, Claudio, removed the cloak and dress he wore over his livery.

'Good luck, Mr Ralph. Kill those bastards,' he said.

'Why? Do you hate them?'

'They took my cousins and killed their parents in Sicily. I have declared a vendetta on them. I would stay and fight if the Viceroy would let me.'

'Do you know who led them?'

'No, I just want them all dead.' Claudio had tears of frustration in his eyes. Ralph put his arm around his shoulder.

'It's time for you to go. We will try and even the score for you.'

An hour later, at the peak of the tide, the six-ship convoy came up to their anchors and set sail. The galleys were nowhere to be seen. They had left as soon as the party had left the Kingfisher. One had headed to Tunis, the other Algiers, both making ten knots with their professional oarsmen hard at work. Their captains were due a bounty for bringing news of the British merchantmen leaving port – especially the black hulled one now called the Annabelle.

The Captain of the one heading to Tunis was the youngest brother of Murat Reis. He would report directly to him. One of the burnt galleys was his and he was particularly keen to exact revenge. There were a number of pirate fleets which operated as a brotherhood and acted as the de facto Algerian navy. They had collectively been investing secretly in more modern fighting ships. They now had seven that would be classified as fifth rates in a

European navy and were sourcing more. He would take command of one in Tunis.

They had four demi-battery ships which had thirty-eight guns. The lower deck had eight 18-pound guns, four to a side mounted two fore and two aft. Between were benches for oarsmen. The upper deck had twenty-eight 12-pounders with another two 6-pounders on the quarterdeck. The other three ships had thirty-two 12-pounders on a single gun deck.

All their guns were French and had limited iron shot. Stone shot was cheaper, and they had topped up their supply with that. Their powder was supposed to have come from Holland, but the last delivery had been intercepted by the British forcing them to top up with locally milled inferior powder.

Their gunners and sail handlers were taken from their own men. They had no formal training except that given by captured sailors who were now slaves. Suffice to say, what they received was what they deserved. They could sail and perform some basic evolutions but, such was the individuality of the men, they were uncoordinated and slow. There were a lot of fingers pointed and blame when things went wrong. Eventually, in frustration, the captains would execute a couple of men to focus the rest's minds.

On the Kingfisher, the already well-trained crew was being honed to a razor's edge. Out at sea they ran sail drills, ran up the top masts and took them down again, and ran gun drills, both in dumb show and against towed targets. During all of this the soldiers drilled with pikes and swords, joined by their sailor cousins when they could to operate as a well-oiled machine.

They had plenty of time; the convoy ran at only six knots during the day and practically stopped overnight. It took two days to get to Marsala on the island of Sicily where they stopped for a day so the merchants could load more goods.

The Barbary pirates were also making good use of the time. Mahmood Reis had taken over his demi-battery ship and was sailing her to Algiers to join up with the other five ships. His brother sailed beside him in their second and would be overall commander of the fleet. He liked the feel of his ship. They had the wind on their quarter, were under full sail and were going with the current. It felt like they were flying along as he watched the coast pass.

Their bronze cannons gleamed in the sun. He had made the crew polish them. The men were getting used to handling the square sails and he had four European sailors who were training them. He watched those men carefully as they were captives; he had promised them an easier life if they cooperated – a promise he had no intention of keeping.

His gunners had been taken from the city defences and were experienced. They had to get used to working on a ship and many were seasick. He smiled nastily; they would get over that fast enough if, no, *when* they found the hated ship that the arrogant Captain and his doomed First Mate Wrenn were on.

He had plans for Wrenn who had killed four of his men – flaying and being buried in salt being his favourite.

Ralph's duties as gunnery officer kept him almost constantly busy. The sewing of cartridge bags, creation of canisters, organisation of ammunition, maintenance of the guns, training, all demanded his attention. He also had to stand his watch. What motivated him was the knowledge they were sailing into a trap, deliberately and with intent.

The Captain had shared his plan with them once they were underway. As soon as there was any sign of the pirates, the merchantmen would scatter and run. The Kingfisher would deliberately choose a course that would let the pirates catch up and engage before they showed their true colours and teeth. They would then have the fight of their lives. Ralph worked the gunners and the midshipmen in charge of the divisions hard, honing their skills and getting the young gentlemen focused.

He and the gunner worked out the most efficient method for getting cartridges from the magazine to the guns. Wooden chests were installed on the deck as temporary storage for four rounds of powder for the main guns and eight for the swivels. This would avoid stray sparks from detonating them. These would be kept topped up by the powder monkeys who would continuously carry cartridges up from below rather than bring one up and wait for the gun crew to claim it. This way every gun would have two cartridges available and a swivel the same.

One of the practices involved the reloading of the swivels which were manned by soldiers. The Captain wanted two rounds a minute of canister. All officers, and non-commissioned officers, whether navy or army, were issued with blunderbusses. Loaded with quarter inch shot, these sixteen-inch barrelled hand cannons were very effective for repelling boarders and easy to reload because of the belled barrel.

Ralph wore his across his back on a strap which was copied by the mids and some of the other officers. He could swing it around and fire it quickly and it left his hands free to use his sword or pistol. He carried three charges of powder wrapped in waxed paper and pouches of balls and wads on his belt.

He could reload in fifteen to twenty seconds – bite off the end of the paper and prime the pan; flip the frizen closed; spin the gun butt down; pour in the rest of the powder then stuff the cartridge paper in on top; grab a handful of balls from the pouch and drop them down the barrel followed by a wad; ram once.

Twelvetrees had a dragon: a blunderbuss pistol with an eleven-inch barrel. The gunner and blacksmith had modified it so he could clip it to his belt with the barrel upright so he could reload it one handed. He primed the pan last, using a horn by tucking the gun under his arm. When he fired, he used the belt hook to slip his hook through to steady the piece. The Kingfisher was a floating fortress manned by the most heavily armed crew ever seen on a British ship.

Off the coast of Algiers, the pirates cast their net. The seven ships spread out across the regular sea-lane flying a variety of flags. Neapolitan, French, even English flags were shown. There was a determination amongst them to revenge themselves on the men that had burned their ships and part of the town of Tunis. They were fired up and ready to fight.

For them it was now a waiting game. The line of ships could see over a hundred miles of sea north to south and their lookouts should spot the convoy twenty miles away.

What the pirates didn't know was that the Kingfisher had raised its topmasts once out of sight of the land and with the extra height could spot the pirates at twenty-seven miles. They set no topsails so it would be impossible for their opponents to see them until their mainsails came up over the horizon.

*Are we the hunter or the hunted?* Ralph pondered as he took the first dog watch. This two-hour watch was from four to six in the afternoon and enabled him to eat with the rest of the off-duty officers in the wardroom. They had been sailing for three days since leaving Marsala and had just passed the coastal town of Annaba.

The helmsman whispered, 'Captain on deck,' and Ralph turned and touched his forelock. They were in what passed for uniform in those days having abandoned civilian clothes once they were at sea. Uniform dress had gained in popularity during the civil war when Cromwell had introduced it for the New Model Army. The navy had copied the army then but, since the restoration of the monarchy, they had diverged. Long coats of blue wool with gold braid decoration, breeches with stockings and a white blouse topped by a tricorn hat edged in silver for lieutenants and gold for the Captain. While not being formalised, their dress differentiated them from the crew and made them easily recognisable during battle.

'All well, Mr Wrenn?'

'Aye, sir. Wind is from the south southeast and we are making a steady six knots. Heading due west.'

'I want to congratulate you on the readiness of the guns and their crews.'

'Thank you, sir.'

'I believe we are probably the most efficient ship in the navy.'

Ralph bowed in acknowledgement of the praise.

Felton joined them on deck, smoking a pipe.

'I was just telling Mr Wrenn that I appreciate his efforts with the guns and their crews.'

'Aye, he has done a fine job.' Felton said.

Off Algiers the seven Algerines tacked back and forth, waiting. The lookouts strained their eyes and the captains paced up and down.

* * *

Two days later, just after sunrise, the lookout hailed down.

'Sails on the horizon, dead ahead! Topsails by the look of 'em.'

'Mr Barnes, please be so kind as to inform the Captain that we have sighted a sail ahead of us,' Cecil Stockley said to the waiting mid.

Felton heard the hail in the wardroom and came on deck at the same time as the Captain.

'Mr Barnes, take a glass up to the tops and report what you see,' he said.

While Barnes was climbing the rigging, the rest of the officers appeared on deck and took up station on the leeward side.

'Deck there! There is a square-rigged ship ahead of us, another four points to starboard and another four points to port.'

'Three square-rigged ships in line abeam?' Felton said.

'Most unusual, don't you think?' Kempthorne said.

'Do the Algerians have full rigged ships?'

'I would not be surprised if they have acquired some.'

'Deck there! I can see a Neapolitan flag flying from the top mast of the centre one.'

'For us to see their topsails from here it must be a bigger ship than anything I have ever seen the Neapolitans use,' Kempthorne said thoughtfully.

An hour later there was another cry. 'Deck there! They are closing up.'

'That confirms my suspicion. Mr Marchant, signal the convoy to disperse,' Kempthorne said. 'Bring the ship to action.'

# Battle of the Seven Algerines

The Kingfisher dropped her topmasts to resemble the merchantman she pretended to be. She wanted the pirates to spring their trap before she showed her true colours and form. The closing speed with the ship dead ahead was close to sixteen knots. They would meet in thirty minutes. The upper-deck guns were loaded with double shot, the lower single.

'Deck! Two more ships closing in from port and starboard.'

'Five ships?' Ralph said as the report drifted down to the lower gun deck. He could see nothing so he stood by the stairs to hear any orders.

'Raise our colours. Run out the larboard upper-deck guns.'

There was a loud thud as the bulkheads were lowered and a rumble as the guns were run out. They turned, and were soon on an even keel.

'Run out the larboard lower-deck guns.'

Ralph had already released the locks on the bulkheads, and they swung up immediately. He looked out of the nearest port and saw a demi-battery ship about to pass them two cables away. It was flying a Turkish flag, which was patently nonsense as the ship was clearly French built.

The guns ran out.

'Fire!'

The larboard guns roared.

'Reload!'

The gun captain stepped forward and covered the touch hole; a second man shoved a worm down the barrel to remove any large pieces of debris; a third swabbed the barrel with a wet sponge; the second dried the barrel with a dry sponge; a cartridge was pushed in and rammed home with a wad on top; a ball manhandled into the muzzle and rammed home with a wad on top by two men. The gun was run forward. The gun captain pushed his pricker down the touch hole to pierce the cartridge and poured fine priming powder into the hole. He raised his arm to indicate they were ready.

*Forty-eight seconds,* Ralph exulted. The hull shook as they received hits.

'Fire!'

On the quarterdeck Captain Kempthorne was taking in the effect of their fire on the first ship they encountered. They had both scored hits on each other, but the smaller balls and ragged shooting of their opponent had little effect on the Kingfisher. The same could not be said for them though. Two full broadsides had done some damage. A spar had been knocked away and there were a number of star-shaped holes in the hull from the lower battery.

He couldn't revel though; the second and third were almost on them and the lookout had reported two more were approaching.

'Five to one, we almost have them outnumbered,' Felton said with a smile.

'They seem to want to fight it out,' Kempthorne said. 'We will go between them as they seem keen to bracket us. Send up the topmasts and set topsails.'

The men jumped to their work with a will and the topmasts were in place in time to manoeuvre against the second and third ships.

'Run out the starboard battery,' Felton cried.

Every gun on the ship was in action, every crewman and a fair number of the soldiers employed. Now their training and expertise would be tested.

'Rolling broadside as you bear!' Felton shouted through his trumpet.

Down on the lower gun deck the big thirty-six-pounders were ready. Ralph waited between the forward guns. He had a thought and stepped forward and stuck his head out the forwardmost larboard gun port, then skipped across to the starboard.

'The starboard ship is slightly ahead. Fire as soon as her bow crosses your guns, aim flat. Larboard side fire when your ship's foremast is in front of your guns. Understood?'

'AYE, AYE, SIR,' the crews shouted.

The shout was heard on the quarterdeck.

'Young Wrenn seems to have his men afire,' Kempthorne said.

'Aye and we will see how they fair after we have been at it an hour or two,' Felton said.

The starboard fore main-deck gun fired followed by the bass roar of the lower-deck gun. The ships were moving slowly, and the guns fired at roughly four second intervals.

Shot hammered into the hull near where Ralph stood. It didn't penetrate. The double planking on their hull was proof against smaller calibre shot. Further aft a ball came through a port when the gun was run back. Incredibly it missed every one of the gun crew and lodged itself in a rib on the other side.

The staggered firing from either side reduced the strain on the ship's fabric allowing the timbers to flex and absorb the shock. Knowing the construction of the ship as well as he did, Ralph's idea preserved their integrity.

'They are going for our rigging with ball,' Felton observed calmly.

'Perhaps they do not have chain or bar,' Kempthorne said.

He was right. The pirates lack of experience was showing. The British were aiming between wind and water as was their tradition since Drake, hammering their enemy's hulls and killing their sailors.

Though Kempthorne wanted the fight to stay mobile, it was inevitable that with so many guns firing they would kill the breeze and eventually it would turn in to a static slugging match.

'Deck there! There are two more ships approaching,' the lookout shouted.

'Seven, bedamned. Looks like we are in for some warm work,' Kempthorne said.

Although Ralph's guns could fire two rounds every three minutes, the mobile nature of the action meant that no more than two broadsides were fired as the ships passed. With four ships blazing away at every opportunity, thick smoke drifted across the sea on the slight breeze.

The demi-battery ships of the Reis brothers joined the fray. Their eighteen-pound lower-deck guns would be more effective against the Kingfisher's hull. Mahmood stood tall on his quarterdeck and sneered at the effect the smaller ships had on the big British. 'It's a frigate!' he gasped as the realisation hit him like a hammer.

'She must have fifty guns!' his first mate said.

'The British intended to trap us, but we will be victorious. They cannot win against seven ships,' Mahmood gloated. His eighteen-pound lower-deck guns would smash their hull. When all four of their larger ships joined the fight, the Kingfisher would be doomed.

They sailed directly for the Kingfisher which was making slow headway as she fought the three 30-gun ships, the frigate's sides belching fire and smoke. The smaller ships were using their manoeuvrability to delay her, passing no closer than two cables distance.

'Load with iron ball!' Mahmood ordered.

The guns ran out. He was getting ready to give the order when a gun fired; that set the rest of them off, and all the guns let loose – early. The shot splashed into the water ahead of the enemy.

'Idiots! Who was that who fired first? I will have you flayed! Reload!' He ran down the line of guns, slapping and pushing the men to make them work faster. He stopped as the hull shuddered. A man screamed from below followed by another. A piece of rail flew past him as an eighteen-pound ball tore a chunk out of the deck, smashing a man to pulp. His men loaded slowly. If he had timed it, he would have seen that it took them two minutes to get the first guns run out by which time the British had fired again. Their second broadside did little better than the first; poorly trained gunners shooting high or wide.

Captain Kempthorne estimated it would take an hour for the two ships coming in from the horizon to get into the fight. His goal in the meantime was to try to neutralise the two demi-battery ships that were already engaged. He focused on the one that was just passing.

'Wear to starboard, we will try and cross his stern. Mr Barnes, my compliments to Mr Wrenn and ask him to hold his fire until we cross. Then to serve him with his starboard guns.'

Any manoeuvres had an element of risk, and he carefully watched the positions and courses of the other ships. The Kingfisher was taking fire from all quarters now and her guns were keeping up a steady fire as one then another of the pirate ships came to bear. The gunfire was having a damping effect on the breeze, and he knew this was probably his last opportunity for any meaningful manoeuvres for a while.

Down below Ralph had the larboard bulkhead lowered as the ship turned – the heel could put the gunports under water. He need not have worried though as they were only doing three knots and the heel was minimal. It did, however, allow him to concentrate on the starboard guns. He took position at the foremost and looked down the barrel. The stern of the target slowly came into view and when it was directly in line he said, 'Fire!'

The linstock came down and the slow match touched the priming powder.

WOOF!

BOOOM!

Smoke and flame obscured the target. He knew instinctively that the shot was true and moved to the next gun.

Murat Reis had just praised his gunners for getting off an almost simultaneous broadside. The ship was shrouded in smoke, and he had lost track of the Kingfisher. A shout from the helm brought his attention to the stern. Out of the cloud of smoke was emerging the bow of the British ship. Their upper-deck guns were firing in turn and the sound of smashing wood and screams came from below. Then the huge lower-deck guns started firing and the deck jumped. His ship shuddered and cried as it was mortally hit time after time.

The British gunners knew their business and aimed low, sending their balls crashing down through the lower gun deck. Guns were hit and spun or upended. The rowing benches were smashed to splinters. Either way, men died. There were eighty men and boys on that deck before they were raked. After, only a dozen or so were left unhurt. Blood ran out of the sides where balls had exited; it stained the sea pink.

'That was good shooting,' Felton said to Ralph. He had run down the stairs to the lower deck to congratulate him. 'Your men have earned an extra rum ration.'

Ralph had to take his word for it as smoke still obscured his view from outside. He was reliant on orders from above and could only let fly a broadside on command. His mouth was dry and tasted of sulphur. He went to the scuttlebutt and used the ladle to take a drink of water.

An eighteen-pound ball smashed through the larboard side showering splinters. Two men staggered as they were hit and Ralph rushed to them. One had a large splinter in his shoulder, the other a smaller one in his side.

'Get them to the surgeon,' he ordered their mates.

'We can get there ourselves,' the one with the wound in his side said as his comrade took him by the arm.

They had been fighting for an hour now and had seriously damaged one ship. Her lower-deck guns would take no further part in this action.

On the quarterdeck there was an air of calm as the Captain and first lieutenant went about their business. Rigging was repaired as soon as it was damaged and their sails had a few holes, but apart from that they had suffered surprisingly little damage.

'We are almost at a standstill,' the Captain said.

'So are the other ships,' Felton said.

He was right. The fight had almost become static, and the Arab ships were taking to their oars, which prevented their lower-deck guns from firing.

'Lookout! Where are the two ships?' Kempthorne called up.

'Three miles out and coming in at around six knots judging by their bow waves.'

The sails shuddered. A gust of wind filled them with a boom and then died.

'We need more of that,' Felton said.

'Where is that second demi-battery ship?' Kempthorne said.

Felton went to the stern and peered into the smoke. He could see nothing to start with then, as it drifted, a gap appeared.

'A cable off the starboard quarter using her oars to turn broadside on. If we can continue to wear, we can hit her.'

He went to the compass binnacle and watched as the heading slowly changed.

'FIRE!'

It was a proverbial shot in the dark but had some effect apart from blanketing them in even more smoke. A pair of the upper-deck eighteens made hits, knocking out one of Mahmood's upper-deck guns and mashing the crew to pulp.

The return broadside was more accurate than most had been and shot hissed across the deck. A ball took a gouge out of the mizzen. Another knocked a chunk out of the rail.

Suddenly a number of heads appeared above the rail on the larboard side. They were being boarded.

Ralph didn't hear the thump as the boat hit the side, but he did see the Arab climbing through the gunport while the crew were reloading. The man raised his sword to slash at the nearest crewman's back. Ralph reacted without thought. He pulled his pistol from his belt, cocked, and fired in a single movement. A red rose appeared in the man's chest, and he toppled backwards. Ralph dropped his pistol, swung the blunderbuss around from its place on his back, and stepped up to the gunport. A boat was alongside full of men. The man he had shot had fallen on top of some of them and they were busy throwing him over the side. He fired the blunderbuss. The balls spread rapidly from the short, belled barrel taking down three more.

He stepped back and a soldier with a pike moved into place to cover the port. Another with a lit grenade stepped up beside him and gently tossed the smoking sphere through the port. He grinned as it detonated, and the grin turned demonic as they heard screams. Ralph reloaded his blunderbuss, retrieved and reloaded his pistol.

The soldiers were dealing with any pirates who made it to the ports. Their wickedly sharp pikes thrusting and twisting in bellies and chests as they appeared in the ports – grenades killing and wounding those on the boats.

A shout alerted him that the same was happening on the other side. The guns were being run out and pirates were trying to squeeze between them and the port. The soldiers cleared them away; then the guns fired. Anyone in the port was blasted by the muzzle flash and shockwave. One was trying to climb up the side of the ship and was in front of the barrel of the gun nearest Ralph when it fired. The smoke was tinged with pink. The two parts of his body landed twenty yards out to sea.

More boats came out of the smoke and Ralph heard the swivel guns on the main deck start firing. Grenades fell past the gun ports trailing smoke from their fuses and occasionally there was a body that would land with either a splash or a thump.

The fact that they had men trying to board the Kingfisher did not seem to stop their ships from firing their cannon. True they seemed to be firing higher than they had been, but more than one unlucky soul was dispatched to paradise by his comrades.

Ralph's biggest concern was the stern. A pair of boats had managed to get up against it and pirates were trying to force entry through the transom windows. They had already smashed the glass and kicked in the frames, so he did not hesitate to fire into their midst before ordering a squad of soldiers to form up and meet the boarders with a line of pikes.

On the quarterdeck it was busy. Pirates were trying to scale the stern and the soldiers were busy pushing them back into the sea. As the sound of smashing glass came up from below, the Captain smiled ruefully; he would have a chilly night's sleep until they were mended. The roar of a blunderbuss from below informed the Captain that Ralph had things under control on the lower gun deck.

'We need a breeze,' Felton said.

'Maybe you should try whistling one up, Granger,' the Captain laughed in reply as he drew his sword and thrust it into the eye of a pirate climbing over the rail.

A ball flew overhead and hit the mizzen. It shattered on impact sending shards of stone across the deck.

'They are firing stone shot!' Felton said.

'They must have run out of iron already.'

'That's good for us. Stone shot will never penetrate our hull.'

* * *

The attack by boats petered out and by some unspoken agreement everyone stopped firing as if to catch their breath. The smoke slowly cleared as the breeze came back.

'They are all still there,' Kempthorne said as one by one the seven ships came into view. All had some damage, but all seemed to be capable of fighting.

The Kingfisher kicked up her heels as the breeze filled her topsails and clewed up mains.

'Target those bigger ships; take us past them at a cable.'

The helm turned and the bow came around. The Kingfisher headed straight into the centre of the seven ships, who, in turn, were trying to manoeuvre to bring their guns to bear on her.

'If they miss us, they will be hitting each other,' Felton said as he watched the shambles ahead of them. 'They have no idea of fleet manoeuvres. What a mess.'

It mattered not to Kempthorne who was set on driving through them.

'All guns, double loads grape over ball!'

The order came down to Ralph and his men ran the big guns in to load a bag of grapeshot on top of the big ball. He took the opportunity to look out the forward port.

'This should be interesting,' he said to the sergeant in charge of the soldiers. 'If you want to give them some exercise, they can help run the guns out once they reload.'

Ralph thought that the seven or so seconds they would save with the extra manpower might make a difference.

'FIRE!'

The larboard guns roared as they passed the first ships and the crews reloaded mechanically. They were feeling the effects of two hours of almost constant fighting. The starboard guns fired in turn. Ralph's eyes stung and his mouth was dry. He had a dull headache from either the fumes or the constant roar. He neither knew nor cared about the cause and ignored it.

Under much reduced sail, they were able to get off four broadsides before they ran out of things to shoot at. The men stood down for a few minutes rest as the ship wore and the bulkheads were lowered. Ralph saw the gunner making his way up to the quarterdeck and was waiting for him on his return.

'How are we for cartridge?'

'Plenty still available. We've used a ton and a half of powder so far. How has it been here?'

'It has been a bit busy.'

'I could hear. Your boys are keeping up a good rate of fire. You had better get them ready. The Captain's making another run.'

Ralph got his men moving and reloading so when the order came to raise ports and run out, they were able to do it as fast as in practice. The enemy must have been better prepared this time as balls thudded into the hull. Most hit above them but one hit the barrel of a cannon as it was being run out, sending stone shards flying through the deck.

One stung Ralph's face and his hand came away bloodied when he checked it. The gun's crew were not so lucky. Two were down and of the other eight five were bleeding. The gun was still serviceable, and two soldiers stepped forward to take the injured men's places. The battery continued to fire at full capacity.

# A Bitter Victory

Kempthorne checked his watch. It was just coming up to noon. They had been fighting for five hours. They had expended a third of their powder and a quarter of their available ammunition. They had ball, chain and bar to spare as well as cannister and grape. Casualties amounted to four dead and twelve wounded so far. All his guns were still serviceable.

As for the enemy, one of the larger ships was out of action after being raked and receiving two full broadsides. Her main was over the side and she was slowly sinking. Another smaller ship had retreated to make repairs and he expected it to return to the fight later. The pirates had relied on their oars which would have given them an advantage if they were sailing galleys, but the fully rigged ships didn't respond as well, and they were at a disadvantage to the well-schooled sail handlers on the Kingfisher.

Kempthorne chose his next target. They were all flying a variety of false colours and one was flying a white ensign next to an Algerian flag on its masts. That one would get their attention next.

The breeze had picked up and could now be classified as stiff. That worked in his favour as he kept it on his beam allowing him to manoeuvre. His intention was to pass through the ships as before but have his starboard guns target just the one flying British colours. As they got to a cable from its stern, he ordered the mains taken in completely. They slowed.

Ralph concentrated on the starboard battery. The larboard were shooting at anything that presented itself but the starboard had a target. The Captain was positioning them to be just three hundred yards off and was matching his speed. Ralph watched through a port as they approached. He spotted a man standing at the stern rail. It was Mahmood Reis.

'Hit her as close to the waterline as you can. Let's see if we can sink the bitch.'

The gunners adjusted their elevation. At that range they needn't take any account of drop. The ships were broadside to broadside.

'FIRE!'

The roar was tremendous, and the ship rocked with the recoil that actually moved her sideways in the water.

'Reload!'

Worm.

Sponge.

Dry.

Cartridge.

Ball and wad.

Ram.

Runout.

*Ninety-four seconds!*

FIRE!

* * *

Mahmood Reis tried to give as good as he got. He had conserved his iron shot and now used it to good effect. At close range his eighteen pounders were scoring hits on the Kingfisher's hull and his upper-deck twelves were targeting the rigging.

Watching the other ship, he saw the tall elegantly dressed figure of their Captain. He went to the aft gun.

'Target their quarterdeck.'

The gun roared and, when the smoke cleared, he was still there looking directly at him.

'Again.'

This time they had to load with a stone ball, having used their last iron one the round before.

Kempthorne looked across the water to the other ship. He could see their Captain directing their aft deck gun to shoot at him. Their first attempt was pitiful; the ball missed by a good six feet. The second hit the rail and shattered. Stone shards and wood splinters flew across the deck.

There was a scream, and one of the helmsmen went down, his body scored by shards.

Kempthorne took the wheel himself and shouted, 'Get a man up here to help steer and get this man below.'

As soon as a man took over, he went to the six pounders on the quarterdeck.

'Load with chain and target their quarterdeck.'

The crews shifted their aim after loading and fired true. Chain howled across the gap. Time seemed to slow as it shattered the rail and stays parted. It continued on slicing through the bodies of the tillerman and Mahmood like butter. Blood sprayed as Mahmood's torso was thrown into the air and his hips and legs fell to the deck. He managed a scream before he died.

'Good shooting,' Kempthorne said.

He looked across the water and saw that his lower-deck guns had opened up a gaping hole at the waterline. The demi-battery ship was doomed. He turned away to look for his next target.

The quarterdeck guns on Mahmood's ship were still in action. They knew they were beaten but also knew they had to avenge their Captain. They loaded with two stone balls and carefully aimed at the stern of the big ship as it sailed away. A wave rocked the hull giving them much needed elevation. They fired.

Kempthorne was about to give the order when the balls arrived. One passed through the rigging harmlessly. The other hit the rail. A section was blasted out and spun through the air at an angle to the flight of the ball. It hit Kempthorne just to the left of his spine, passing through his body to emerge from just below his lowest left rib. He looked down in surprise.

'Well, I be damned,' he said.

Felton saw him crumple to the deck from the corner of his eye as a helmsman shouted, 'The Captain be hit!'

Felton rushed to his side, but Kempthorne was already dead. The splinter had pierced his heart. Felton immediately reacted as the trained officer he was.

'Get his body below. I want the officers on the quarterdeck now.'

The guns would keep firing as targets came into view even without their officers in attendance for as long as this would take. So, he waited, evaluating their position and what he would say to them.

They arrived and he called Midshipman Highcliffe into the group as well.

'The Captain has fallen.' He allowed the men to express their shock. 'I am therefore taking command as the next senior. Mr Twelvetrees, you are now the first; Mr Stockley, the second and Mr Wrenn, the third. Mr Highcliffe you are now the fourth.'

They all nodded and muttered, 'aye, aye.'

'We have sunk two but there are still five left. I intend that we finish the job. You all know your posts, get to it.'

Ralph took his post on the main deck. He had charge of the forward half and Stockley the after. Highcliffe had taken over the lower gun deck. Twelvetrees was sailing the ship and Felton looked after the tactics.

As Kempthorne had, he focused on the larger of the five ships. They seemed to have decided to work together and were approaching in line astern. The two smaller ships were working their way around to try to come down the other side of the Kingfisher.

'Looks like they finally got organised,' Twelvetrees said.

'Too little too late,' Felton said. 'We will take them down the starboard side that will give us the wind gauge. Double shot the guns.'

'Won't they be too hot?'

'Hmmm, maybe you are right, load grape over ball.'

The grape was in mesh bags hung on the hull either side of the gunports, so all the loaders had to do was reach out and grab one. The only problem was the bags weighed more than a solid ball.

At first sight Felton's plan seemed insane. He was steering his ship to run a gauntlet, taking fire from both sides. But he had studied the pirates' weapons and tactics and knew that, while they may take a few casualties, the Kingfisher could take the punishment and deal it back fivefold with more effect.

* * *

The crew were ready and, although they had been fighting now for six hours, they were still keeping up a steady rate of fire when asked. Ralph walked down the starboard and back up the larboard battery to the mainmast. He knew the men were ready. They would start a rolling broadside as the forward guns passed the bow of the first ship.

He looked forward. The ships were following each other about half a cable apart. That was too close. The navy taught that a cable was the correct spacing for line of battle.

They slowed.

'Ready!'

The first ship on the larboard side, one of the twelve-pound 30-gunners, came up. The forward gun started the ripple of fire as she passed. The starboard ships came up a little later and the first broadside targeted her foremast. It was not that they aimed for it but rather used it as a firing point which meant that many of the balls crashed through in roughly the same place. By the time the forward gun was ready to fire again, they were almost to the mizzen. They fired as soon as they were ready.

The ship was wreathed in smoke. Incoming shot was causing casualties and Ralph picked up a splinter of stone in his cheek. He left it. The surgeon could dig it out later.

If he thought the fight would end soon, he was wrong. The foremast of the first ship broke with a crack and went over the side causing her to slow and veer to starboard. Because the second ship was only a hundred yards behind, the gap closed before they could fully react, and they ended up passing behind the first. The result was the gunners aim on both ships was spoiled by the unexpected manoeuvre and both it and the Kingfisher only suffered minor damage.

On the larboard side the first of the three 30-gun ships lost the top half of her mainmast. The second took a full broadside and smoke started to rise from below deck. The third sailed wide putting on sail while firing its guns wildly.

'Are you well?' Twelvetrees said, looking at Ralph's face with a concerned expression.

'I'm fine.'

'You look like the red death. Go and see the surgeon.'

He had at least thirty minutes if not longer while the ships sorted themselves out for the next engagement. The surgeon's domain was on the orlop deck, and he climbed down the two flights of stairs to get there. Inside it was dimly lit by lanthorns and reeked of the smell of blood. The surgeon had just finished taking the lower leg off an unfortunate crewman and was wiping his hands on a bloody rag. There were at least a dozen wounded, lying on the deck, a blanket between them and the wood the only comfort.

'Young Ralph! What can I do for you?'

'Got a shard of stone ball in my cheek.'

'Let me see, come sit on the table.'

One of the loblolly boys had just washed the table down and rubbed it dry with a rag.

'Eric, bring that lamp closer,' Weston said. 'Aah, yes, there it is.'

He took a pair of forceps and Ralph braced as he took a grip on the piece of stone. He pulled.

'I think it's embedded in the bone.'

'Hurts like hell now.'

'It will hurt more.'

He took a firmer grip and pulled at a different angle.

Ralph's eyes watered as he gritted his teeth.

The shard came out.

'Hold out your hand.' Weston dropped the offending shard in his palm. 'Souvenir, now hold still while I check it's all out.'

He probed around inside the hole and then flushed it with raw alcohol.

'FUCK!'

Weston laughed. 'I thought that might sting a bit. You can thank you lady friend for that.' He selected a small needle and threaded some silk thread.

'I will make nice neat little stitches so you have a rakish scar.'

It was the longest three minutes of Ralph's life, but it was finally done.

'Try not to have any more holes made in your body. I will take the stitches out in ten days.'

On deck it was quiet as the men rested. They were beating their way back to the five remaining Algerines. The one with the broken fore-mast had cut it loose and was back in action. The thirty-gun with the broken topmast was also looking like it was still in the fight. Smoke still rose from the other damaged thirty-gunner.

'You're back,' Twelvetrees said. He turned Ralph's head with his hook so he could see the wound. 'That will leave a nice scar for you to woo the girls with.'

Ralph held up the shard which was shaped like an arrowhead.

'It was embedded in my cheekbone.'

'Ouch.'

'Yes, hurt like hell when he pulled it out.'

'Officers to the quarterdeck!' came the call putting an end to the chat.

The Algerines had lined up in two columns again, but this time had put their two biggest ships at the front and their smaller lined up behind. They were learning and had spaced out at cable intervals.

Felton had no intention of running the gauntlet again.

'We will make it look as if we are going to pass down the centre again. However, this time I intend to go head on with the starboard line. We will approach at speed. They will not expect this, and I think they will turn to try and force us down the centre. We will turn with them, forcing them to continue their turn. We will parallel their course serving them as many broadsides as we can. The upper-deck guns to load with chain and bar to take down their rigging. If we succeed and disable them, we will turn our attention to the nearest accessible target. I want sharp sail handling. Make it happen.'

The officers went to their stations and prepared the sail handlers for their task. The foremast gang would have to be particularly sharp as they would need all the push on the bow they could get to pull this off.

'Set the mains.'

They were two miles away. The Kingfisher responded.

'Ten knots and a fathom.'

*That's a closing speed of fifteen knots; he will turn in around twelve minutes.* Ralph stood with the handlers of the forecourses, the sails that would provide the most turning power.

'Ready, lads?'

'Aye, sir.'

Ralph looked back to the quarterdeck ready to give the command on the signal from Felton. The clock ticked slowly down.

Felton raised his arm.

'Standby.'

The arm dropped.

'Haul the forecourses! Clew up the fore main.'

The ship turned and a glance to port showed that the pirate had done exactly what Felton expected. The Kingfisher slowed to match their speed and paralleled them at a cable.

'Fire!'

The broadside roared. the chain and bar howling as it shimmered across the gap. Its enormous destructive power shredded the other ship's sails and rigging. Orders came thick and fast.

'Reload. We will hit them again. Aim lower this time! Two reefs in the topsails.'

They were in danger of overtaking the ship and needed to slow down.

The guns fired again. Her main was canted over and her mizzen shot in half.

'One more and she's dead in the water.'

The third broadside was her death. The main went and smoke started up from below. It was soon streaked with flame as the fire took hold.

'Set mains and topsails!'

They would go looking for their next victim.

Throughout all this the Kingfisher had taken fire and suffered damage. None that would cause them a major problem or couldn't be repaired on the run but, when this was all over, she would definitely need a refit. For now, they would mend and make do. Men spliced and tied, plugged, and patched as they came about and started for the remaining demi-battery ship – the one with the broken foremast.

Two of the thirty gunners made to protect it; a third headed to the burning ship.

'They are trying to delay us. Look, she is running,' Ralph cried.

He was right, the last demi-battery that had flown the Algerian flag throughout was turning away and making sail. She was heading straight for the port of Algiers.

Felton ordered them to concentrate their fire on the most damaged of the two with the intention of sinking her. The other he looked to dismast.

Two full close-range broadsides did for her, the thirty-sixes blowing a series of holes on and below her waterline.

'Prepare to board!'

Ralph spun and looked at the second ship. Her masts were still standing but her rigging was a mess. She was almost dead in the water.

'Prepare grapnels,' Ralph called. 'Arm yourselves.'

The men growled; they had been fighting this battle for long enough and they could see an end to it. The ships came together with a grinding crunch and the grapnels flew. With a howl the boarders leaped across to the other ship, their officers in the lead.

Ralph had his blunderbuss at the ready and as he jumped onto the rail; he fired it into the massed men on the other deck. He let it swing around behind him as he leaped forward, sword and pistol in hand.

Not far along the rail from him, Twelvetrees fired his dragon, then threw himself across the gap to the other deck. The two ended up almost side by side. They hacked and slashed, thrust and parried, clubbed, punched, and kicked. It was deck fighting at its most ferocious. No quarter asked and none given.

Boarding pikes stabbed and gouged soft flesh, tomahawks removed fingers and stove in heads. Men fell and were trampled. Inexorably the jack tars pushed the pirates back.

Twelvetrees cried out and fell. Ralph stood over him protecting him as well as he could. He took a cut to the left arm. It hung useless, the muscle cut through, but he stood his ground.

Then it was all over; the pirates had fought to the death. In the end there was not one standing. Any that were wounded were summarily killed. The dead were thrown over the side. The Kingfisher had won the day. The Golden Rose was theirs.

Two sunk, two burned, one captured and two ran away.

# Leghorn

Captain Felton decided they would sail to the free port of Leghorn where they could sell their prize and affect repairs. He had read Kempthorne's orders where it was listed as one of the preferred ports after Naples. Ralph thought he had just wanted a change of scenery, but it turned out that Kempthorne had been born there and wanted to be buried there as well.

Kempthorne's body was placed in a barrel of wine as they needed to preserve it prior to burial. Twelvetrees had taken a spear thrust to the thigh. It was hoped he would recover, if the rot stayed away, but it put him out of action, and he had to stay in his cot.

Cecil Stockley had been killed, his head split open by a huge Arab with an equally large scimitar. The scimitar had stuck in his skull enabling two crewmen with pikes to avenge their lieutenant's death. One recounted, 'We must have put ten holes in him before he went down. Even then Bill had to slash his throat to finish him.'

The butchers bill added up to eight dead, including Kempthorne, and thirty-eight wounded, in which Ralph was counted. His wound was stitched and bound. He had his arm in a sling but was mobile. He took over as first lieutenant. Highcliffe, who got away without a scratch, was acting second.

The shortage of officers meant that they ran a modified watch list. Ralph had the forenoon watch and the second dog watch and he prayed for fair weather. He was exhausted but had to keep going.

The prize was manned and commanded by Midshipman Barnes. It had a skeleton crew and would be burned if attacked. They had six hundred miles to make before they made port.

The dead who'd wanted to be buried at sea were consigned to the deep with all due ceremony. A solemn service but one appreciated by the crew.

'A cup of beef broth, sir?' Standing, the wardroom steward, said and offered Ralph a cup.

'Thank you, Standing. Most kind of you,' Ralph said. He had the watch and would be having a late dinner.

'How long before we get to port, sir?'

'Oh, we should make landfall in the morning and be in Leghorn by noon.'

Ralph sipped the broth. It was laced with something. 'What's in this?'

'I put some of that sweet sherry you picked up in Porto in it.'

'Tastes good! Better than broth on its own.'

The broth was made by roasting then boiling the beef bones from the preserved beef. The bone marrow gave it a particular flavour.

They made landfall as he predicted and entered the port. There was a British Navy ship in the harbour and Felton went across with the written reports to be taken to London for Admiral Allin. He returned slightly worse for wear having been dined by the Cambridge's captain. The third rate was heading back to England the next day and they were celebrating their last night in port.

* * *

The first thing they did was get the wounded ashore and into hospital. There was one near the harbour run by an order of Franciscan nuns who took the men in and cared for them.

The funeral of Captain Kempthorne was a solemn affair. They bought a coffin worthy of his status and six bosuns, dressed alike in white shirts and blue trousers, were pallbearers. The service was at the church of Saint George, and he was buried in the English cemetery on the via Para.

The men started repairs after a thorough inspection that revealed just how much fire the Kingfisher had taken. Twelve-pound iron balls were embedded in the hull. The double layer of oak that made up the wooden walls of the ship had absorbed the impact in a lot of places, but the timbers were damaged and would have to be replaced. In other places she had been shot through. Her rigging was a mass of splices and repairs and needed replacing. Once into dry dock they discovered that the rudder had a large chunk missing. The dockyard estimated it would take at least two months if not three to make all the repairs.

The crew were happy; they got to stay ashore in a barracks that was quite comfortable and had their pay and prize money from the sale of the Golden Rose. The warrants stayed with the ship of course and the officers took up residence in a tavern close to the docks.

Ralph kept himself busy as acting first lieutenant by visited the ship on a daily basis and used his knowledge of her construction to help the shipwrights.

Felton fell ill after being ashore a month. The doctors said he had the flux and confined him to bed. Over the following days, his condition deteriorated despite the bloodletting the doctors insisted on. He died quietly in his bed.

Twelvetrees recovered from his wound, but his leg never recovered its full use, leaving him with a pronounced limp. He invalided himself out of the navy and took passage on a merchant ship back to England. That left Ralph as de facto Captain – a position he felt unready to fulfil but took on all the same.

Leghorn had its attractions. Ralph, as the Captain of a British warship, received invitations to dine with the British families who lived there and even the occasional ball. He dallied with several women, but none were Maaike who he missed terribly. He went to the opera and theatre and had a rare time of it.

That all stopped when in October, just after the Kingfisher came out of dry dock, the Nonsuch came into harbour. She was a thirty-six-gun fifth rate and was designed as an experimental fast sailing ship by Anthony Dean. Her captain, Francis Wheler, had orders to take command of Kingfisher.

'Mr Wrenn? Francis Wheler. I am to assume command of the Kingfisher,' he said as he came aboard.

'Welcome aboard, sir.'

'I have orders for you as well.' He looked around at the side party, noting the lack of officers.

'Are these the only officers left?'

'Yes, sir.'

'I am told there are replacements on their way but until then you will stay as first. After that, you are to assume temporary command of the Nonsuch.'

He handed Ralph a packet of orders with the fouled anchor seal.

Ralph read the orders in the wardroom. He was to take command of the Nonsuch until its return to England where he would re-join the Kingfisher as first. The two ships would be under the overall command of Wheler.

He chafed as they waited for the replacement officers. The Nonsuch was a beauty, and he couldn't wait to get his hands on her. He was, however, to be disappointed.

'Mr Wrenn, Captain's compliments, sir, but would you be so kind as to attend him in his cabin,' Midshipman Teddington-Smythe said.

Ralph was in the wardroom off watch and had heard a boat come alongside. He hoped it was delivering the replacement officers.

'Lieutenant Wrenn, Sah!' the sentry on the Captain's door announced.

'You wanted to see me, sir?'

The Captain stood which Ralph thought odd.

'I have some bad news. Crowberry, the lieutenant that was supposed to take over as first, had an accident on the voyage down and broke his leg badly. Consequently, I am asking you to stay on as first. I know it will be a bitter pill but needs must, you know.'

Ralph's heart sank. He could see the Nonsuch out of the transom window.

'Who will get the Nonsuch?'

'Thomas, the first, will command her temporarily until we can find an alternative. Look, you were my preferred man for first lieutenant. The Admiral was seeking to reward you for your service by giving you the Nonsuch, and I am in no doubt you deserve it, but your knowledge of this ship is invaluable.'

The Captain was trying not to sound like he was pleading as Ralph would be well within his rights to insist on taking his commission. Ralph sighed inwardly; he would have to wait.

'I would be pleased to be your first, sir.'

'Excellent, excellent. Let me call the new officers in so you can meet them.'

The two new officers came in along with Highcliffe.

'Mr Wrenn, may I introduce Peter Salisbury, the new second, and Anthony Trowbridge, the third. Gentlemen this is Mr Wrenn, the first lieutenant, and you have already met Mr Highcliffe the fourth?'

They nodded. Salisbury was a stocky landowner's son from Wiltshire. Ruddy faced, with a shock of brown hair, and in his late twenties, he had the bearing of a man that had come up the hard way. Trowbridge was a different kettle of fish entirely. Red haired, trending to fat with puggish features, he was probably in his early twenties and had a belligerent look about him.

'Welcome to the Kingfisher. She is a good ship and efficient. All but a handful of the crew have been on the ship since she was commissioned and know their business. We had to replace a dozen who were killed or invalided.'

'We were told you were involved in a battle with some pirates,' Trowbridge grunted.

'The ship and her crew did themselves credit,' the Captain said before Ralph could respond. 'They took on seven fifth rates and came away victorious, destroying four and capturing one.'

Ralph felt that he should say something.

'The ship took a lot of damage; the Captain was killed, the second was wounded and disabled and the third killed. We lost eight crew in the fight and another thirty-eight wounded. This is an excellent ship that has proven itself. Remember that when you work with the crew.

'Do not underestimate the Algerians. They are learning fast how to handle European ships and have acquired enough expertise to cause problems.'

'Thank you, Mr Wrenn. Gentlemen, I invite you all to dine with me tonight. We will sail on the tide in the morning.' The men were dismissed.

'Mr Wrenn, indulge me a moment,' the Captain said. 'What is the ship's preparedness?'

'In all respects ready to sail, provisioned for three months at sea.'

'Thank you, you may attend to your duties.'

The dinner was a relatively quiet affair. Ralph was asked to recount the story of the battle, which he did with the minimum of embellishment. Trowbridge drank steadily and more than the others but seemed to be able to take it. Highcliffe said little, unused to being part of the officer group. Salisbury showed he had wit and amused everyone with stories of his previous ships.

The next morning Ralph was on the quarterdeck with the Captain.

'Take us out, Mr Wrenn.'

Ralph took a deep breath and prepared to give the commands. The crew were ready and watching him expectantly.

He would need to get the ship turned to be able to use the square sails.

'Bring us up to the anchor, prepare the headsails and spanker.'

The capstan clinked and the ship moved forward until the anchor cable was vertical.

'Anchor up and down.'

'Avast the haul. Set the headsails.'

The crew drew the canvas taught so it was applying pressure to the bow.

'Up anchor, set the spanker.'

The capstan clinked again, and the ship broke free and turned to the opposing pressures from the headsails and spanker.

'Set topsails and gallants.'

The sails boomed as they tightened. The ship accelerated.

'Rudder's bighting, sir,' the helmsman said.

'Steer two points east of south.'

He looked forward and shouted through his trumpet. 'Mr Trowbridge, have a care with your trim.'

Trowbridge, who had been idly watching the men work without interfering, jumped as if stung.

The course settled to where Ralph wanted it.

'Set the mains.'

The Captain stepped up beside him.

'I see the men do not require starting,' he said referring to the practice of bosun's mates using a ratan cane to strike the back of anyone who didn't move fast enough.

'They are eager enough.'

'The punishment book was relatively empty.'

'Captain Kempthorne only used the cat as a last resort. He was a leader who led his officers by example.'

'Are you comparing me to him?'

'Not at all, sir.'

Ralph recognised the danger signal and left it at that. He cast an eye around and saw the Nonsuch fall in behind them.

'Will we be performing evolutions in concert with the Nonsuch?'

'Yes, she will accompany us. Set course for Algiers.'

Ralph kept a straight face even though he was surprised. He expected this to be a shakedown cruise to bed the new officers and crew in and to test their repairs. It was apparent this Captain wasn't one to share his plans even with his first.

As soon as they were out of the harbour Wheler started a series of sail evolutions, then gun drills. Ralph felt the men did well, meeting their previous times. However, he was somewhat disturbed by the fact Wheler never once tried to change the ships appearance and, with the Nonsuch in attendance, he was pretty sure no Algerian ships would come within a sea mile of them.

The Nonsuch mirrored them, a little slavishly in Ralph's opinion, and without the Kingfisher's efficiency. Her performance was average to say the least. Wheler sent signal after signal to correct them.

They reached a point that was one hundred miles from Algiers when Wheler gave the order. 'Signal the Nonsuch to fall back two miles off our port quarter.'

Ralph raised a single eyebrow as he ordered Midshipman Marchant to make the signal. The Nonsuch acknowledged and reduced speed. They also slid out to windward by a mile. Wheler was being very precise with his instructions to their consort.

One of the penalties of being first lieutenant was the paperwork. He effectively ran the ship on a day-to-day basis and had to make reports for everything from the number of stores used to feed the men, to the condition of every piece of rigging. These were taken by the Captain and used for his reports to the Admiralty. He also had to keep his personal log. In it he noted the behaviour of the junior officers and their performance, leadership capabilities and willingness. His opinion of Trowbridge was not high and he struggled to be fair.

The ship that had delivered the officers also delivered their mail and he had a number of letters to go through. None of them were from Maaike. There was one from his father and another one in his mother's scrawling hand. Another had no sender's address which was unusual, and only a plain seal, so he opened that first.

It was from Admiral Allin. It had the usual Admiralty lead in. The meat of the letter said,

I was exceedingly pleased to read of your success against seven Algerine ships of the fifth rate. I read of Captain Kempthorne's death with some sadness and I was also saddened by the later revelation that Felton had died of the flux.

Your new captain has earned his promotion to a fourth rate and has proven his worth in his handling of the Nonsuch. I have recommended that you get the captaincy of the Nonsuch until a new captain can be found as the first lacks in imagination and initiative.

*That explains the signals.*

Of the new officers the new first, William Thomas, is the best I could find. Salisbury is also a good man but if you should have to work with Trowbridge be on your guard. He has strong and politically powerful sponsors and isn't afraid to use them to get his way.

*Oh wonderful!*

# The Salé Pirate

They sailed to Algiers and, as Ralph had predicted, not a ship could be seen outside of the port.

'We will follow the coast west, Mr Wrenn. Signal the Nonsuch to close up to a cable astern of us,' Wheler said with a look that spoke volumes. The detailed signals continued for a week as they slowly made their way down the coast. Several times the signal had to be repeated or redone before it was understood and Wheler got more and more frustrated.

'Mr Wrenn, sir. Captain's compliments and could you attend him in his cabin.'

Ralph went down after handing over the ship to Salisbury.

'You wanted to see me, sir?'

'Ralph, take a seat.'

*Ralph? That's a first.*

'I have been considering the efficiency of the ship and am most pleased with the performance of the crew. However, I cannot say the same for the Nonsuch. Her performance seems to have degraded since I left.'

*What's coming?*

'Consequently, I have reconsidered my decision to keep you aboard as my number one. To be honest, I am finding myself spending more time commanding the Nonsuch than the Kingfisher.'

He pushed a packet across the desk.

'This is your commission. Heave to and get the Nonsuch alongside, transfer over and take command. Thomas is to come over and take over as number one. Is there anyone you wish to take with you?'

'Midshipman Marchant if I could, sir.'

Wheler nodded, then stood and held out his hand. Ralph took it.

'Return the Nonsuch back to the efficiency I expect from her. You may take up position three miles off my port quarter.'

Ralph thanked him and went to his cabin where he asked the steward to pack his sea chest. He also found Tim and told him to pack and meet him on deck.

'Heave to. Signal the Nonsuch to come alongside and the Captain to report aboard.'

Wheler appeared on deck as the Nonsuch came alongside. Ralph waited until Thomas stepped across and met Wheler. Trowbridge seemed to have guessed what was going on and looked at Thomas with a nasty look on his face. Thomas saluted Wheler and returned to the Nonsuch to come back fifteen minutes later with his chest.

Ralph had his sea chest sent over along with Tim's and waited for Wheler to come to the side.

'Captain Wrenn, I congratulate you on your commission. Make me and the Admiral proud.'

'Thank you, sir,' Ralph said and boarded.

He read himself in.

'By the Commissioners for executing the Office of the Lord High Admiral of Great Britain &c and of all His Majesty's Plantations &c.

To Lieut. Ralph Alphonsus Wrenn, hereby appointed Master and Commander of His Majesty's Ship, Nonsuch.

By virtue of the Power and Authority to us given, We do hereby constitute and appoint you Master and Commander of His Majesty's Ship, Nonsuch, willing and requiring you forthwith to go on board and take upon you the Charge and Command of Master and Commander in her accordingly. Strictly Charging and Commanding all the Officers and Company belonging to the said ship subordinate to you to behave themselves jointly and severally in their respective Employments with all the Respect and Obedience unto you, their said Master and Commander; And you, likewise, to observe and execute as well, the General printed Instructions as what Orders and Directions you shall from time to time receive from your superior Officers for His Majesty's service. Hereof, nor you nor any of you may fail, as you will answer the contrary at your peril. And for so doing this, shall be your Warrant. Given under our hands and the Seal of the Office Admiralty, this 20th day of September in the one thousandth seven hundredth and ninety-eighth Year of His Majesty's Reign.'

By Command of their Lordships

He made no speech. The crew looked resigned and a little bored by it all. He decided to change that immediately.

'Set top sails and gallants, Helmsman two points to port.'

The officers looked surprised.

'Jump to it!'

He glanced back at the Kingfisher. Wheler was at the side on the quarterdeck and raised his hat in salute with a grin. Ralph returned the salute and returned his attention to his ship.

Three miles behind and a mile off the Kingfisher's port quarter, Ralph put the Nonsuch through her paces. Not a single signal came from the

Kingfisher. He had them raise and lower the masts, while changing sail configuration; run out the guns in dumb show; change main sails without losing speed. He made notes on a slate, then called his officers to his cabin leaving Tim, who had been made senior mid, in charge.

'Gentlemen, you have had a taste of what is to come. I will expect this ship to operate efficiently and eagerly in all situations. Mr Harris, you were second I believe?'

'Aye, sir,' Harris replied with a strong Aberdeen accent.

'You are now first.' Ralph turned to the next officer.

'Mr Parker, you are now second. Mr Clarke, you are third. We will not have a fourth lieutenant. Midshipman Marchant will perform those duties. Any questions?'

'Do you have new standing orders for us, sir?' Harris said.

'I will issue a new order book once I have examined the existing one and the other ship's books. Anything else?'

He waited ten seconds then said, 'Who has the watch?'

'I do,' Parker said.

'Then return to your duties. I want to be informed if there is any signal from the Kingfisher or change of course. The rest of you are dismissed.'

The ship's books were a mess.

'Call my clerk.'

A small man with a long beak of a nose arrived.

'Jeramiah Forester, sir,' he said.

'Did you write up these books?'

'No, sir, Mr Thomas did that himself.'

'I want these redone in a fine hand. I can barely read them. When you are done, I will have more for you to do.'

Taking that as his dismissal, Forester took himself to his desk and set to work, seemingly happy they had a proper captain again.

* * *

After a couple of days of exercises, the ship had regained some of her efficiency. His officers had settled into their new roles and the men seemed happy. However, there were always dissenters and he noted that there were a group of hands, landsmen, who seem to resent being ordered around.

He noticed a black look at Tim's back by one when he gave an order to latch on and haul. The man moved slowly.

'Bosun! Start that man.'

A ratan cane came down across the man's shoulders and he spun around with his fists clenched.

'Master at Arms! Put that man under arrest and bring him to me.'

He would nip this behaviour in the bud.

The man was dragged to the foot of the quarter deck stair. Ralph stepped down and looked him over.

'You seem to have a problem taking orders. Would you care to explain why?'

The man just stared back sullenly.

'Master, do you know this man?'

'Aye, sir, he be Carl Smith, landsman, came aboard at Leghorn. He says he was able. The Captain put him with the waisters as we didn't need any topmen.'

'Did he come with any others?'

'Aye there were four of them. They said they wanted to join the navy, but we think they'd all run from merchant ships and had run out of money.'

'Well, Mr Smith, you will find that I do not stand for insubordination, either active or dumb, on my ship. You will receive twelve lashes in punishment. If you want to continue with that behaviour, then the next will be twenty-four and I will put you ashore at the nearest landfall.'

He stared the man down.

'Rig a grating and serve the punishment.'

The Kingfisher continued to lead them up the coast and Ralph noted she had lowered her topmasts then they hove-to to change bowsprit. While they were doing that the Nonsuch sailed out to the horizon. They were approaching Morocco and Ralph wanted to see what was ahead as they entered the Alboran Sea.

Spotting a sail, Ralph called up to the lookout. 'Can you identify it?'

'Could be a snow.'

*That's worth investigating,* Ralph decided.

'Make a signal to the Kingfisher, "Investigating strange sail". Fire a cannon to get their attention.'

'She's acknowledged, sir,' the signals mid reported.

*I must learn their names. Is that Jennings or Smethurst?*

'Make all sail, raise an Algerian flag.'

The Nonsuch fairly flew across the water. This was the first time Ralph had the chance to loosen the reins and he was loving it. She heeled over in the stiff breeze and threw up a moustache of foam at her bow.

'Steer to pass her a mile away.' Ralph looked at Harris who was looking equally exhilarated.

'Sails like a witch, doesn't she,' Harris said.

'She does that.' Ralph laughed.

The strange sail was in fact a large snow. Ralph could see her hull up and her mast configuration was plain to see. Two masts, the aft taller than the fore, both carrying square sails. A short third mast close behind the mainmast carried a gaff sail. She flew a strange flag.

'What flag is that?' Ralph said, focusing his telescope on a green flag that looked to have a pair of scimitar blades in a V coming out of a single hilt.

The sailing master, Geoffrey Byrne, a veteran sailor who looked to be carved out of gnarled elm, stepped forward.

'I believe that be a Salé flag, sir.'

'Salé?'

'A town on the west coast of Morocco. Proper haven for pirates.'

Ralph grinned.

'Gentlemen, bring us to quarters; this sheep dog is about to show its teeth.'

They sailed past the snow as if they hadn't seen it and got upwind of it. A mile past Ralph ordered, 'Wear ship! Bring us about, Mr Harris, and run out the starboard guns.'

The Nonsuch fairly spun on her heel.

*Whoohoo!* Ralph exulted as the manoeuvre was performed beautifully.

'Run out.'

The ten demi-culverin eight-pounders were trundled out. The range closed to three quarters of a mile, the extreme for those guns.

'Bring our broadside to bear. Raise our colours.'

The union flag streamed out as the ship swung her bow to port.

'Fire as you bear!'

The guns fired a ragged broadside.

*Needs a little work,* Ralph noted.

Shot splashed around the snow that turned east and ran.

'Perfect, keep us this distance behind. Lookout, let me know when the Kingfisher is hull up.'

He turned to Harris. 'Prepare to loosen the main course. I want it to look as if it has broken free.'

The minutes ticked by.

'Kingfisher is hull up,' the lookout shouted down.

Ralph looked at Harris who picked up his speaking trumpet and bellowed, 'Let her loose!'

The sail suddenly flapped and curled up to foul the foremast as they let go the starboard sheet.

On the Kingfisher, Wheler heard the gunfire and thought, *that young whippersnapper has taken on a prize!* He had to revise that thought a minute or so later when the mainmast lookout called, 'Deck there, a snow making directly for us.'

'What the hell?' He looked at the other officers who shrugged or looked blank.

'Deck there. The Nonsuch is a mile behind the snow driving her towards us.'

'Bring us to quarters!'

*Damn, if the boy isn't bringing her to me!*

The lookout could see that the Nonsuch was just hull up when her main course suddenly flapped, and they slowed.

'Deck there. Nonsuch has lost her main course and slowed. She is turning into wind.'

'So much for their efficiency,' Wheler heard Thomas mutter.

'Dolt! He is setting a trap!' Wheler snapped.

The snow, seeing the Nonsuch apparently in irons and an undefended merchantman ahead of them, did what any good pirate would do and went for the prize.

'All guns double shotted and ready,' Thomas reported.

'Let's see which side he decides to take us. Wear ship, make it look sloppy and merchant-like.'

The ship turned around, only just shy of going into irons. The snow was catching up fast.

'What's the Nonsuch doing?'

'She has miraculously regained control of her sails and is circling around to windward of us,' Thomas said.

Wheler could see the snow was going to go for their larboard side to maintain the wind gauge.

'Wait until the snow's bow is up to our stern before running out.'

'Sir, won't that be too late?' Thomas said.

'You are about to see how a well-schooled battery operates,' Wheler said. 'Watch and learn.'

'Run out!'

The larboard gun ports opened, and the guns ran out before the snow was halfway along. She was just two hundred yards away.

'Fire as you bear.'

The well-trained gunners made sure their shots counted. Rigging fell and the snow's hull took a pounding.

The snow returned fire with her ten 12-pounders. At two hundred yards they couldn't miss, and men went down as the balls smashed into the upperworks. Her captain knew what he was doing but he didn't expect the thirty-six-pound lower-deck guns that knocked big holes in the side of his ship.

Ralph had the Nonsuch prove she deserved the title of fast ship. Carrying as much sail as she could handle, they raced around in an arc to take the snow on the other side to the Kingfisher. As they approached, he saw a different opportunity.

'Reduce sail, the Kingfisher has taken her mizzen. We can get across her stern,' Ralph said referring to the small mast that carried the gaff sail.

They slowed and Ralph had them steer to cross the stern of the damaged snow.

'Back the foresail.' The Nonsuch came to a halt right across the stern of the ship just one hundred feet away.

'Fire.'

'Well sailed!' Wheler crowed as the Nonsuch delivered a killing broadside. 'Right up the arse!'

The snow was in real trouble.

'Bring us alongside, prepare to board!'

The crew armed themselves as the ship came up alongside. Grapnels flew, tying the two ships together. The men swarmed across. The fighting was fierce, but the pirates had been thinned out by the Nonsuch. Their captain was dead and they fought to buy their place in paradise.

Wheler walked through the ship when the fighting was over,

'It looks like a damn abattoir,' he said.

There was blood and body parts all over the deck, guns were turned around and on their sides. There was a groan and he walked towards the sound. A man in Arab dress was impaled by a two-yard-long piece of timber. He leaned against the hull.

Wheler eyed him cautiously, checking his hands were empty from a distance before approaching. The man looked at him, blood dribbling from the corner of his mouth.

'Didn't go so well for you, did it?'

The man just looked at him.

'You will pay for your heathen, pirate ways in hell.'

He grabbed the end of the timber and twisted it viciously; the man gasped, and his eyes rolled.

'This is for my father.'

He wrenched the timber free and a gout of blood fountained out of the body. He was about to ram it home again when, with a rattling breath, he died.

Wheler spat on the corpse and threw the timber to the side. There was a step behind him.

'Your father?' Ralph said.

Wheler turned, looking the deck over, then at Ralph.

'He was killed trying to stop these bastards raiding our village in Devon and they impaled him for his efforts. His body was still there when I arrived three days later from Portsmouth.'

'Some revenge then.'

'A little but never enough.'

Ralph nodded and led him back up into the fresh air.

The ship was sinking; the hull was full of holes and her shattered stern further weakened her hull. The British got off and watched her go down until all that was left was a bloody stain in the water that was rapidly dissipating.

# Recall and Refit

The Kingfisher continued to cruise the Mediterranean accompanied by the Nonsuch for another two years with some success. The pirates had learned that any ship looking like the Kingfisher was to be avoided at all costs. After reading the reports, the Admiralty decided they had done enough. The recall came along with a new captain for the Nonsuch.

Ralph handed over to Henry Teasdale, a newly promoted captain who handed Ralph a packet of orders. Ralph read them before leaving the ship. He was to return to the Kingfisher as first lieutenant for her journey back to Chatham where she would be refit. He noted the orders were signed by the secretary to the First Lord of the Admiralty, Charles Cornwallis.

He reported aboard and saw that Thomas was noticeably absent. Wheler greeted him at the entry port.

'Welcome back, Mr Wrenn. Good to have you aboard.'

'Pleased to be back, sir. I understand we are to return to Chatham.'

'Yes, our job here is done. It's time for the Kingfisher to return to the fleet.'

'The Nonsuch is staying here on convoy escort duty.'

'That's their orders? I am surprised. I thought she would be coming with us,' Wheler said.

'May I ask what has happened to Mr Thomas?'

'He chose to resign his commission; his father has died, and he will take over their estate. He is better suited to the life of a country squire. He left as soon as he was notified by the Admiralty that his resignation had been accepted. The second has been running things for the last month.'

Ralph wasn't surprised by the candid comment.

His first task was to get the Kingfisher back to her old self. Thomas and whoever had stood in for him, had not been one to impose himself on the ship and, as sailors were inherently lazy, the standards had slipped somewhat. Tim had come with him, and he put him back in charge of the mids. He had a new second, Frederick Arundell, Peter Salisbury having been sent home invalided after the Salé pirate engagement. Arundell was the fifth son of Baron Arundell of Wardour in Wiltshire, and he outranked Ralph by some way socially.

Ralph called the lieutenants together.

'Good morning, gentlemen, I see you have had an easy time of it under Lieutenant Thomas. As of now that will change. I have very high standards for my ship, and you will all meet them. I want this ship cleaned from stem to stern; then I will carry out an inspection. You are dismissed.'

He intended to let them know he wasn't happy with the state of the ship and that it had to conform to his and navy standards. He succeeded; by the midday meal the deck had been holystoned, washed and swabbed, brass was polished, and ropes flaked down neatly.

He changed into slops and went up into the rigging, inspecting the standing and running gear minutely; he was joined by Arundell.

'You were Captain of the Nonsuch for a couple of years. How come you are back here as first?' he said with a hint of a sneer.

Ralph took that as a criticism.

'I will forgive your impertinence this time but that is the last time,' he warned. 'I was given temporary command of the Nonsuch when Captain Wheler got the Kingfisher. Lieutenant Thomas had the command, but the Captain deemed him better as first on the Kingfisher and asked me to take over until the Admiralty sent out a new captain.'

Arundell looked slightly abashed at the admonishment but nodded.

'Now, this stay has frayed and needs replacing, and the top gallant halyard needs attention as well. All these blocks need to be greased.' The inspection continued and the list of faults grew longer.

'When will we be ready to sail? Wheler asked as they sat together in his cabin going over the lists.

'Tomorrow, that stay will have been replaced by this afternoon; then we will take on water. The tide is right for us to leave at six bells.'

'Excellent, we should be back in Chatham in two weeks or so then.'

'Weather permitting.'

Wheler laughed, then sobered.

'How are you getting along with Arundell?'

'He was a little casual in our relationship to start with, but I think he understands now.'

'He got the second due to his father's position. He is actually quite inexperienced.'

'I noticed, I had to explain what a stay was.'

Wheler shook his head. 'The system of interest is not the best for the navy.'

'I agree a meritocracy would be better, but we have what we have.'

Even though Ralph knew he had benefited from interest, he also felt he had earned his position and it wasn't an accident of birth.

Arundell's education continued. Ralph made sure he learned all the basics. It had started in the rigging and continued throughout the inspection. Once they set sail, he tested his knowledge of the running of a ship.

'Mr Arundell, be so kind to assist the master in taking the midday sighting,' Ralph said when they were alone in the wardroom.

Arundell looked worried.

Ralph said quietly. 'If you are to command a ship you will need to know how to navigate. Have you had any education in navigational mathematics?'

'I must confess that I have had very little.'

'Meet me in my cabin when you come off watch.'

Arundell duly appeared.

'Have you been taught any spherical navigation?'

'No, sir.'

Ralph shook his head. 'Then you must learn.' He pulled out his copy of The Arte of Navigation by John Tapp.

'You can use my copies, but I would advise that you get yourself copies of Master Wrights Errours of Navigation, Master Tapp's Seaman's Kalendar, The Arte of Navigation and Master Gunters Workes. Study them and practice taking sights with the master. It is not good for the men's respect if they see you are bettered by the mids in this. Do you have a quadrant?'

He did and Ralph ran him through the procedure for taking a sighting. Over the voyage, with Ralph's gentle coaxing and help, he developed the knack of taking a sighting and learned the basics of the mathematics of navigation.

The voyage home was uneventful which gave Ralph time to make sure all the officers were up to scratch on their skills. By the time they got to Chatham, he was confident that any one of them could take over from him if needed.

Chatham had not changed. It was still the same busy place it had always been. They anchored in the river Medway and Wheler reported to the Port Admiral.

'We were expected,' he said to Ralph on his return. Their lordships want the Kingfisher put back to a fourth rate as soon as possible. We are to unload all our stores and guns; then she will be taken into dry dock.'

'Will the men get leave?'

'They will be lodged in the barracks. The officers can take leave for the duration. I have to go to London.'

The Kingfisher was warped to the jetty and offloaded all her stores. Water was pumped over the side. The powder had already been offloaded at the powder dock before they anchored. Ralph decided that he would rather stay and oversee the changes.

'I will stay with the ship during the refit. You can have leave. You will be informed when to return. Make sure we know where you are staying.'

'How long will the refit take?' Arundell asked.

'At least three months, according to the master shipwright, but that depends on what they find once the tar is stripped off. Now be off with you and enjoy your leave.'

Arundell hung back; Ralph raised an eyebrow in query.

'You have something on your mind?'

'It doesn't seem fair that you do not get any leave, sir.'

'Thank you for your consideration, but it is my choice.'

'You have no family to visit?'

'Still asking impertinent questions, Fredrick?'

'I meant no offence but if an officer needs to be here, I can take part of the duty.'

*He is learning.*

'That is very generous of you. If you could delay your leave for a couple of weeks, I could see my parents.'

'I can be here for the first month at least.'

Ralph held out his hand and Frederick took it.

'Thank you, then I will return in a month. Make the best of your time here and learn how this ship is put together. If you get a chance, mingle with the craftsmen. You will be surprised at how much knowledge they have.'

Ralph returned home to the family manor house outside of Sharnbrook in Bedfordshire. It took three days by coach to get there, and he had to walk the final three miles from the village to the house. It hadn't changed; the gardens were neat and tidy, and Alf Smith was still the head gardener.

'Mr Ralph! Welcome home,' Alf cried as Ralph passed him on the drive.

'Hello, Alf, still keeping everything shipshape I see.'

'I be at that, though I ain't getting any younger.'

'Are those boys of yours helping?' Ralph said, referring to his two sons.

'Tommy be, but Eric took an apprenticeship with the local saddler.'

Ralph looked towards the house. He had been spotted and his mother and father were standing framed in the front door. He sped up and, when he got to the steps, his mother rushed down and hugged him.

'You look well, son,' his father said.

Ralph untangled himself from his mother and shook his father's hand.

'I am, did you get my letters?'

'We did, did you get ours?'

'The last one I received was dated three months back.'

'Come inside,' his mother said, 'and we can all catch up. How long are you staying?'

As he stepped inside the door, the smell of the house induced a wave of memories. Bridge, the butler, had a young man take his bag up to his room. His mother kept up a constant chatter asking questions that he barely had time to answer before she asked the next one.

'Now, Martha, let the boy recover from his journey. He can bring us up to date over dinner.'

Ralph went to his room to strip off his uniform and change into civilian clothes. As he sponged himself down he saw the scars on his body from the battles and for a moment was lost in memories. He was startled when the door opened and a maid walked in with a pitcher of hot water.

She had taken three steps into the room when she realised he was naked.

'Ooooh, my lord!' she squeaked and blushed bright red.

Ralph wrapped a towel around himself to spare her modesty.

'You should have knocked,' he said, gently as she just stood there wide-eyed.

'I, um, yes,' she said and, recovering her wits, put the pitcher on the washstand which brought her close to Ralph.

She turned, keeping her eyes down then realised she was looking at his groin. She looked up and saw the scars.

'Did you get them fighting?' she said.

'I did.'

She reached up and ran a finger over the one on his arm.

'Who gave you that?'

'A pirate, an Arab with a great big scimitar.'

'Did you do for him?'

'I did. What is your name?'

'Peggy, sir.'

Ralph's stay at home was comfortable, restful, and full of warm nights with the more than willing Peggy in his bed. She knew it was nothing more than a dalliance, but Ralph was strong, good looking and a good lover. He also took care not to get her pregnant.

His family wanted to hear of his adventures, and he spent many a night recounting the battles. He also told of Maaike and his mother noted the hurt in his eyes. Relatives appeared and marvelled at his tan and the bleached colour of his hair.

He walked the hedgerows with a gun and his father's spaniel and rode to hounds with the local hunt luxuriating in the lush green countryside despite the English weather. He wrote to Twelvetrees who came and stayed for a couple of days. He was in good spirits despite walking with a pronounced limp. He had found a position with a merchant house as their manager of all things nautical. He allowed that he was satisfied with life. He had found a good woman and was to be married the next spring.

Ralph's brother, Ian, and his wife came to visit. She was pregnant and waddled, being close to term, her cheeks rosy and glowing. Ian was making a name for himself in London with the East India Company and was, according to his father, making a fortune.

However, all good things come to an end, and he had to leave to relieve Arundell. Peggy gave him an extra special send-off the night before his departure. His father insisted on having the family coach take him back to Chatham and it was waiting for them after breakfast. His father wanted to see his ship and declared he was coming with him. His mother cried and hugged him.

He looked up through the coach window as it started off and spotted Peggy in his bedroom window. She waved a handkerchief in farewell.

At Chatham the coach was able to take them right up to the dry dock. The Kingfisher was high and dry, her false bulkheads and masts removed. Ralph escorted his father aboard. The sound of carpenters working echoed. The smell of wood and tar, almost overpowering.

'She is bigger than I expected,' his father said.

'One hundred and ten feet at the keel and thirty-three feet across the beam, six hundred and sixty-three tons burthen,' Ralph said, then saw Frederick approaching. He laughed. Frederick was dressed in the leather apron of a carpenter.

'Well met, Fredrick. Have you found a trade?'

Eyes shining in amusement, Frederick bowed and said, 'I must allow I am a dab hand with an adze. You were right, I have learned much about the ship I didn't know before.'

'May I introduce my father. Father this is Frederick Arundell, my second.'

'Arundell? Are you related to Lord Arundell of Wardour?'

'My father, he is rather prolific, and I am his fifth son.' As Mr Wrenn started to bow, Frederick held up his hand. 'Please, no ceremony. On this ship I am just Lieutenant Arundell.'

The two gave Ralph's father a tour of the ship's hull. He exclaimed when they showed him a timber that had been removed that still had a plug in it where an eighteen-pound ball had penetrated. Ralph turned it over and showed him where the wood had splintered.

'That wounded two of my men.'

His father would tell the tale in the local tavern for months to come.

The refit proceeded apace. Her hull was made as sound as it was when it was new and coated in brown stuff. Brown stuff was a mixture of Tar and Pitch called black stuff, with added brimstone. It was deemed more effective than black stuff alone. Gunport lids were refitted, and the guns would be replaced with new ones.

The stern was refitted, the gingerbread and scroll work restored, gold leaf applied. At the end of the three months, she was ready to have her masts re-stepped. This was done with the hull afloat and ballasted, with lifting barges tied along both sides. Around a third of the crew were back on board and as each mast was dropped into place, stays were fitted and tensioned, and the rest of the standing rigging fitted.

The full crew were brought aboard, and the running rigging rove, new guns fitted, and stores loaded.

Ralph hadn't seen hide nor hair of Wheler nor received any letters. He was beginning to wonder what was going on when a new captain appeared. Thomas Hamilton took command and read himself in. He called Ralph to attend him in his cabin.

'Is the ship ready to sail?' he asked.

'Aye, sir, we only need to load powder and we can put to sea.' Powder was loaded at the powder dock well downstream from the dockyard.

'Good, we have a mission.'

# Argyll's Ringing

'The Earl of Argyll has rebelled against the King. We have orders to proceed to the Cowell peninsula and lay siege to his castle.'

The Cowell peninsula was on the west coast of Scotland, north-west of Glasgow. It would be tricky to approach the castle which was on the bank of Loch Goil. The loch was accessible from the Firth of Clyde. Tricky sailing all the way in and especially out.

They called the master and discussed the best course to take.

'The armada went up the east coast and around the top of Scotland but to get into the Firth we are better to go around the south of England, up St. George's Channel and through the Irish Sea. If we time it right the tide will carry us into the lochs.'

'Even if we do not, we can anchor in the Firth and wait for it,' Hamilton said.

The decision made, he ordered Ralph to take them to the powder dock and fill their magazine. That done, they set sail for Scotland.

The weather on the south coast of England was rough. An Atlantic storm had come in and the wind was south by south-west. In danger of being blown onto a lee shore they beat their way out of the English

Channel and made as much southing as they could before turning west.

'Lovely night,' Trowbridge quipped when Frederick reported on deck to relieve him. 'Wind is from south by south-west and brisk.' The ship lurched and they both grabbed a stay. 'Sea is running eight-foot waves which are hitting our larboard bow. Oh, and it's raining.'

'I hadn't noticed,' Frederick said as a wave sent spray showering down on them.

Below it was damp and uncomfortable as the ship worked and water seeped through the deck. Ralph's dreams were full of images of Maaike. He woke for his watch just before dawn feeling muzzy and unhappy.

'Where are we?' he said, looking up at an overcast sky as he came on deck.

'Somewhere off Hastings according to the master,' Frederick replied.

'Is that all? Christ this voyage is going to take forever.'

'Look on the bright side, we are at sea and close to home.'

'Get thee below Satan.' Ralph laughed.

They eventually reached Land's End and could make the turn north a month after they left Chatham.

'This is more like it!' Hamilton said, as they sped up. The wind was on their stern and the current was with them so they fairly flew along. The waves were also on their stern, so the Kingfisher had a chance to dry out when the sun came out.

Their course was a point east of north to the west of the Isle of Man. At their speed they would be there in a day and a half.

'We could call in at Douglas and rewater,' the master said. 'That would allow us to catch the tide into the Firth.' He had consulted his almanac and spoke with a firmness that almost bordered on insistence.

The Captain gave him a long slow look which made the master flush under his tan.

'Any other reason to stop in Douglas?'

'No sir, just to rewater.'

'Hmm. What do you think, Mr Wrenn?'

'I think our master may have a wench stowed away on the island,' Ralph said. The master's colour deepened.

'You may have hit a chord, but it does make sense. Make it so, Mr Wrenn. I will be below.'

Ralph adjusted their heading a point more to the east. The island came up off their larboard bow. Re-watering took hardly any time and they sat in port waiting for the right moment to leave to catch the tide into the Firth of Clyde. The master never left the ship.

They entered the Firth on time and passed the Isle of Arun on their larboard side. It was an hour before dawn and the only light was the setting moon. There was no pilot but they had found a Manxman who knew the waters.

Donal Quayle was as gnarled a sailor as you could imagine, his face wrinkled and lined by the weather in the Irish Sea. His hands were thickly calloused. He stood only five feet tall, but his presence made him seem taller.

As they entered the Clyde before dawn he stood on the quarterdeck watching the Rebh' an Eun beacon.

'The Little Cunbrae be on our starboard bow. Keep the light on our larboard bow for now.'

They made a mere four knots over the tide, and Ralph watched the shadow of the island pass by. Then, as the beacon came up on their beam, Donal growled, 'A point to larboard.'

Ralph glanced at the compass. They were heading due north. The sun rose watery and weak, and the shore was revealed, sliding silently along beside them. They reached the point where the Clyde turned east but they maintained their northerly course and slipped into Loch Long. They were well and truly in enemy territory now and the ship went to quarters. The upper-deck guns were run out, a clear signal they meant business.

The air was crisp and clear; the smell of heather drifted down from the hills.

'A damn good job there's no castle on these bluffs. We would take a pounding,' Hamilton said.

Ralph had to agree; they were at a real disadvantage at the moment to anyone taking pot shots at them from the surrounding heights.

'Two points to starboard,' Donal growled. 'Loch Goyl is the west fork ahead.'

'Masts ahead,' the lookout called, 'and a castle.'

'We will anchor in mid-channel and commence a barrage,' Hamilton commanded. 'Prepare to set the best bower and prepare two kedge anchors to be run out astern.'

Ralph bellowed the orders and the ship came to a halt as the foresails were backed. The anchor splashed down and cable ran out. The ship started to move backwards under the pressure of the backed foresails and when they had run out a full cable, they dropped the first kedge. The second was carried in a boat and set off the larboard quarter. The sails were reefed, and the capstan pulled them forward half a cable. Springs were set.

The castle was a big target with a curtain wall, a keep and a great hall. It was clearly occupied as there was smoke rising from a chimney and men appeared on the wall. Shouting drifted across the water.

'Mr Trowbridge, please assemble a cutting out party and take that ship,.' Hamilton said. 'Mr Wrenn, commence the barrage as soon as she is clear.'

The ship was identified as the Sophia. One hundred and forty-five tons burthen and twelve guns. Her crew were ashore, and Trowbridge and his men had no opposition. She was warped out from the dock and anchored ahead of the Kingfisher.

The field of fire cleared; the guns roared a full broadside. Smoke erupted from the side laced with flame and balls which slammed into the wall and keep.

'Good shooting, keep it up until the castle is raised,' Hamilton said.

Broadside after broadside pounded the castle. The guns got hot and jumped on the recoil. The walls gradually succumbed and breeches opened up. Men fled into the hills. A fire started and the roof of the keep burned, but the pounding continued all day until what was left was no use to man nor beast.

'Mission accomplished, Mr Wrenn,' Hamilton said when the guns finally fell silent. 'We will stay here for a few days to see if they try and come back – an extra rum ration for the men.'

The officers had dinner that night of fish caught in the loch and a suckling pig from the manger. The conversation centred around the future.

'I was told that you are likely to get a ship of your own on our return,' Hamilton told Ralph. 'The Centurion, a fourth rate of forty-eight guns.'

The other officers cheered, and a toast was given.

'That is good to know, sir. Thank you,' Ralph said but wondered why he hadn't been told before. Something must have shown in his face because Hamilton leaned forward and said softly, 'Orders.'

He wondered what the future would bring and where it would take him.

# Epilogue

The Kingfisher returned to Chatham and there waiting for Ralph was his new ship. She was beautiful. His orders were sending him back to the Mediterranean, but he would have been happy to go anywhere.

He took Tim with him and had him take his lieutenant's exams before they left. He passed with flying colours. While they were in dock, Ralph was summoned to London to present himself to the First Lord with all speed. He took a horse and arrived at Admiralty House three hours later. He was shown straight to his offices.

'Captain Wrenn, good to see you. Your arrival is timely. Come, we must go to see the King,' Cornwallis said and led him right back out again.

*What the hell is this all about?* Ralph thought as they took the fifteen-minute walk to St James' Palace. He was dressed well but the journey had taken its toll on his appearance. Cornwallis ignored it, was tight lipped and said little. They entered the palace and were taken deep inside to a reception room. There were a number of people gathered there, milling around and talking. Ralph was led through them to where King Charles stood talking to a tall man dressed in regal clothes.

'Your Majesty, Captain Wrenn of the Centurion.'

Ralph gave his stateliest bow, his hat in his hand.

'Aah, Captain, I have heard a lot about your exploits on the Kingfisher in Naples.'

'Highly exaggerated I am sure, Sire,' Ralph replied modestly.

'Not at all,' a familiar voice said and Maaike stepped from behind the well-dressed man.

She was stunning and he stood looking at her, lost for words. She smiled and said, 'Ralph, may I present my husband, Duke Archibald of Westphalia.'

Ralph regained his wits. Her father had always threatened to arrange a marriage for her and now he could see the truth of it. He made a bow over her hand and another to her husband, who, it turned out, didn't speak English – a mighty relief. Maaike translated when the duke said, 'I understand you saved my wife's life when she was wounded. I thank you for that.' He shook Ralph's hand and told him he would be welcome to visit their palace in Dusseldorf if he happened to be there.

After small talk with the King, they were able to have a moment together.

'Does your husband know we were lovers?' Ralph asked.

'Of course not, silly.' She smiled. 'He only knows you saved my life. I haven't told him anything about us in Naples.'

'Why are you here?'

'Archibald is an emissary for the Dukes of Bavaria who are his two older brothers. They want a trade agreement between Bavaria and England.'

'And me?'

'You are here because I mentioned to the King that you were my knight in shining armour and that I would love to see you again.'

'I wish it could have been different.' Ralph sighed.

THE END

# Historical Notes

The Kingfisher was a real ship and was built exactly as I have described. She was a fourth rate, laid down in Woolwich. The action against the Algerian pirates was also real and can be seen on Wikipedia. Ralph Wrenn was a lieutenant on the ship and survived the battle.

*Painting signed by Peter Monamy, and dated 1734, which was probably intended to depict Kingfisher's fight with seven Algerines*

A race-built galleon was effectively a cut down galleon that only had one gun deck and no forecastle. It had the usual main and fore masts but in addition two mizzens. The rearmost was shorter and lighter than the forward one. It was a favourite of privateers and pirates.

Murat Reis was a real pirate. He had a large fleet of ships based in Algiers and could well have been one of the captains that faced the Kingfisher in their epic final battle. There is very little about the actual battle that has been published so the entire battle is fiction apart from the result.

Campyon is a predecessor of the modern game of Rugby Union. Played with fifteen players a side and a cricket ball sized ball, it was violent and extremely good fun. Players passed the ball hand to hand and tried to score on one of two goals set up at the end of the field. The other team tried to stop them of course.

A taille is a woodwind instrument of the oboe family. In modern instruments it is known as a tenor oboe.

Kempthorne was buried in the English Cemetery in Leghorn or Livorno as it is now known. He was born there as written.

Salé is on the other side of the river to Rabat and was a notorious home to Barbary pirates.

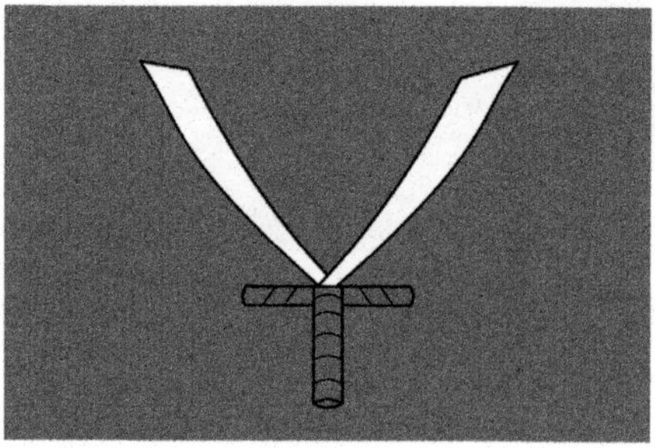

*Their flag.*

The real Ralph Wrenn stayed in command of the Nonsuch and stayed in the Mediterranean where he took over the Centurion. Later he distinguished himself in the Norwich and became a commodore on the Jamaica station. He died in 1692 from fever in Barbados. I have modified his history so he could continue with the Kingfisher to the end of the book and have closure with Maaike.

# Glossary of Sailing Terms

Arquebus – a portable long-barrelled gun dating from the fifteenth century: fired by a wheel-lock or matchlock.

Bowsprit – a spar projecting from the bow of a vessel, especially a sailing vessel, used to carry the headstay as far forward as possible.

Cable – A cable length or length of cable is a nautical unit of measure equal to one tenth of a nautical mile or approximately 100 fathoms. Owing to anachronisms and varying techniques of measurement, a cable length can be anywhere from 169 to 220 metres, depending on the standard used. In this book we assume 200 yards.

Caravel – a medium sized, fast ship bearing a forecastle and stern-castle – though not as high as those of a carrack, which would have made it unweatherly – but most distinguishable for its square-rigged foremast and three other masts bearing lateen rig.

Gripe – to tend to come up into the wind in spite of the helm.

Ketch – a two-masted sailing vessel, fore-and-aft rigged with a tall mainmast and a mizzen stepped forward of the rudderpost.

Knee – a natural or cut, curved piece of wood. Knees, sometimes called ships knees, are a common form of bracing in boatbuilding.

Knot – the measure of speed at sea. 1 knot = 1.11 miles.

Leeway – the leeward drift of ship, i.e. with the wind towards the lee side.

Mizzen – 1. on a yawl, ketch or dandy the after mast.

2. (on a vessel with three or more masts) the third mast from the bow.

Prow – an alternative to bow, the pointed end of the ship.

Ratlines – lengths of thin line tied between the shrouds of a sailing ship to form a ladder. Found on all square-rigged ships, whose crews must go aloft to stow the square sails, they also appear on larger fore-and-aft rigged vessels to aid in repairs aloft or conduct a lookout from above.

Rib – a thin strip of pliable timber laid athwart inside a hull from inwale to inwale at regular close intervals to reinforce its planking. Ribs differ from frames or futtocks in being far smaller dimensions and bent in place, compared to frames or futtocks, which are normally sawn to shape, or natural crooks that are shaped to fit with an adze, axe or chisel.

Sea anchor – any device, such as a bucket or canvas funnel, dragged in the water to keep a vessel heading into the wind or reduce drifting.

Stay – A *stay* is part of the standing *rigging* and is used to support the weight of a mast. It is a large strong rope extending from the upper end of each mast.

Sweeps – another name for oars.

Tack – If a sailing ship **is tacking** or if the people in it **tack** it, it is sailing towards a particular point in a series of lateral movements rather than in a direct line.

Wear ship – to change the tack of a sailing vessel, especially a square-rigger, by coming about so that the wind passes astern.

Weather Gage – The weather gage (sometimes spelled weather gauge) is **the advantageous position of a fighting sailing vessel relative to another**. It is also known as 'nautical gauge' as it is related to the sea shore.

Printed in Great Britain
by Amazon

58872901R00169